Grey Dawn

A Continuation of *The Churning Cauldron*

Ronald Dahle

2013

You can contact Ronald Dahle at the following internet connections:

http://www.facebook.com/RonaldDahle?ref=hl

https://twitter.com/chrningcauldron

http://churningcauldron.com/

Editor: Ella Medler
Cover Artist: Patti Roberts
http://paradoxbooktrailerproductions.blogspot.com.au/
Text Design: Rita Mills
www.BookConnectionOnline.com

Printed in the United States of America

Dedication

This book is dedicated to my wife Gail,
who left this world for a better place
May 24th 2002.

Gail dutifully played 'second fiddle' to the Army and
my whimsical nature for much longer
than she should have.

She deserved more out of life than I gave,
but being a true 'trooper' never complained.

We all miss you Gail.

A Special Thanks

*Special thanks go to the following friends
who helped make this a better book.*

*David Smith, my Medic on ODA-335 in the 70's.
Dave's SCUBA skills and SADM training
added immeasurably to the UN/East river Scenario.*

*John Simmons and I go back to the early 60's.
John is a repository of good to know information
about damn near everything.
He offered up, Gunny and Rodney the rattler, as well as
other information woven throughout this story.*

Introduction

Dear Reader,
In an ideal world, you would already have read The Churning Cauldron and Grey Death prior to embarking on this phase of the journey of the Deacon and his Geriatric Warriors.

This adventure is event and character driven, and you will be totally lost without some basic facts on the personnel involved and a general knowledge of how they got where they are now.

I will start out with a roster of key players, along with some of their more endearing traits, as you will be spending a lot of time with most of them.

Ron, alias The Deacon
There are those who are so impassioned with an ideal or concept that it consumes their very soul. The Deacon, a retired Green Beret, is one of these people. He has determined that America is in rapid decline, and he plans to save it from a completely destructive administration, as well as a myriad of other problems, by whatever means necessary. He has teamed up with several old friends with similar backgrounds and they have set out to—in their words—"Save Lady Liberty." In their quest to accomplish this goal, there are no sacred cows; anything and anyone is fair game. The Deacon has named his force "The Geriatric Warriors." Ron retired after 25 years in Special Forces.

As he says, he was a Green Beret before it was cool to be one. He held every position on an A Team, and went on to become the Group Operations Sergeant Major. Ron retired and spent 20 years running his own photo studio.

A driven, cold taskmaster, Ron knows what he wants, and gets it. He has a strong affinity for hand grenades and goes nowhere without at least a couple of them.

Dirty Joe,
Skill sets: professional hit man, cold, calculating, ruthless, borderline sadist. Intelligence specialist, trained in light weapons, quick kill qualified, and an excellent pistol shot. Joe recently retired from the CIA but the Deacon knows things about Joe the Agency never did.

Filthy Fred,
Skill sets: heartless, indifferent, excellent physical condition, expert demolitions man, with both conventional munitions and expedient explosives. He assisted the Deacon on a torch job of the residence of a friend in Georgia. "Shit happened" and two deaths were associated with the fire, making it a capital crime. The fire was determined to be an accident but three people knew better. The Deacon was one of them.

Larry Montclair,
Skill sets: Pilot, IFR, Prop, Jet and multiple engines qualified. He is now the director of flight operations at LaGuardia Tower. A strong conservative, he is extremely disturbed about where America is heading. In a weak moment he admitted to the Deacon that he, and Bert Wilton, were forced to kill two DEA agents in the 70s when they were running drugs out of Columbia for the Columbian cartel.

Bert Wilton,
Skill sets: Multi-faceted pilot. Currently owns three aircraft used for parachute jumping at a major parachute center in his native state of Texas. Bert is also a skilled sports parachutist, and never one to turn down an opportunity to mix it up or do what he thinks is right. Bert was part of a two-man operation involving the killing of two DEA agents. Although Bert did not do the killing, he was there at the time. He was also known to have been involved in gun running into South America.

John S,
Skill sets: A construction engineer and project manager. He is also a cold-blooded killer, and a serial rapist predisposed to necrophilia. The only value John has going for him rests in the fact he is totally dedicated to making America great again. Served with Ron in Germany in the early 60s and has been a close friend ever since. He has major health issues (heart problems; he has a defibrillator and pacemaker along with 13 stents), all of which govern what he can do. However, what he does, he does as well as anyone who walks. Ron is comfortable sacrificing John in the "We the People" operation in the event that it comes to fruition.

Steven Stein,
Skill sets: one of Ron's medics in Special Forces, Steve is now a working physician's assistant, capable of performing a wide variety of minor and some major surgeries, an expert in triage and treatment of trauma victims. The Deacon witnessed Steve administer fatal dosages of drugs to a couple of black dopers who came to him for help. Steve is a closet racist, and has little tolerance for drug addicts, especially black drug addicts.

David Schmidt,
Skill sets: HALO, SCUBA, SADM qualified, has multi

engine pilot's license, IFR VFR qualified. He is a prior member of the Golden Knights Army Parachute Team. David, the newest member of the Warriors, served with Ron on ODA-335. As the assistant medic, he worked with Steve Stein. David is younger and stronger than most of the Warriors. Known for his singing and dancing routine, and his magic act. Before this story ends, he will be known for a lot more than that!

B obby Fogel,
Skill sets: Tenth degree black belt in karate, deadly, enjoys inflicting pain and knows many ways to do it, trained by masters in Korea and Japan. Bob is retired and enjoys travel; he is an extremely close friend of the Deacon. It was Bob's wife and stepdaughter who were killed in the fire in Georgia. The whole house was gone in an instant. Bob appeared to be visibly shaken. Three weeks later, over lunch, he looked at Ron and smiled—no, it was more of a grin—as he told him that, between his wife and stepdaughter, he was in line for a 1.5 million dollar life insurance settlement. Ron looked for a sign of sadness or remorse on Bob's part, but there was none.

B ob H,
Skill sets: A highly skilled operator, Bob's health keeps him from ground operations. He is, however, a computer genius. There is nowhere he could not hack into while remaining totally undetectable, a skill set that Ron knew would be of use someday. Currently Bob is refining personnel records to help select ex-service members the Deacon may be able to recruit when the situation warrants it. Bob goes back to the 60s with Ron in Laos and Cambodia.

T he Dief,
Skill sets: Excellent physical condition, follows directions to the letter of what he is told, experienced demolitions man,

trained sniper, electrician, great mechanic, silent kill trained, has no conscience. Lined up an entire village in Cambodia and participated in killing all of them in 1967. The Deacon arrived and witnessed them finishing up. He asked the Dief what in hell he was doing, to which the Dief replied, "I don't know, Sarge; it just felt right." The Dief is currently a recovering alcoholic; he has not had a drink in three years. He was just recently informed that he has an inoperable brain tumor. He calls it "his brain bubble." Another volunteer for the "We the People" operation.

Vince McCullough,
Skill sets: An ex-Navy Captain who was drummed out of the service by Congress. He witnessed Ron, Fred, and the Dief take two jetliners down with Stinger missiles. The planes were carrying the heads of state of Iran and Syria. Vince recorded the act with a reconnaissance drone he was testing for the Navy.

Mary Jane: Ron's long time girl Friday, who started out as a photography client in the 1990s. She ultimately went to work for him and has become a permanent fixture in Ron's life for the past twenty years. Within the past couple of years, she has become Ron's love interest, as hard as he tried to avoid it.

Kim: Kim has a long history with Ron that goes back to 1988, when he took her senior class portraits. Ron was immediately smitten with her charm and grace, to say nothing of her incredible body. Ron pursued Kim for years, until he finally had her meet him in Vegas a couple of years ago. The downside to this interlude was that Ron realized that in his eyes Kim was still a little girl, the daughter he never had. He could not bring himself to violate her.

Throughout the book, you will find references to operations conducted by Ron and his crew from the book "The Churning Cauldron." They are referenced in order to give you a feel of what the "Geriatric Warriors" have already accomplished to get to where they are now. A thumbnail sketch of some of these operations is provided below.

Ron, the Vice President of Operations for a defense security company has long been dissatisfied with the direction America was headed. His disdain reached a point of critical mass when the current administration took office and started America galloping headfirst into socialism. Ron knew he had to do something, however little it was.

Ron started to establish contact with numerous old Army friends of the same mindset. It was over breakfast with one of these friends, John, when Ron suggested that while John was dying, he could still contribute to the betterment of America. All he had to do was to kill his senator, an idea that John jumped at; he now had a purpose in life.

Ron then acquired four Stinger surface to air missiles which he used to take out an Iranian and a Syrian jetliner that had their heads of state and their entire delegation aboard, enroute to a meeting at The United Nations.

Based on intelligence Ron received from a close ally in Homeland Security, Ron and his crew, "The Geriatric Warriors", mounted an operation which took out an Al Qaeda sleeper cell located in Logan, Utah. This resulted in capturing tens of millions of dollars packaged for shipping to Pakistan. Ron smiled, as he realized that the Warriors just got a new lease on life. They now had a lot more flexibility to execute operations.

The company Ron worked for had an opportunity to start a Top Secret training camp and Ron was invited in as a partner, as he had just acquired over 1000 acres of relatively desolate woodland in central New Hampshire. Seeing the potential for this to dovetail with his other operations, he jumped at the opportunity.

The story goes on to include numerous operations directed against Jihadists in Mexico, as well as in New Mexico. Part of the booty from these operations was a Libyan cargo plane full of weapons, both conventional and WMD.

Finally, what is a story featuring testosterone and adrenaline driven ex Green Berets, without a judicious sprinkling of all types of sex?

To get more on the backstory I recommend you stop reading right now and get your copies of The Churning Cauldron and Grey Death. Read them before you continue with this installment of the saga of "The Geriatric Warriors". They are both available at Amazon in print and in the Kindle format.

This novel is written in the vernacular particular to each individual character within it. You may like the characters or in some cases they may disgust you. However, if you are a red-blooded American Patriot, you will have to love their stated goal—"Returning Freedom and Liberty to America." In addition, this story may tend to raise a question whenever you pass an elderly gentleman on the street, for now you realize you never really know who is under that grey hair and hiding behind those wrinkles.

I hope you enjoy reading this book as much as I enjoyed writing it for you.

Best Regards,
Ronald (Deacon) Dahle

Chapter 1 — Confusion
29 February 2012

Jimmy was in that transition between having a bad dream and awakening. Far off in the distance he heard a faint knocking on a door that kept getting louder and louder. "Jimmy Paxon, this is the Police, open up!"

The knocking and hollering got progressively louder until Jimmy finally awoke and realized that the beating on the door was not a bad dream. He looked through the peep hole and saw two uniformed police officers plus an FBI agent whom he knew as Ralph Summerall. He opened the door only to be immediately overpowered and handcuffed by the DC Police officers. He was read his rights and informed that he was under arrest for the murder of Melinda Cambridge. Jimmy's bad dream just turned into his worst nightmare.

His mind was racing, in an attempt to make sense of what was going on. The fact that he had a hangover didn't make the task any easier. The name, Melinda Cambridge, raced through his mind. Jimmy tried hard to associate a face to it. Bingo, he recalled that he had a hooker named Melinda to his apartment about a week ago. He knew he did not remember her departure and recalled that she didn't even take the $100 bill he set on the nightstand for her. However, she did steal his laptop computer that was on his worktable. A theft never reported by Jimmy, as that would have opened up Pandora's Box within the FBI, and that, he did not need.

The police retrieved his weapon and un-cuffed him to allow him to get dressed before they took him to central booking. Upon arrival at central booking, they arrested him for murder and set up an arraignment date. During his processing, Jimmy underwent close examination by the crime lab. They paid particular attention to the remnants of his scratches and bite marks, photographing and taking scrapings from all of them. Jimmy changed his clothes one more time this morning; only this time, after being strip-searched, he put on an orange jumpsuit. They put him into solitary confinement, as was standard procedure for law enforcement personnel, for their own safety.

Chapter 2 — The Rest of the Story
17 Days Earlier

The Deacon, Joe and the most of the "Geriatric Warrior" chain of command had just left Larry's office after sitting through the dog and pony indoctrination given to all new CIA agents and vetted CIA contractors. Now, at least the "Warriors" had the cover of being associated with the CIA to fall back on if the shit hit the fan, which it had before and, more likely than not, it would again one of these days.

Joe was enroute to Columbia, where he was the supervisor of an indigenous training camp during the winter months. In the summer months, the training relocated back at the Academy the Deacon had built in Wolfeboro, New Hampshire. Joe had but one minor mission prior to flying to Columbia. He had to tend to an FBI Agent named Jimmy Paxon.

It would have been so easy to just kill Jimmy and get it over with, which is what Joe would have done under normal circumstances. The problem with killing an FBI agent, is that it is akin to letting loose the dogs of war. The FBI is relentless in pursuit when chasing down the killer of one of their own. That is not what concerned Joe, though. The real problem was that every case Jimmy had ever been associated with would come under extreme scrutiny, and within the labyrinth of cases there was the possibility of linking many of the jobs the Deacon and his "Geriatric Warriors" had pulled off. Jimmy Paxon was on the verge of putting the pieces together when Vince McCullough found out about it and reported it to the Deacon. This…is what precipitated this action.

Joe received a briefing on Paxon from Vince McCullough of Homeland Security and from Larry Neider from the CIA, both of whom are sympathetic to the cause of "The Geriatric Warriors."

Joe now knew more about Jimmy than Jimmy did. He knew that, as a result of some questionable decisions and a spate of bad luck, Jimmy was now a pencil pusher for the FBI, and that totally dampened his career aspirations as an FBI Agent. This led him into depression, to drink excessively on a frequent basis, and he was predisposed to pick up hookers and bring them back to his apartment. All of which caused Jimmy to be looked upon with disdain by his co-workers and superiors.

Joe had already located Jimmy's apartment and inspected it for surveillance cameras, which were nonexistent. He had also watched Jimmy arrive at his home carrying his computer and briefcase, usually around 1800 hours. As a rule, Jimmy would spend most of his time in a local bar a block and a half from where he lived. Invariably, he would get drunk, and frequently pick up a hooker and take her home with him.

Joe did some shopping around and found a gorgeous upscale working girl named Melinda Cambridge with whom he immediately struck up a business relationship. Joe told her he was only going to be in town for a week and asked what she would charge to spend that week with him. Without batting an eye, she told Joe that for $10,000 she was his to do with as he pleased, barring beating, for the week. Joe, being cautious, said he would go along with that under the conditions that he paid her $3,000 initially and $1,500 every night thereafter. She made out better that way, and Joe was confident he would see her every day and that she would not disappear after receiving the money. This was the beginning of what appeared to be a great deal for each of them.

Ron Dahle

Actually, Melinda proved to be a delightful partner for Joe both in and out of bed. On one hand, she was a skilled lover, and on the other, an intelligent woman that was conversant in a wide variety of topics and just plain fun to be around. Joe was thinking that likely someday she would have made someone a great wife.

On the fourth night of their arrangement, Joe asked Melinda if she would like to receive an additional $1,500 that night. She immediately got suspicious and asked what she would have to do for it.

"It is simple; I have a close friend who I want to screw with. I want you to go home with him and screw him like he has never been screwed, real bites, scratches, the whole nine yards. Once you have made love to him a couple of times, you need to slip him a Mickey with his drink. As much as he drinks, he will likely pass out within a couple of minutes. At that time, leave him there, grab his laptop, and get out. Leave his door unlocked when you depart. I will be waiting across the street and we can go to my place for the rest of the night."

"Why would you want to do that?" Melinda asked.

"He is an old friend, we go to the same gym at noon time whenever I'm in town, and I want to rag on him about his scratches and bites. He always tries to play the role of a preacher. I just want to bust his balls. He and I went to school together; believe me, this battle has been going on forever. I am going to replace his hard drive with one that has a bunch of crap on it and I will sneak it back into his apartment before he wakes up. This isn't shit; you should see some of the shit he has pulled on me in the past."

"I suppose I can pull that off. You guys, I swear sometimes you act like ten year olds."

———

When Melinda walked into the bar, she knew that Jimmy was hers, for the taking, just by the way his eyes followed her across the room, all the way to the other end of the bar, undressing her with every step she took. Like a dog in heat, Jimmy approached her and asked if he could buy her a drink, an offer she eagerly accepted. It was but a few minutes, when she sensed that Jimmy was already a little on the drunk side, so she decided to make her move while she was sure Jimmy could, and would, comply with her sexual advances.

Melinda was happy to leave the bar with Jimmy, as it was a dingy dive and not the least bit what she was accustomed to by any stretch of the imagination. Jimmy's apartment was an improvement from the bar, but just barely.

They were no sooner in the apartment when Jimmy started undressing. 'A real class act', Melinda thought. She took a deep breath as she also started to get undressed, albeit very slowly, to torment Jimmy who was, by now, panting like the dog he was.

The lovemaking was the least painful part of the evening, as Jimmy was finished before she had really started, and he was a little strange. He withdrew from her and finished by masturbating and ejaculating on her breasts, which he then rubbed in. She realized that, to cause the damage Joe wanted her to inflict on Jimmy, she would have to work fast on the next round.

'And oh, what a round it was', Jimmy thought to himself. He had unleashed a tiger, never having experienced a woman this passionate in his life. He was a mass of scratches and bites and he savored every one of them, as it was proof, to him at least, that he was a virile sexual beast in his own right. This time he ejaculated inside her and promptly collapsed.

Melinda served him a drink after round two of sex . As he drank, he was anticipating round three and started feeling woozy. He realized he needed to lie down but managed to last long enough to have a second drink, all the time admiring Melinda's dancing.

———

Ron Dahle

"I deserve a tip!" Melinda said to Joe as she got into his car with Jimmy's laptop in tow.

"That bad, huh?" Joe replied.

"Worse, you can't imagine. This is precisely why I work the hotels I do; they cater to a totally different clientele. This dude rated high in crass and low in class."

"Well, we will see if we can salvage your night for you," Joe said to Melinda as he reached over and rubbed her thigh.

On the way back to Joe's room, he suggested they stop by the reflecting pool for a drink and a romantic stroll in the moonlight. Joe pulled over and poured them both a glass of Champagne to celebrate. Melinda smiled as she looked at Joe and said, "This is what I mean about class." She finished her second glass of Champagne while they were getting ready to take that romantic stroll around the pool.

———

It was about 9:30 the next morning when little Jamie's parents heard him hollering from the woods. They ignored him at first, as this was normal behavior for Jamie, a very hyperactive four year old. He got their attention when he came out of the woods, beside the reflecting pool, covered in blood. He took his parents into the trees and showed them the dead woman hidden in the bushes.

The crime scene revealed little other than the fact that this was where the murder happened, based on the volume of blood present. The victim had her throat slit and her jugular vein severed in what appeared to be one continuous movement; obviously inflicted by one who had done this before.

———

Joe was cruising at 35,000 feet enroute to Columbia about the same time Melinda's body reached the city morgue. He was excited to be going back to work. He had to be at the Academy in Columbia in order to segregate as much C-4 and Det Cord as possible upon the closing of the academy for the spring. Bert would fly in, pick Joe and the munitions up and take them straight to Wolfeboro when he was finished.

It only took the FBI lab a couple of days to process the DNA from under Melinda's fingernails and from the sperm samples collected from all over and within her. As suspected, it was a perfect match to Jimmy Paxon. The lab also found traces of GHB in her system. Things did not bode well for young Jimmy, thought Agent Summerall, who worked alongside the DC police during the entire investigation. The FBI entered the case from the beginning, as Melinda had one of Jimmy Paxon's business cards in her clutch bag when they found her. The DNA evidence coupled with finding the empty Champagne bottle with her fingerprints on it under the seat of Jimmy's car, all of which was topped off by finding the bloody knife used to kill Melinda under Jimmy's bed made this case a slam-dunk. True, Jimmy had a record of drinking and was a known womanizer, but this shocked even his most ardent critics.

Chapter 3

Ron (the Deacon) had almost fully recovered from the gunshot wound he received on Christmas Eve during the Martinez operation in Mexico. As well he should be, he had Steve, the resident team's Physician's Assistant who had taken as many lives as he had saved, checking on him several times daily. He also had the constant doting by Mary Jane who had turned from "a girl Friday" to an office manager who then turned lover and now a full time nurse. Although he had seen better days, he had also seen a lot worse, Ron thought with a smile as he remembered days recovering in a hospital from a wound and being cared for by a nurse that didn't give him any pussy.

Ron was in the middle of lunch when Joe called him. "Hey, Top, I just arrived in Columbia and wanted to check in and see how you are doing."

"Hell, I'm going stir crazy. Did you take care of the business you needed to tend to in DC?"

"Hell yes. You would have been proud of me. I will tell you all about it when I get back. Duffy and crew did a good job on their own down here. They are starting the last class tomorrow. Duffy and his instructors will be leaving here in about a month. They plan to take two weeks off before they return to Wolfeboro. By then, I should have closed out the logistic end of it here and will also be on my way back."

"That's good, as we are scheduled for an additional twelve instructors the first of April. The first class will arrive on Sunday, the 15th, and it just goes on from there. Larry D has been informed that I am taking over the entire CIA contract as of 15 April, and he has a royal case of the ass over that, especially since our mission and staffing has just doubled.

"With the additional instructors, they are going to run the classes back to back with no break in between. The Buffalo will bring in a new class when it comes to pick up the graduating class. That was why I was in such a rush to put in our additional bunkers last fall. I knew we wouldn't have time to do it unobserved this year.

"Serf just hit another cash return on the border. This will be the fourth one he has policed up, with an average of $400,000 per score, not bad at all. It keeps us in Cognac and pussy anyway.

"No word on the paperwork we are waiting for from Fred yet, but I expect it before you get back here."

"I assume I will be starting my worldwide tour when I return?" Joe asked, hoping for an affirmative response.

"As a matter of fact, you will. Bob has already started creating electronic accounts around the world. 'Operation Bankrupt' will be well underway by the time you return.

"As for here, we are preparing the cadre quarters to accommodate the additional team members. We have five billets in the cantonment area; we are putting two cadre members in each building in private cadre rooms. We are furnishing them now, so we haven't really been sitting on our asses either."

"Ok Top, just wanted to give you a status report and catch up with your end. Have to run; I have a lot of catching up to do here. We'll talk later."

Ron poured another cup of coffee as he was pondering the past year. Overall, he had to categorize the year as a great success. Five major operations, all successful, only sustaining three losses and one being wounded.

Through his relationship with an ex-team leader and friend, Larry N, Ron was awarded the CIA contract to run the Academy. The mission of conducting clandestine operations along the Mexican border was part of this new arrangement.

Additionally, the academy was doubling in size and scope this year in cadre, students, and in number of classes. This equated to millions of dollars in contractual payments from the CIA. But the real benefit was that now Ron was able to divert more weapons, ammunition and explosives from each class to equip his envisioned Army of freedom fighters.

One of the operations resulted in Ron acquiring a Russian-built cargo plane, the Antonov AN-12, in a raid in Mexico. It was loaded with numerous RPG-29s with ammunition as well as many SAM missiles. The plane and all of the weapons had been smuggled out of Libya before the government fell. There was also a large quantity of VX nerve gas as well as Mustard gas on the plane, and last but not least it had three lead-encased containers, all marked with the universal symbol indicating the contents were radioactive. The plane was now resting in Bert's hangar, and the bulk of the weapons in Ron's underground bunkers.

The formalization and vetting of Ron's operation with the CIA resulted, among other things, in Ron and all of his remote operators receiving secure satellite phone links, which were a great asset. Larry N insured that Ron and his operators had their own dedicated cypher keys for the phones, as Larry did not want any possibility of anyone else tapping in on them. This would be especially convenient when Joe goes off on his global tour to set up accounts in banks all over the world, a key component of "Operation Bankrupt". Filthy Fred was handling the thirty sets of passports and identification Joe will need to pull off that caper.

The Deacon has decided the most effective way he could help prevent the President from being re-elected was to leave all his major donors as well as the world's leading advocates of Globalism flat broke. Ron, with help from Larry N and Bob H in California, had figured out how to accomplish that. Bob had already established in excess of 150 offshore numbered accounts. Joe was going to set up an additional 150 accounts around the world.

Larry had had a team of the Agency's best forensic accountants gathering account numbers and access codes to all of the individuals on which Ron had provided data. When the operation kicked off, in a two day period all of their accounts would be electronically drained and the monies would start a journey through a labyrinth of over 300 different electronic accounts, never resting anywhere for more than a day. There were several switchbacks and safeguards built into the system to make tracing the money impossible. Larry and Ron estimated that, at its peak, there will be in excess of $670,000,000,000 traveling through cyberspace at the speed of light, stopping off just long enough to split and change directions. The program was designed to split monies from a particular source into separate bundles of $20,000,000 and send them on different paths where they again split and are forwarded; this process would continue until, ultimately, the money will come to rest in ten separate numbered accounts. Bob claimed that from the beginning until the end there would be over five million separate transactions involved in masking the final destination of this money.

Adding insult to injury, this event will fall under Homeland Security, who will pass the investigation off to the CIA. The same group of forensic accountants that facilitated this operation would insure it is never solved.

As Ron was sitting there, pondering the scale of the entire operation, it finally dawned on him that, once initiated, he would become the single richest man in the world. That was a long way from the days of being a private in the Army drawing $68.00 per month with a wife and child to support.

———

　　　　　　　　　　　　　　　　　　　　Ron Dahle

Chapter 4

Serf called with his weekly situation report. "Hey Batman, how's it hanging? I want to thank Steve for the medical supply drop he made on us. Wilson was tickled to death with it, as were we all."

"Not a problem, we're here to serve," commented the Deacon sarcastically. "What's going on in your area of operations (AO), anything I should know about?"

"Tommy and Wilson took out another drug return last night; it netted $472,000—a big one. For the first time, there were three personnel on the return—two carrying the rucksacks and the other was just tagging along. Additionally, they were more heavily armed than they have been in the past. I am not sure what that means."

"I'll tell you what it means; they are obviously tired of getting hit and losing the money. You need to stop the cash recovery operation for a while, and just lay low; I don't want to conduct another body recovery operation just for the sake of money. Bring Tommy and Wilson back across the border and I will arrange with Bert to get you guys and the money back here for a while. You should now have the cash from four different hits, if my memory serves me right. Remember, as far as Tommy and Wilson know, this cash must be turned in to the CIA.

"When we reinsert you, I want maximum emphasis placed on Hezbollah and Hamas agents. We've just received word that we lost an entire team that we trained last summer. All indications point to a combination of Mexican cartel members and Hamas as the ones responsible for taking them out. This is the only business where we bury our mistakes; remember that on your cross border ventures."

"Ok, Batman, I will get on bringing Tommy and Wilson back here. That may take several days; I'll let you know when they close in on my location."

"Sounds good. Keep me posted. Later, dude."

Ron had no sooner hung up with Serf that he called Larry N. "Hey Larry, I just want to inform you I am pulling Serf and his crew back here for a couple of weeks. We need to re-orient them in what their primary mission is. They are still chasing drug smugglers, which is ok. However, I want to get it across to them their major role is pursuing Hezbollah and Hamas agents.

"Personally, I think they are still a little gun-shy after losing Gentry the way they did."

"That could well be the case, Top. When you get them back at the academy, give me a call. I will come up and we can have a pow-wow about the Mexican operation, to include its priorities, and what impact it can have on America."

"I was hoping you would come up with something like that. We have gone too far to screw this up now."

"So true. Other than that, Top, what is going on in your world?"

"I talked to Bob H today and he already has 150 numbered offshore accounts in place. I am contemplating bringing Joe back early and having him kick off his whirlwind world tour as soon as Fred comes through with the passports and IDs. The downside of that is I have no one to take his place in closing the Academy out. Of course, I could always go myself."

"Hey, the break could do you good. Why don't you grab Mary Jane and head on down to Columbia? That will free Joe up to start as soon as we can kick this SOB off. My people have all the information Bob needs to make it happen. Have you ever figured out what in hell you are going to do with all that money?"

"No, I haven't, but I assure you it is all going back into America and saving her from the course she is on now. As far as my going to Columbia, you have a good idea there; I think I may just do that. That will kill two birds with one stone. I'll plan to depart right after we meet with Serf and his crew. By the way, Bob H just called and asked for another mainframe so he could have a redundant system in the event of a problem. I told him to go ahead and get it. That old man has compiled more computer power in his house than NASA has online in Houston."

"If that's what it takes to do the job, by all means get it. Shit, get him two," Larry said jokingly. Ok, Top, I've got to get off this phone and get some work done. Give me a call when Serf is due in."

Ron paged Mary Jane to drop down to the war room. She arrived with two cups of coffee. "What's up, babe?" she asked.

"Thanks for the coffee, hon. Just for curiosity's sake, is your passport up to date?"

"Yes, why do you ask?"

"I am thinking of pulling Joe out of Columbia for a different mission. If I do that, I will have to go down and replace him and I thought you might enjoy the trip. We would be there about one to two months if we go. Are you interested?"

"Well, yeah…what a stupid question that was. It's February in New Hampshire, dummy, why in hell wouldn't I want to go to the tropics? Where would we be staying if we go?"

"In the Commandant's Villa, complete with maid service and a private cook, I might add."

"And you thought you had to ask me if I wanted to go? You are such a…man. Why in hell would I not want to go?" asked Mary Jane again with a smile.

"Ok then, transfer all your working files and payroll data to your laptop so you can handle them from there. This works out great; now I won't have to buy any pussy while I am there."

Mary Jane just glared at him. "If you plan on getting laid while we are there, that may be the only way you will ...asshole."

Ron set his cup down, went over, hugged Mary Jane, and asked, "Ok, so how much do you charge anyway?"

"That depends on how much you piss me off on a daily basis; on a good day you might get a freebee, but on a really bad day it would bankrupt you," Mary Jane smiled.

"Ok, hon, we will plan for that. I have Serf and his crew coming up soon for a pep talk. We will plan to head out as soon as that is over. It should be an enjoyable trip. I have a couple of weeks' work to do spread over the time frame we will be there, depending on how much Joe gets done before we arrive, and then we can take a short vacation afterwards.

"Right now, I have a major project set up in Fayetteville next week. The headhunter I have been dealing with has over 40 people for me to interview for the additional group to come up and join the Cadre. You should probably accompany me on that, as I intend to make my decisions while I am there. I already have their resumes, and the status of their security clearances."

"That works for me; that way I will be able to get a head start on initiating the paperwork for their security clearances," Mary Jane said.

The interviews went well. One of the prospects Ron decided to hire was Ronnie Mac, with whom Ron served at Fort Devens in the early eighties. Ronnie Mac retired as a Command Sergeant Major, which did not surprise the Deacon at all, since he was a hard charging young buck sergeant when Ron retired, and there was no doubt he was going to excel. The rest of the choices weren't that easy, although he eventually got the twelve prospective candidates selected, along with four alternates. Mary Jane got all the information needed for the payroll, as well as to update their security clearances. They would be ready to roll as soon as they arrived.

———

Serf, Tommy, and Wilson were already at the Academy by the time Ron and Mary Jane got back from Fayetteville. Ron immediately called Larry to arrange for him to come up later in the week, after the Mexico crew had a chance to relax a bit. One of the first orders of business was for Ron to collect all the monies captured on the cash return operations that they conducted. Ron had long since run out of space for this cash; this is what the secret room was for in the last set of bunkers John had built. The only problem was that it was full of VX and Mustard gas that everyone thought got dumped last summer.

There were in excess of fifteen million dollars in it before the proceeds from the past four cash return operations Serf had just turned in. The Deacon realized that, when John came up this summer, he needed to build an underground walk-in safe that was only accessible from the war room. We probably need to put that safe on order now, as it will definitely need to be custom-built, thought Ron.

———

The meeting with Larry was a low-key attaboy affair congratulating the crew for their many successes. At the same time he stressed the shifting of priorities back to their primary mission of identifying and eliminating members of radical Islamic movements.

"This is the largest threat America has right now, although the administration refuses to acknowledge it. We need to keep it under control as much as humanly possible before it gets too large to contain. You, Warriors, are our front line in this battle. The Columbians and Nicaraguans we are training at the Academy are having limited success, but realize they are only stopping part of the infiltrators. We lost an entire team a while back so, as you know, it is no game. It's up to you to get who our graduates miss," Larry said.

Ron interjected, "I have studied the after action report on the death of Gentry in great detail. It is my opinion that from a team point of view there is absolutely nothing you did to cause that to happen. We don't have the specifics of Gentry's actions leading up to the capture, but I assure you your actions were sound. There is nothing that could have been done differently to alter the outcome. Sometimes you can do everything right and it still goes to shit. Remember, we are running a low-tech boot-on-the-ground operation here. I am amazed at the successes we have enjoyed. Cool your heels around here for another week and get ready to go charge them again. America is counting on you."

"Deacon, I think I speak for all of us, we are ready to return to the mission ASAP. We have already been off station over a week as it is," Serf said with the others nodding in agreement.

Ron had Mary Jane arrange for their travel back to Deming the next day. She also booked Ron and her flight to Columbia in three days.

"Damn, Top, I just got unpacked and you are shipping me out again," Joe said smiling.

"Joe, you need to stick around for a week or so to help me get my feet on the ground here and show me the ropes as well as what you have been working on."

"Top, you need to know that we have received a report that someone has been watching the Academy for a while now. I am not sure who or why."

"Ok, set up a concrete maze barrier at the front gate and close off all of the other gates. Double the guard on the gate and have the students carry their weapons and ammo with them at all times while they are on the compound. That means for classes, PT, everything."

"Wilco, Top, will start on it immediately."

Ron was a little surprised and disappointed that Joe had not taken that action on his own. Assignments like this can lull one into a false sense of security, Ron thought, and Columbia is not the place to be caught napping.

Ron was getting the hang of the operation and the methods Joe was using to divert explosives that Ron would bring back to the Lodge. Actually, it was a piece of cake. Mary Jane was spending more time on the payroll and proposals than Ron was spending at his job. Although she totally enjoyed having her own maid and cook.

―――――

"Hey, babe," Ron said to Mary Jane, "how about we take Joe out to lunch tomorrow as he is leaving tomorrow night for the Lodge. Freddie just told me Joe's paperwork will be in within a week."

"That sounds like a great idea to me. Is there anything you want me to do?"

"Just be your ravishing beautiful self during lunch. And, oh yes, there is one other thing, you can give me some pussy when you have a chance," Ron said with a grin.

Mary Jane smiled, grabbed Ron and tugged him toward the bedroom. "This is the best thing that is going to happen to you all week," she said as she was unbuttoning her blouse. (Little did either of them know just how true that statement was.)

―――――

Mary Jane, Joe and Ron were walking back to the compound after lunch when, just as they were abreast the barrier, Ron saw a truck accelerating towards the gate. Ron instinctively drew his pistol and shot the driver four times. The driver slumped to the left, steering the truck away from the gate. Ron grabbed Mary Jane, threw her over the barrier, and jumped over it right after her. Joe was already there. Ron had no sooner landed that the truck exploded.

Mary Jane stood up, fairly well bruised all over, looked at Ron, and said, "So this is what you do for a fucking living!? I often wondered," with a hint of a nervous smile on her face.

Ron was happy to see that she was able to maintain her composure and even a hint of a sense of humor after this event as he took her in his arms.

A quick inspection showed that the truck had driven through a deserted warehouse and exploded in there confining the blast to that structure, which was nearly demolished.

"Joe, there is a minor change in plans. I want you to supervise the entire crew in beefing up the security of this compound. Redouble the concrete maze, do it on the inside of the front gate also. I want a double layer of razor wire along the top of the fence and a triple layer razor concertina barrier around the entire internal perimeter of the compound as well as a roving patrol at night.

"It is obvious someone has figured out who we are and what we are doing," Ron said to Joe and Dewey. "This isn't a game changer, but we will have to start paying a little more attention to what's going on around us on a regular basis.

"We need to double up on the security until the new barrier and the fencing is in. I will discuss this with our host nation counterparts tomorrow. Joe, you go ahead to the Lodge, Dewey can handle this, plus I am here. I really need you to start on your trip."

"Quite a vacation you are taking me on, old man," quipped Mary Jane. "I must say this is the first time I have ever had the opportunity to be blown up on vacation."

"Hell, babe, stick with me. You ain't seen nothing yet."

"I know, that's what I'm afraid of."

"I doubt we have anything to worry about; by the time they can regroup, the class and cadre will be gone and there won't be any reason to strike.

"I have about a week of work here closing the camp out and then we will take a week to do some travelling. We will have to come back here to pick up some stuff that we have to bring back to the Lodge with us. Hell, by the time we get back the new instructors will start to trickle in. Steve knows what to do with them till I get back."

Ron was thinking that Joe did a great job of segregating C-4 and Det Cord for the Warriors. There were over 300 pounds of C-4 and 3,000 feet of Det Cord, including both electrical and non-electrical blasting caps with wire and fuse. This would do well to replenish the supplies used on the Mexican tunnel and warehouse job they conducted several months ago. Now it was just a matter of packaging it all and getting it to the airport when Bert arrived.

Ron and Mary Jane talked about the relative security in Columbia and decided that they would go back to the Lodge as soon as Ron was finished. Mary Jane had had all of the Columbian excitement she wanted for a while.

Chapter 5

Bert landed right on time. Ron and Mary Jane were there, waiting with their cargo, and were really happy to see Bert. Once the cargo was loaded, Ron brought Mary Jane back to the gun turret and showed her the hole in the skin of the plane that the bullet that wounded him on Christmas Eve made. She just glared at Ron and went forward to grab a seat. Ron took the radioman's seat and Mary Jane sat in the navigator's seat. Peter was co-piloting today. Bert determined that, unless it was under dire conditions, the Albatross definitely needed a co-pilot.

The flight was uneventful; it was flying under CIA mandate, which allowed it to bypass international airports, thereby avoiding customs. They did land in Clovis, New Mexico, to refuel, and then flew straight to Wolfeboro. Steve and Joe were there to meet them. Joe had just returned from picking up his identities and passports from Freddie and was flying out to London in the morning. He had an itinerary that would make one dizzy just looking at it. He had 90 legs to his journey, in some cases scheduled to hit two countries in a single day, and often setting up several accounts in the same city under different names. Joe told Ron that Bob wanted him to call him as soon as he returned.

Both Ronnie Mac and Dewey were already there. They knew and liked each other, so that was one issue that wouldn't have to be dealt with. Nothing is worse than a pissing contest between two Sergeants Major.

Ron called Bob to be brought up to date on "Operation Bankrupt".

"Hey, old man, you got that other mainframe on line yet?"

"Hell yes, I had ordered it before I even asked you, and it's a good thing I did. Instead of a redundant system, I am utilizing them in tandem to speed this whole process up. Once the actual transfers start taking place, we will need all the computer power we can get."

"Is that a hint for two more?" asked Ron.

"It wasn't, but that wouldn't hurt either. It would allow for the level of redundancy we really need."

"Go ahead and order them, they will pay for themselves in the long run."

"That was a wise decision, my friend. As for this end, I have created 150 separate numbered accounts all over the world. I have completed the algorithms that will accomplish the actual transferring and re-bundling of the cash. All of these transactions are to be processed in a circuitous series of servers located in the Cayman Islands, Singapore, Thailand, and Vietnam. There is no way to trace it back to here. Basically, the only thing I am missing is the input from Joe."

"Could you start the withdrawals and transfers before you get Joe's data? He will be able to update you daily with his new accounts via the sat-link."

"Who said you were a dumb ass? Yes, that would definitely work. My only concern is one which we have discussed before, and that is causing a banking crisis here in America with so much money being withdrawn in a short period."

"I have considered the same thing, and while at one time I thought that pacing the withdrawals was the way to go, I have changed my stance on it.

"If we go at it slowly, we will tip our hand and they may stop all electronic withdrawals. If we do it overnight, it may well put the banks into a chaotic position, but so what? That is just more fodder to support the claim that the President has screwed up the entire economy. Basically, it is a win-win situation for us.

"You have done well. Proceed with the operation as soon as the other two mainframes are on line."

"That will take a week or so, as I am ordering these two from separate dealers, one on the East Coast and one in the Mid-West. I don't want to raise any flags in the system.

"By the way, I trust you won't object to my drawing most of my cash out of the bank?" Bob asked smiling.

"Not at all, that's probably a good idea. I may do the same. Keep me posted, my friend.

"The next project I want you to look into once this gets cooking is the best way to convert the bulk of this money into gold and silver bullion and coinage and get it back here. I expect the dollar to take a nosedive shortly, and I want to be protected."

Ron then called Larry N and Vince and appraised them on the progress of the operation. What he failed to tell them was how soon this was going to happen. He did suggest that they consider diversifying their portfolios at the earliest possible date, and to consider gold and silver coins for a large part of it.

During his conversation with Vince, he told Ron he had some maps he wanted him to check out. "They are in the National Forest near Deming. The Forest is closed for the sake of security due to the illegals in the area, but we have coverage of a trickling of illegals passing through it with some holding up within the forest.

"On several occasions, we have picked up heat signatures of a single person that seemed to be scouting the area. When you have a chance, maybe this is something Serf and his crew can check out."

"This may well be a good confidence builder for them; I will be waiting for the photos."

Ron sat back and realized that he had not been back at the Lodge for 24 hours yet and he was already up to his neck in the war for the heart and soul of America.

In a meeting with Duffy and Ronnie Mac, Ron divided the leadership responsibility between the two of them equally on all issues. That sat well with both of them, especially with Duffy, as he knew Ron and Ronnie Mac went back a long way. The rest of the instructors were due in tomorrow and the next day. Ron told the two of them that, as soon as they got the cadre settled in, he wanted a meeting with them. He also advised them that in addition to being the head medic, Steve was going to be working as his assistant during Joe's absence.

———

Ron called Serf after the photos arrived from Vince and brought him up to speed on what he knew about the situation.

"Shit, Batman, this will be a piece of cake. We will get on it starting tomorrow. I will send Tommy in with a sniper rifle and a couple of claymores to see what he can come up with. Hell, we may just stumble across another sleeper cell."

"Yeah, well, be careful. That Forest belongs to the cartel and God only knows who else. I am also interested in this lone soul who wanders around in there. See what you can come up with for me. I will have the photos to you tomorrow afternoon." In the meantime, the Deacon gave Serf the GPS coordinates of several sightings from the photographs so they could get started on the operation.

———

Ray MacDonald was traversing the side of a hill looking for the man he had sighted a while ago. Based on his initial sighting, his quarry was a Mexican, likely a cartel watchdog. Ray moved silently through the forest, a befitting example of his Apache warrior heritage. His tracking skills could not be learned, they were part of his heritage. His Indian name was Light Shadow. He could remember his grandfather telling him that no one can see a light shadow. Ray thought that based on some of his experiences in Iraq and Afghanistan his grandfather may have been on to something. He'd had five tours between the two of them and came out pretty well, unscathed, with only two minor wounds that were treated locally, a feat which was totally unheard of for a Marine with that many combat tours.

He suddenly came to a complete halt. He spotted his prey approximately 450 yards to his left front and about 100 feet lower on the hill than Ray was. He studied him with his binoculars and determined that, yes indeed, this was an illegal Mexican who was armed with an AK-47.

Ray silently brought his Model-1891/30 Mosin Nagant to his cheek, steadied the rifle against a tree, and set his elevation on the scope for 400 yards. Carefully centering the crosshairs in the low center of the chest cavity due to the downward shooting angle, he ever so gently squeezed the trigger. As soon as he felt the trigger break, he watched as his prey fell in his tracks. This makes seventeen, Ray thought as he headed back out of the forest.

Ray never believed in his heart that he would be able to reclaim the National Forest, but he was determined to give it a good try. This land was special to Ray since most of it was part of his ancestral grounds.

He headed back to the location where he had parked his truck and then drove to his great-grandfather's small farm where he was staying. It was austere, but felt akin to a palace when he considered some of the conditions he'd lived under in Afghanistan.

He had mixed emotions about his tours in Iraq and Afghanistan. Ray was a Marine through and through. A third generation combat Marine and not afraid of telling anyone how bad he was. This characteristic led to the only problems he had in the Corps. He was jealous of the missions he saw the Special Forces go out on, on a regular basis. He believed most of those missions should have been assigned to the Marines, but instead the Marines were guarding the Special Forces. This led to several encounters between Ray and the Special Forces. It got to the point that Ray's commander had to give him a direct order to avoid the Special Forces troops.

He'd retired two years ago as a well decorated Master Gunnery Sergeant. He wished his father and grandfather had lived to see him retire. He got ready to turn in for the night, as he had to get an early start in the morning, to continue his mission.

"Hey, Top, you never told me when you offered me a trip around the world where I wouldn't get to see anything except the inside of trains, jets, taxicabs, and banks. At some point in time, you owe me a real vacation," Joe said laughing.

"Yeah, I know you are pressed for time. How are you doing overall?"

"Great, I will wrap up Europe tomorrow, then to Southeast Asia and that region, and then off to the Caribbean and South America. I am keeping Bob posted on what I am doing."

"That is great. He is expecting his additional mainframes in this week; we will be able to kick this operation off shortly. Joe, you keep up the good work. We need you back here too, you know. We have a major personnel flap I am going to have to get involved in tomorrow. Talk to you later. Get a little Asian pussy for me, too, while you're at it next week."

The entire cadre was seated in one of the classrooms when the Deacon arrived.

"Good morning, men. We have students arriving in four days. Do all of you feel confident in what your role is in this operation and where you fit in in the overall scheme of things?"

One man raised his hand. "Sir, my name is Otis Neilson, and I have a grievance I would like to air. I am a retired Lieutenant Colonel in the US Army and I resent working under two ex-enlisted men. Additionally, the billets I have been assigned to in the troop area is not befitting of my position. I really feel I should be afforded the respect of a room in the Apple Cabin, as you call it."

"Well, Mr. Otis Neilson, your problem is nowhere near as big as you think it is. First, there is no rank here! I have two men in charge who have earned my respect and full confidence! Since you brought rank into the picture, let us look at it a minute. Like Dewey and Ronnie Mac, I, too, am a retired Command Sergeant Major. You are only a retired Lt. Colonel. Do the math! For a CSM to get to his level, he has to be recommended, evaluated, and judged a total of ten times. To make Lt. Colonel, you are evaluated a total of four times! I call it the wall locker syndrome. You lock a private and a lieutenant in a wall locker for fifteen years, open them up, and you have a private and a Lt. Colonel.

"As I told you at the beginning, your problem is not nearly as dire as you suggested it was. When this meeting is over, I want your bags packed. In the morning, you will be provided transportation to the Manchester airport. You are released from this assignment effective immediately. My secretary, Mary Jane, will get your travel information from you and have your ticket tonight.

"Are there any other questions or points anyone would like to bring up? If not, I am looking forward to seeing you in the training area."

Ron called Larry N and apprised him of this situation. "For some strange reason that doesn't surprise me one bit, Top, you always had a bit of contempt for rank. That is one of the qualities I liked about you, you wouldn't back down if you were right. Is there anything else I should know?"

"Yeah, Joe is wrapping up the European swing tomorrow, then it's off to Southeast Asia for him. Bob is receiving his additional mainframes as we speak. He anticipates being able to start withdrawing by Saturday morning. By Monday, there will be financial calamity across America, no, in reality—the world. We will be able to relocate and divide the funds faster than they can track them until suddenly they will run into programmed dead ends. At that point, my brand of Cognac will change."

"Top, I have to hand it to you, if this works it will go down as the biggest banking scheme in history. Do you have any idea what in hell you are going to do with all that money?"

"Hell, the same thing the Democrats would have done, buy a President! At least, mine will have the best interest of America in mind. I also plan to replace most of Congress and the Senate. If you have been in office over eight years…pack your bags.

"There are many worthwhile causes out there that could really benefit from an anonymous donation of several million dollars. And lest we forget, if push comes to shove, I have a revolution to fund," Ron said with a grin.

"I know, that's what worries me."

"The one thing we do know is this caper will never be duplicated. By the time the smoke clears on this, the banking industry, or what's left of it, will have more safeguards in place than you can count. This is going to be a one of a kind operation, so we may as well go for it with gusto!" Ron said, leaving Larry to contemplate on the actual scale of this caper and questioning what he had facilitated.

In the meantime, Bob was making the final connections between his mainframes and testing them out. He was excited about what was about to happen. He had been a closet hacker for over 20 years now, and boasted in private that he had hacked into every network in the DOD, to say nothing about foreign governments, and still has not been caught. He fully realized this operation would put his abilities to the ultimate test.

He was thinking about the one account he had set up that no one else knew about. He had no intention of being greedy, since at his age there wasn't much he could do with a large sum of money anyway, but it was good to know it was there in the event he ever needed it.

Chapter 6

Tommy had studied the maps intensely. He had discovered a network of trails throughout the forest that were likely man made, as had they been game trails they would have been laid out much more efficiently.

He had been watching this younger Anglo tracking the area, hunting Mexican drug runners. Tommy had witnessed him kill three to date, and it looked like the fourth was about to occur. He was damn good, thought Tommy. He expected the answers to his identity to be cleared up as soon as his photo, GPS coordinates of his cabin, and license plate number that Tommy sent in yesterday were tracked down.

On one occasion, Tommy followed him to his cabin about 30 miles from here. He figured this was one dedicated son of a bitch to make that drive daily to kill a stranger, and then go home just to come back the next day and do it all again.

Tommy was not as dedicated. He discovered a cave on the hillside, well off the beaten path. He was spending his nights in there, getting up early enough to spot "the stalker", as Tommy had named him, "coming to work" as it were. He was wondering how long the stalker could get by with his activities before he screwed up. Granted, he was good. No, he was excellent, but Tommy knew we are all fallible and it only takes one mistake to end a life in this business.

Raymond was fixing himself a batch of canned beans and sausage for supper and thinking about today's activities. It was a clean kill, but something had been bothering Raymond. For several days, he'd had the feeling he was being watched. He thought back to his grandfather's teaching: "Remember, Light Shadow, you come from a long line of fallen warriors and you carry the protection of them whenever you go into battle. Never forget, you have the blood of the greatest war chief who has ever lived flowing in your veins." Ray was wondering if he was sensing the presence of his ancestors as his grandfather had told him he would.

But there was more to it and Ray doubted his ancestors' spirits would be able to help with that one. He pondered his current path and the fact that, while killing a man was the hardest thing he'd ever had to do, in the case of defending his grounds he felt a complete inability to stop. He didn't know if it was his strong desire to reclaim the tribal lands which were now denied to him by a murderous band of Mexicans, and some from the Middle East, or if the urge to kill ran deeper, as he recalled the enjoyment he derived as a sniper after a kill.

After supper, he cleaned his Mosin-Nagant rifle. It was his pride and joy, given to him by his father. Ray had it chambered for the more powerful 30.06 caliber that almost doubled the effective range on it. It was as accurate today as the day it came off the line.

———————

Tommy got up and put on his Ghillie suit that had served him well over the years. He grabbed his Winchester Model 70, checked the scope zero, and set out to find the stalker since he knew it was about time for him to show up. He was walking higher on the hill than the stalker usually did. He was in a protected stand, just watching, when he saw three armed Mexicans walking lower on the hill, taking up a position to observe the lowlands. The first thing that came into Tommy's mind was ambush. Tommy saw the stalker before the Mexicans did due to his altitude. As soon as he saw the stalker, he set the range on his scope for the Mexicans and drew a bead on the one in the middle.

When the stalker came into the Mexicans' view, they started to position themselves to shoot him. That was as far as they got. Tommy took two of them out before the stalker realized there was a problem. Then Tommy took the third out and stood a moment to make sure they were dead.

Ray saw Tommy high on the hill. Their eyes met and Tommy saluted Ray and disappeared into the forest as if he was part of it. Ray could tell he was an older man, but he had seen him a thousand times. He was definitely a Special Forces soldier, Ray could tell that by the way he carried himself, to say nothing of making three successive 350 yard downhill one shot kills.

Ray took off to find Tommy, but had no luck, although he was able to find the vacated cave Tommy had stayed in.

———

Serf and Tommy were debating on what to do about the "stalker". "Obviously, he is on a mission. Not sure what his end game is, though. It sort of dovetails with what we are doing. He would be a lot more effective working the Mexican side of the border, though. What do you think?" Serf asked Tommy.

"I've watched him up close and personal. He is good, he glides through the forest like a cougar, attacking at will on an unsuspecting prey. I checked his cabin out one day after he had left for the hunt. He lives a very Spartan existence. I would guess that his can opener and his rifle are the two most utilized articles he has at the cabin. If there is one area he splurges on it is with his reloading equipment. He is set up to reload both 30.06 ammo as well as ACP .45 calibers. He uses only the best rounds available, and top notch brass; he takes his shooting seriously. I also saw two different pattern Ghillie suits there and he left with one. If I were to venture a guess, I would pick him as a person who is totally predisposed to kill, and very possibly enjoying it; the question is why?"

"Hell, he sounds like a lot of our friends. Maybe the Deacon will be able to fill in some of the blanks for us once the data you collected gets processed. Shit, we may have us a new recruit if he checks out ok. That could allow three of us at a time to handle the Mexican side of the border."

———

Chapter 7 — Power Up

The Deacon was waiting to hear from Bob, as today was the big day. Bob was going to initiate "Operation Bankrupt." Bob selected early Saturday morning for the beginning, since the financial world remains closed until Monday morning, giving the process a longer time to work, at which time all hell would break loose. Joe had already established over 70 separate accounts that Bob integrated into his matrix. Joe wrapped up his SEA tour with Bangkok that same day, and then he was off to Singapore.

Ron was thinking that this'd better work, as he had over $350,000 tied up in this project already, with more to come, but that paled in comparison to the potential of this operation.

Bob called. "It's too late to turn back now," he said. "I kicked it off fifteen minutes ago, All we can do now is let the machines do their thing and see what comes out in a couple of weeks, when everything finally lands. I have calculated approximately one point three trillion dollars it is going to be shuffling throughout cyberspace. That does not mean we will get that much, as some accounts may have additional safeguards built into them that got by me. All we can do is wait and see."

"That is a hell of a lot more than we discussed earlier, basically double. Why the increase? Bad estimates or greed?"

"A little of both," replied Bob. "When I started looking into the accounts, I discovered quite a few that had a lot more in them than we had estimated initially. Apparently, some of the "elite" have a lot more than they own up to. It gets interesting when you start on their offshore accounts. We are going to put Hollywood and the pro sports world into cardiac arrest."

"It will be interesting to see how this turns out in the end. At the beginning, I was quasi joking about this project, not ever imagining it was remotely possible," Ron said.

"Ah, but you forget, my friend, that the light bulb started out as an obscure dream, too. You underestimated my ability when it comes to hacking as well as the ability of Larry N to provide us with the basic data we needed, enabling us to put it all together to kick this off. Then there is you, whose foresight and gut instinct said to go for it even though your head said no. That trait, my friend, is called leadership, gutsy, but leadership nonetheless! Risk aversion is not one of your traits, which oftentimes is a good thing. We have a government full of sheep that wouldn't make a decision under any conditions.

"I am getting more accounts from Joe daily, which serves to widen our footprint in cyberspace. We now have a high number of unlinked innocuous sites all over the world where we can float this money in as long as we want to.

"With help from Larry N, there is virtually no chance of getting caught. What will do us in is any unaccounted lavish spending. That will raise red flags with the FBI and possibly the Rico Commission. So, while we may have it, we cannot squander it, at least not frivolously or beyond our ability to substantiate the income. Now, my friend, I have to monitor my pet project. Later."

———

Ron just sent the information to Serf about their mystery man. Contingent on what drives this Raymond character, he may be of use to Serf and his crew. Time will tell. It will take several face-to-face meetings before that determination can be made.

On the other hand, there is no indication that Raymond would be the least bit interested, as he may well be a loner. If so, more power to him, he is doing a good job, but he almost came to the end of his winning streak yesterday, Ron thought.

Chapter 8

The delivery Tommy and Serf had been waiting on just arrived. There was more excitement over its arrival than you would expect from a bunch of kids on Christmas morning.

As they pored over the documents, they were intrigued by what they read.

It seems the stalker, Raymond McDonald, was a third generation Marine. He retired at 22 years of service as a Master Gunnery Sergeant. The only blemish on his record was a letter of reprimand for allegedly numerous fights with Army Special Forces soldiers. It went on to state that Master Gunnery Sergeant McDonald was given a direct order to avoid all contact with Special Forces soldiers.

Well decorated, having received a Silver Star, two Bronze Stars, and two Purple Hearts during his career, he'd been a sniper on all of his tours to Iraq and Afghanistan. He is a descendent of Santana, the Great War Chief of the Mescalero Apache Tribe. Through the generations, his great grandfather's marrying a white woman forever diluted his heritage. While she was a jewel of the apache nation with her olive skin, large brown eyes, and long flowing black hair, she was the source of shame by Raymond. He resented the fact that his pure lineage was broken.

"This may well be why he is waging his own war in the National Forest, as that was all Indian land at one time. He may feel, rightly so, that his lineage is again under attack, this time by Mexicans and Arabs. I can fully understand that scenario," Serf stated.

"So where do we go from here, Serf?"

"I think I am going to give the Deacon a call and get his feelings on it before we proceed any further on this."

"Hey, Batman, how's it going, you still hanging in there?"

"Serf, you didn't call me to check on my well-being. What is going on in your AO?"

Serf recounted the information Tommy and he had collected about the stalker and how it fitted in with the documentation the Deacon had sent to them. "We are at a quandary on where to go with this; he could be a hell of an asset if we can get him to see the big picture and bring him on board. I question if he just isn't so obsessed with working in the Forest that he won't entertain an offer."

"Well, Serf, I am not sure I want to extend an offer yet anyway, at least not until we get to know a lot more about him. I am willing for you to give him a broad-brush idea of what we are doing. No specifics, though!

"I could consider providing him with aerial coverage of the forest every two weeks or so based on Vince's schedule. Let's try that and see what he does with it and we can take it from there."

"That sounds like a doable plan. I will send Tommy to meet him with a copy of the set of maps we already have, and we will take it from there and see what develops."

"I want both of you to go, armed and in Gilley suits. I want him to be able to relate to you on an equal footing, plus there is safety in numbers. We don't know what his reaction will be and I would rather play it on the safe side."

"That sounds like a reasonable approach, Batman. I just fucking knew we kept you around for a reason. We will initiate contact with him this week and get back with you on it."

"Sounds like a plan. Just watch your step, as I don't trust this mother fucker yet."

―――――

Ray was a little late leaving his cabin this morning. When he got outside, he noticed the two men leaning alongside his truck. Both in Gilley suits and both armed.

"Good morning, Gunny, got time for a cup of coffee?" said the one he recognized from the Forest.

"I suppose I have. That was one of the areas Special Forces really excelled at, drinking coffee."

Serf could not let that go unanswered. "True, when we weren't out saving dumb-asses' lives!"

"Come on in, I'll brew a pot. So what cause puts two old men in Gilley suits and has them take up arms?"

"Like you, we are driven to a goal, saving America. We are part of a larger group and concentrating in a completely different area than you. You were brought to our attention and we decided to check you out to see if you were friend or foe," said Serf.

"And did I pass your fucking test?" Ray asked arrogantly.

Tommy piped in, "Well, I killed three Mexicans who were getting ready to ambush you. This was after I watched you kill three other Mexicans on different occasions, so I guess you passed...since I decided to pull my trigger and save your ass."

Ray realized what he'd just heard and decided to knock off the belligerent attitude and see what these two were really up to, as he was stumped.

"Ok, guys, I have to give you that and I do appreciate it. So, what are your real motives?"

"Like I said, you were brought to our attention and we wanted to check you out for our own sake. We ran a very extensive background check on you and determined that you were not a foe. It remains to be seen if you are a friend.

"You have been playing a game of Russian roulette the way you have been hunting your targets. You have been targeting people who were using the same path. In a short period, you took out three within a two-mile radius. You drive in every day and some day that will bite you in the ass. You already established one pattern. The Mexicans figured that out and set up the ambush. You know the rest of that story.

"If you are going to do this, you need to be smarter and target different areas at different times. If you want, we can provide you updated aerial map coverage of the parts of the Forest you want to concentrate on about every two weeks."

"And what do you expect from me in return?"

"Simple, check your bodies. If you come across any goatfuckers, take any documents they may have and give them to us for processing. There is a large contingent of Hezbollah and Hamas just south of the border. They have been trying to infiltrate into the US. So far, we have done pretty well at stopping them, but we know that some are getting through in spite of our efforts."

"Ok, guys, I don't know who in hell you are, but you have yourself a deal."

"And you may well not know who we are for a while; just realize we are all on the same side. I am going to give you this set of maps for right now, they are current as of three weeks or so. I will get current ones to you as soon as possible. As for you, we have nicknamed you the Stalker."

"The Stalker, huh…I like that. I am looking forward to working with you guys…I think."

"Till later, then," said Serf. "By the way, before you go out, replace the firing pin in your rifle; it's on your windowsill. See you soon," Serf said.

Ray went into the house to check his rifle and was totally dumfounded that they could get in and do that without waking him up. He checked his windowsill and there was no firing pin there. He then checked his rifle and the firing pin was in the bolt where it belonged. "Those Bastards!" he exclaimed as he went out the door only to discover they were nowhere to be found; the only trace he saw was a phone number written on a piece of paper.

"So, what do you think?" Serf asked.

"Not really sure, I don't know if anything we said sunk in. Frigging jarheads, they can be bullheaded as a motherfucker. I hope for his sake he thinks about what we said, reference to establishing patterns. That would get him killed faster than anything else. He is fighting a different war than he did in the sandbox. We are back to Nam tactics with the assholes here."

"Time will tell. We will see what happens in a couple of weeks."

"If he is able to last that long."

"In the meantime, Tommy, I want you to head south and link up with Wilson and see what's going on there. It has been a while since we have talked to him."

———

Ron Dahle

Chapter 9

"Hey, old man, are your eyes crossed from looking at that system yet?"

"No, not yet, but only because I won't watch it. All four of the mainframes are sizzling, though. They probably will be for a couple more days at least. I expect the last batch in from Joe tomorrow. That will give us a grand total of 382 different accounts in the matrix, all humming along in an absolutely insane pattern, or should I say non-pattern, at a dizzying speed.

"We will have three accounts in Europe, two accounts each in Asia and SEA, and four different accounts in the Cayman Islands, one account in Boston, and one in Monterey that we will have direct access to. The other accounts will be deleted as soon as they are drained, but I am going to keep half of them active for storage. I have a feeling there will be too much to put in just a handful of accounts. The European accounts are in Germany, Switzerland, and Austria, as they are the only stable countries there. Those accounts are all listed under Corporate Names. The Cayman Island accounts have tens of billions of dollars destined for each of them, as they are strictly numbered accounts. As we tap them, we will replenish them from some of our other accounts."

"Do you have a feel for how much money is actually involved?"

"To be perfectly frank with you, Ron, I couldn't come up with an estimate that would be within two or three hundred billion dollars. Everything happened within a six hour time frame and has been constantly traveling and splitting ever since it started.

"Hell, there are still many individuals who don't realize they have been drained yet, but the groundswell is happening. The banks are showing signs of panic. It has been kept pretty low key till now, but you can only hide an elephant in your dining room so long."

"Ok, old man, ya done good. Your next problem will be to figure a way to convert the bulk of it to gold and silver, preferably in coinage. I fully expect a collapse of the dollar in the coming year, partially as a result of our action but mostly by the failure of government."

"I will give that some thought, but right now I have to tend to my machines. Talk to you later."

———

"Hey, Top, got a mission for you to ponder. The cartel has had a nationwide series of clandestine radio towers and repeaters for a couple of years now, giving them good voice communications throughout Mexico. Well, NSA has picked up transmissions in Arabic that sound like they are coming over the same systems, only on different frequencies. We suspect they are using the same towers. We are going to try to get a fix on the repeating stations and may just see if we can take them out and kill two birds with one stone. I just wanted to run it by you for your take on it."

"Shit, Larry, that sounds like a chapter right out of the Special Forces playbook. The one thing that could really help is if you could get us some C-5. That would make a big difference, as it is a lot more malleable. It would be a lot easier molding it on the girders and braces than C-4 would."

"That shouldn't present any problems; I will get on NSA's ass to come up with coordinates for you."

"That would be good. Once I receive them I will get aerials of the areas surrounding them and see what we are really up against. I will issue a warning order to Serf just to get him thinking 'blowing towers'; it's a mindset thing, you know."

"Ok, Top, I will work on the C-5 and the coordinates. I will let you know when I have something. Do you have an estimate on the amount of C-5 you will need?"

"Since we are going into this blind, let's try for 1,000 pounds of C-5 and 3,000 feet of Det Cord and 200 each of electrical and non-electric blasting caps. It sounds like a lot, but ribbon cutting charges can eat up some demo. And this needs to be a one shot operation for each tower, as we won't likely want to go back."

"That is great; it won't take too many towers to totally disrupt their communications, at least for a while. I will be getting back to you. By the way, don't use any of this C-5 in your stateside escapades, as it can be traced by the chemical markers used in the manufacturing process."

"Ron, glad you called. I have four days of imagery of the forest for you. I will mail them out this afternoon. And what are you up to, sir?"

"Just a notice, that shortly I will have a series of coordinates south of the border that are going to need to be looked at. Seems the Hezbollah have piggybacked on some communications towers that the cartels have been using, so now we have two groups that are using them. As soon as NSA pinpoints their coordinates, we are going in to take them out, but I would like a better idea of what we are getting into, if you know what I mean."

"Oh, I know. As soon as you get the coordinates, send them to me and I will see what we can do. By the way, I am getting vibes that a number of Iranian terrorists have just landed in Argentina. We are concerned that they may be heading to the US to pull off something. The CIA has diverted all of their remaining classes you guys put through last summer on this. They have to be stopped at any cost. I wouldn't be surprised if this is why the pressure on the radio relay sites."

"I'll keep that in mind. We will probably wind up in the middle of it before it is over.

"Thanks on the tip to convert to gold. My stocks are in the crapper right now, as are everybody's."

"It is amazing what can happen to the financial market in a matter of a couple of days. I need to call Bob and see how our project is cooking. I will give you a holler when I get the coordinates. Later, sir."

Christ, Ron thought, I haven't even had breakfast yet and it seems like I have done a day's work already.

The first class landed yesterday, without a doubt wondering what they got themselves into by now. The first three days will be hell. Especially since now, with a larger staff, they will be able to alternate drill them indefinitely. Ron was pondering the classes and their importance in the big picture when Mary Jane arrived.

"Hey, old man, you feel like taking a lady to breakfast?"

"Hell yeah, where is she?"

Mary Jane gave the Deacon the finger. "If you want to go, let's get it in gear, I still have a lot of payroll data to input; remember, this class is twice as big, to say nothing of the cadre. That reminds me, the replacement for LTC Otis Neilson is due in this afternoon. One of the cadre is picking him up in Manchester at 1600 hours."

"That's good; I hope this one doesn't have a chip on his shoulder.

Chapter 10 — Back in the Forest

Ray was sitting at the base of the tree stump he had adopted, pondering the conversation he'd had with the two old men from Special Forces. And while it hurt his pride, he knew they were right; he had lulled himself into a degree of complacency that almost cost him his life.

Their offer of supplying him with current aerial photographs of the Forest was extremely attractive. They would enable him to be proactive instead of reactive. He would actually be able to plan his actions and strike like the cougar he was, only on his terms and at his leisure.

He had killed four people, all in different areas, since he moved into the Forest. Two of them were from the Middle East and had a collection of documents that he felt sure the two old men would want. He decided to work his way back to his truck and go home for a week, as he had a wife and three teenagers, two boys and a girl, to raise, in addition to answering his own calling.

His wife, being Indian, accepted his plight. However, the children questioned his frequent periods of absence. His sons were brought up to understand Indian ways and culture, but his daughter was a lost cause, he thought, although he still loved her dearly.

Ray decided to call the two old men and make arrangements to meet with them to give them his booty taken on the kills. Hopefully, they would have updated map coverage for him.

Ray had been home three days when he dialed the number the men had left with him. "Hello," answered a voice on the other end.

"Hello, this is the stalker. Do I have the right number?"

"Yeah, Gunny, we were wondering if we would ever hear from you again. What's up?"

"I have some documents you said you wanted, we need to meet somewhere so I can give them too you."

"Let's try the Café in Deming about 1300 today, will that work for you?"

"That will be just fine, I don't live too far from there."

"I know," Serf said, "see you then."

———

The stalker was sitting in the corner in the Café when Serf arrived. They shook hands and Serf finally told him his name. "Tommy, the other one you met, is working south of here right now.

Serf was feeling comfortable with Ray's demeanor, so he suggested that they go to the safe house in Deming to conduct their business. Ray agreed and told Serf he would follow him.

On the way to the safe house, Ray wondered where he was being led, but he realized that if these men wished him harm he would have died at the hands of a trio of Mexican drug runners a month ago.

They arrived at the safe house and the first thing Serf did was to put on a pot of coffee. "This is all we do, right?" Serf said with a smile.

His next action was to pull out the map coverage he had for Ray and helped him interpret the night IR coverage. "This is where we find out where they are concentrated at night. An invaluable tool once you learn to interpret it.

"Let me show you something," Serf said. "Here, notice this heat signature here on the three photos. It is from a single person, while all the others you see are multiple sensings. I would be willing to bet that this is where you are sleeping. If that is so, you are staying in one place too long, and that will make your wife a widow."

Ray said nothing but it was apparent that what Serf just said sank in. He handed Serf the documents the Hezbollah agents were carrying and could not help but notice how happy Serf was to see them. "I will get these off to headquarters first thing in the morning," Serf said.

"And where is Headquarters?" Ray asked.

"A long way off," Serf replied. "But these are precisely the type of documents we are looking for. When do you plan to head back out?"

"By the end of the week, I expect. I want to take time to study these maps and pick a new area to patrol. I stay out two weeks at a time and then back in for a week."

"Here," Serf said, as he handed a satchel which contained four hand grenades and two claymore mines to Ray. "You never know when these will come in handy."

"Holy shit, Serf, I don't know what to say!"

"You don't need to say anything, just stay alive. Now you know where our team house is. Just give us a call before coming to make sure we are in. See you later, Gunny. Keep your head down."

On his way home, Ray pondered what just happened at the safe house. Granted, they wanted something from him, but they actually seemed to be concerned with Ray's welfare. Ray never thought he would wind up aligned with a couple of ex-Special Forces soldiers and enjoy the experience. The cynical side of Ray kicked in and reminded him that this relationship was in its infancy. There was no telling what the future would bring.

The one thing he did know for sure was that he was going home to study the maps Serf gave him and select a series of new MSS's (Mission Support Sites).

He really wanted to take his two boys along with him on one of his treks, but he knew they were too young, and although he had tried to maintain their Indian heritage and the Indian way, they would likely never understand his actions. He did at least derive satisfaction from the fact that they only dated Indian girls. He had help in this endeavor from his wife, a full-blooded Apache, who was living on the reservation when they met. At least she understood his plight and supported him fully. In her eyes he was, and always had been, her warrior, first during his career in the Marines and now in his endeavor to regain control of their hallowed ancestral grounds.

Chapter 11

Ron was anxiously awaiting Joe's return, but it appeared that Joe started thinking with his dick and made the decision to take a couple of days off on the world-wind tour he had just finished. That didn't bother the Deacon one bit, as Joe had been going non-stop for three weeks. Ron received word from Bob two days ago that Joe wrapped up his mission and would be home within the week.

The phone snapped Ron out of his quasi daydream. "Top, got an information overload for you. I have a shitload of coordinates for you to check out; I will mail them to you today via next day Nat Express. There are two sets, the ones in red are Arabic stations and the ones in black are the cartel. The numbers beside each indicate the average number of transmissions per day that site averages. The cartel network is much more extensive than the Arabic system. Keep me posted on what you find out."

"Okay, we will. By the way, Larry. Any word on the C-5 and Det Cord we requested yet?"

"It will be delivered to you by Buffalo later this week. Just remember, only out of CONUS with it."

"No problem, you wouldn't want to know how much C-4 I have on hand," Ron said smiling.

"I shudder at the thought. Are you hearing anything about the possibility of the Iranian agents we talked about?"

"Not a peep, but all ears are open and listening. That's the last thing we need to worry about, especially with the threats those bastards have been making."

"Ok, Top, I've got to run. Keep me posted, I'll do the same."

Mary Jane walked in the room. "What's up, anything hot?" she asked.

"Not really, just talking to Larry about the Mexican radio system we are trying to track down. How about you?"

"I was just wondering if you wanted me to fix you lunch or screw your ears off." she said.

Ron pondered a second and suggested that the ear task would go a lot better on a full stomach.

"You should have run for office with as much bull as you sling. Ya talked me into it, the place is dead, everyone is in the White Mountains on a land navigation course, so I figured this would be a good time to play house."

"I have always had a lot of admiration for a woman who was capable of deep analytical thought," Ron said just before Mary Jane bit him on the neck.

———

National Express delivered the coordinates from Larry today. The first thing Ron did was secure fax them to Vince and then call him.

"Good morning, Vince. I trust you got the coordinates ok? The ones in red are from Arabic speaking sites, the others being cartel stations."

"I will get on them tomorrow; the birds are already programmed for today. I will send them directly to you when they get in. How were you able to get on these so fast?"

"The Army deployed 15 ASA Vans to work on the monitoring and triangulation. Also, there are some NSA assets deployed, but I don't know how many or where."

"Nor would I expect you to; they hold their cards tight to their vest, which is a pretty good idea. How about your guys, are they ready for this?"

"I am pulling them in today and issuing a warning order, that's about all I can do until we know what we are up against here. Depending on what we are facing and how far away it is I may try to get some Agency choppers to assist in this operation."

"No problem, Sergeant Major, just keep those maps to yourself; I definitely don't need the CIA snooping into my business."

"You know that's a given, Vince. There is no way I would risk compromising our working relationship."

Serf, Tommy, and Wilson were cooling it at the safe house, waiting for instructions from the Deacon, when Gunny called. "Hey, I have more documents for you. I was wondering if you were at the safe house."

"Sure, bring them over. I'll put a pot of coffee on."

"What's that all about?" asked Wilson.

"That is the Indian Tommy and I told you about. He has some more booty he captured. I don't know what anyone else is thinking, but it seems there are a lot of goatfuckers holding out in that forest."

"Yeah, I know, it makes you wonder just how deep the shit pile we are walking through really is."

Ray pulled into the parking area and Serf went out to meet him. "Come on in, there is another member of our crew here that you haven't met yet and you need to get to know him, as we take turns staffing this place."

Ray entered and met Wilson. He gave his documents to Serf who looked at them and immediately packaged them and handed them to Tommy and told him to get these off to Langley, as there was time to make the local Nat Exp drop. This would put the data in an interpreter's hands tomorrow, he said.

Ray perked up a bit when Serf mentioned Langley. That sort of gave him an idea of the level his newfound acquaintances were working at.

"Ok, Gunny, we appreciate your motivation for what you are doing in the Forest, and can't fault it at all. If you ever get bored, let us know and every now and then we have some ass kicking operations across the border which may just prime your adrenaline pump if you are the least bit interested," Serf said. "Every now and then, a little younger blood wouldn't hurt, either. In case you haven't noticed, we average ten to twenty years on you."

"If I went along with this, what capacity would I be going in as? I don't have the time or the inclination to be anybody's flunky or rear echelon lookout."

"Gunny, if and when you ever deploy with us, you just make sure you are locked and loaded. We don't have or want the luxury of flunkies. Everybody on the team is a warrior with a specific mission, that's how we roll.

"There may be something hot coming up within a week or so. If you are interested, let me know. Realize this hinges on the approval of the Deacon."

"And just who is the Deacon and where does he fit in in the picture?"

"The Deacon founded this organization and has brought it to the level it is today. When he is ready, you will meet him."

"Yes, count me in if you have a need for me. I will be hanging around with my family for a bit, at least until I get a new update on maps."

"Looking forward to working with you, Gunny. The reason you don't have current maps right now is that our assets are working the area we are looking at going into. We will keep you posted."

Ray pondered the events of the morning and was wondering what he was getting into. While Serf did mention Langley, there was little else said to show their hand. They were very closed-lipped, right down to the identity of the Deacon. Ray knew how Special Forces worked, in as much as no one knew what was going on until everybody was in a locked down situation. He could not fault this for the sake of security. He was anxious to see what irons they had in the fire.

———

The anticipated aerial photographs came in and on the surface proved to be a bit disappointing, as there were no towers shown on the photos. The closest indicated tower was about twelve miles south of the border, but nothing beyond indigenous vegetation showed on the map. The only point of interest was an elevated mound in the middle of nowhere about 65 miles to the south. What made it interesting was the fact that it handled more traffic than the rest of the sites combined. Ron asked Vince to try to get some better imagery of that one site to include infrared sensings at night.

Ron called Serf and said he was going to send him the maps and he wanted Serf and his crew to check it out and see what in hell was going on.

At the same time, Serf mentioned the meeting with Ray and told the Deacon that they had sent some documents directly to Larry in Langley as they all had agreed was prudent, in the interest of saving time. Serf also mentioned inviting Ray along on a mission.

Ron suggested this tower search, it was low key and it would give them an opportunity to evaluate Ray's tactical awareness in a low-pressure environment.

Serf called Ray and asked him if he could be ready to deploy the next day.

"Don't waste any time, do ya?" Ray asked.

"This just came down the pike right after you left."

"No sweat, I'll be there early morning."

Gunny showed up at 0600 hours, only to find everybody sleeping. He walked in and Serf hollered out he would be right out to put a pot of coffee on. Gunny said "screw it" and made the coffee while asking Serf if this was why he was invited along.

"Hell no, Gunny, it's just a matter of the definition of early," Serf said. Serf gave Gunny a breakdown of what they were going after. "I know this doesn't seem like much but it could make a world of difference in the big picture.

"Tommy is going to take us to the drop off point this evening. We will infiltrate by foot to the exact spot that repeater is supposed to be and see if we can figure out what in hell is going on. There are no tracks or trails in the area, but we will all be in desert Gilley suits.

"We will be going in with M-4s with two CMAGs each, night vision goggles, squad radios, IR beacons, strobes, four canteens each and four hand grenades. In addition to that we will all carry two MRE rations.

"We have the rest of the day to zero our weapons, and pack. I want everyone to drink plenty of water all day, as I want to start out well hydrated.

"More than likely, we will hold up somewhere during the day tomorrow for the sake of security. We will rendezvous with Tommy at the pick-up point designated on the map."

Gunny interjected."You know, it would be good to have a sniper rifle along, just in case. I can kill flies out to 1000 yards with my 30.06. Damn sure can't do that with an M-4."

"Gunny, you probably have a point there. Ok, you can carry your 30.06. It isn't like we haven't watched you use it," Serf said with a grin.

Tommy dropped the team off at dusk, wondering what they had ahead of them.

The traveling was easy, relatively flat with a good surface, enabling them to make excellent time. They took turns on point, with every move of Ray being watched and judged for future reference.

Their GPS indicated that they were within 25 yards of the tower, but there was no tower there.

Ray approached an eight-foot rockrose bush only to find that it concealed a tower painted the same dark green as the bush. It had an antenna on it and a battery at the base, connected to the repeater. A cable led from the battery, underground, to a solar panel that kept the battery charged. They took the repeater and the solar panel and started the trek back.

On the way back Serf was thinking that Ray had passed his first outing with flying colors, as it was doubtful that either he or Wilson would have discovered that antenna. When asked why he found it, Ray said that the rockrose bush appeared straighter than it would normally be. This was a result of tying it off to the tower, to conceal it.

While travelling, Ray felt good, as he knew he was the reason for the success of the mission. It was highly unlikely that a white man would know to look for that little discrepancy. Ray knew that he had proven his worth to the team, and for that, he felt equal to a Special Forces soldier for the first time in his career.

———

They put up in a small draw during the day, taking turns pulling guard and sleeping. At dusk, they headed towards the pick-up point. Serf called Tommy and gave him a heads up.

Tommy was waiting at the pick-up point as scheduled. They all got out of Dodge as soon as possible. Back at the safe house Ray asked what was so special about that repeater they recovered.

"Ok, Gunny, look at it this way. This is the closest repeater to the border. The entire Trans-Mexico network into the US is effectively shut down until it is discovered and replaced. What that does is buy us time. We have strong indications that there is a cell of Iranian terrorists working their way to our border. The problem is, we don't know their mission. The more we can do to slow their progress, the higher the likelihood we can find them before they get here.

"We have ASA and NSA working both sides of the border, trying to figure out the location of the US point of contact. Our big issue now is that these repeaters and relays are going to be a lot harder to locate based on the way this one was camouflaged. We may not have found it if you weren't along."

Serf called the Deacon and updated him on the situation with the repeater, and what they found.

"Shit," the Deacon said , we don't need 1000 pounds of C-5, we need a pipe wrench and a hacksaw from the way it sounds.

"You can look forward to seeing me tomorrow. That mound that I had Vince reshoot is an adobe structure, mostly underground. A lot of radio traffic in and out, picked up ten heat signatures within the building and several outposts guarding it. There is something serious going on in that building. Larry is going to be at your place tomorrow, and we have to figure out what to do about it. So my friend, I suggest you get a good night's sleep, it is going to be a busy couple of days. By the way, how did Gunny work out?"

"Shit, we wouldn't have found the repeater if it hadn't been for him."

"Do we want to take him along on the next phase of this operation?"

"I will check with him and see. For my money, I would say yes."

"Hey, Gunny, this hole is about to get a hell of a lot deeper, are you up to jumping in it with us? The Deacon will be here

Ron Dahle

tomorrow and our Boss from the CIA. There is some shit out there we need to get, and we're not sure how we are going to go about it; that will be determined tomorrow."

"Shit, if you want it done right I guess I have to go," the Gunny said with a big grin.

"Hey, fuck you," Serf said.

Chapter 12 — Operation Deep Thrust

Ron and Steve left first thing in the morning to get a flight to DC out of Boston. It would put them in DC at 0945 hours when Larry would meet them for the second leg of their trip. Larry had a small jet booked into Deming. It was just going to drop them off and would return to pick them up when the mission was completed.

"Ok, guys, this is a hot operation. We have clearance for all the air support we think we need. Ron, you have studied the map coverage. What do you think is our best approach to this?"

"If you can get the support, I see an air invasion with Apache Longbows. They can be configured to carry 16 Hellfire missiles, in addition to their 30mm chain gun. The accuracy of the millimeter wave guidance system for the Hellfire missile is incredible; it is truly a fire and forget system.

"I would like three Apache and a Black Hawk. One Apache used to take out the command center with its Hellfire missiles. The other two-eliminating the guard posts with their chain guns. I want the Black Hawk carrying in a command and control element consisting of you and me, along with a bomb damage assessment (BDA) and recovery team to go through the bunker to see if there is any intelligence they can police up.

"On our way out, I want to target all the known relay sites with the remaining Hellfires. The Apache will easily be able to identify them. We may as well make a night of it and make it tough for them, we damn sure can't get to them by foot and if we did there is nothing saying we would recognize them."

"That BDA mission is a bit bold, Top. You'll have no way of knowing if everyone in the bunker is dead."

"The Apache has incredible optics and sensors, I trust them. If push comes to shove, that is why we have both Wilson and Steve along, to pick up the pieces and patch them up."

"I hear you, but remember we have a history of flying around the Mexican desert and getting shot up, or have you forgotten ?"

"No shit. That is the last thing Mary Jane harped on me about as I left today."

"Ok, I am going to call Clovis and lay on our air support. I will have them report to Serf's safe house. They will likely have to refuel at Deming Municipal before we kick the operation off."

Steve looked at the Deacon and said "Top, I don't want you out of that Black Hawk. You are still recovering from the last time you were here, and your knees will be a hindrance. We have no idea what we are heading into and I don't want to have to worry about you along with everything else that will be happening."

"That is all worthy of consideration, Steve, and I will give it some thought."

"You cantankerous old mother fucker, you just said no, and you damn well know I am right."

Ron was thinking of his long history with Steve, from Nam to Fort Devens, and now in their latest ventures. Ron had been known to say that a better Special Forces medic has never existed, and he truly believed that. When Steve left Ft. Devens, he joined the Golden Knights parachute team along with David Smythe, the other team medic. After that, Steve was appointed to the Warrant Officer program and transferred to the 75th Rangers. Steve was involved in the invasion into Grenada and distinguished himself there. Steve giving Ron shit was nothing new, he had been doing it for over forty-five years, and will likely continue, Ron thought as he smiled.

"Ok, Top, I just got off the horn with Langley and Clovis. Our air assets will be at Serf's at 1500 hours tomorrow. We need to brief them as well as provide them with all the coordinates of the antennas spread across a 50 mile radius from the bunker. They will feed that data into the Apaches' targeting system. The rest is just a ride.

"They will stay on location with us and fly covey while we are on the ground. Once the Black Hawk takes off they will depart and take out the other relay sites."

"So, tell me, Larry, why isn't the Mexican government involved in this operation? You would think they would be."

"It's a matter of security, Top. No one knows who can really be trusted there, and the potential yield for this mission rules out their involvement. At the highest levels, the Mexican government knows this and turns a blind eye to these types of operations. Our State Department will brief them after the fact. The one sacrosanct rule is that we have no military boots on the ground. That is a ruling from our side of the house, not theirs."

"And what, prey tell, is the rationale for that?"

Larry looked at Ron for a minute. "It's simple, it is easier to explain the death of someone who doesn't exist, than a member of the military. That's the easiest way to say it."

"I sort of knew that all along, so nothing has really changed, has it?"

"Nothing has changed," Larry said.

They landed at Deming Municipal, and Serf was there, waiting for them. On the way to the safe house Serf gave a rundown on the known history of the Gunny and his performance on the operation they'd just completed. "The only downside I picked up on, and it may not be anything, is that he is overly attached to his Mosin Nagant sniper rifle. He took it on the operation stating that we may have a need for a sniper rifle and I could see his point, so I let it go."

They pulled into the safe house and went in. Everyone was introduced around, and showed to their rooms. One thing John did well on this structure, he had two bays with four beds each in addition to the regular three bedrooms that were part of the original plan. He envisioned launching out of here and provided for it.

Ron gave the mission brief and the task assignments. "Gunny, you are going to have to trade that sniper rifle in for an M-4 carbine. There is no call for a sniper rifle on this mission. If anything, it will be a hindrance."

"No problem sir, I fully understand."

"That's good. By the way, call me Top, or Deacon, or even asshole, but don't call me sir!" the Deacon said with a smile.

"Ok guys, we have no idea what is in that command bunker. Whatever it is, we want it, so do as good a search as you can considering the shape it is likely to be in after the strike. Take any documentation you can find on bodies present. In the event there is anyone still alive get Steve on him asap, we want him! Take it easy for the rest of the day, pack, put fresh batteries in your optics, squad radios and beacons. Take this opportunity to check the zero on your weapons. You are going to have to be at the very top of your game when you step out of your helicopter. Larry and I will be circling in the blackbird to assist the Apaches in providing cover. We will come in and pick you up when we receive your signal."

All missions accomplished, a couple of them were still cleaning their weapons, and the rest had gone to bed as they had a serious day ahead of them and they all knew it.

The air support arrived right on schedule. After the obligatory introductions, they all went into the safe house for an operational briefing. The head of the flight component, a Chief Warrant Officer 4, stated he didn't see any reason for concern on the briefing they'd just received, his only question was if there were any friendlies in the area they would be flying.

Larry assured him that the area was barren, and there was no one there that was a friendly.

"That's good," the Chief said, "as we intend to vaporize any sign of life we see. The last thing we need is an asshole popping up and firing a SAM at us in the name of Allah. The Apache scans once a second and is capable of tracking 235 targets simultaneously. With three of them doing this, it is highly unlikely anything will get past us."

They departed at 0915 hours. The pilots decided to fly an indirect route for the sake of deception. In unison, all of the choppers banked hard, the primary Apache heading straight as was the Blackbird well behind him. The other two Apaches circled one to the left and one to the right. The Lead Apache fired three Hellfire missiles at the bunker five miles out. The other two Apaches then engaged the noted sentry positions with their chain guns, eliminating them with one burst each. The two secondary Apaches started circling while the lead Apache went in to take a look at the bunker.

"Black Hawk leader, this is Apache Chief, be advised I see what appears to be one person still alive in the bunker, do you want me to take him out?"

"Negative on that, Apache Chief, we will try to take him alive; he could be holding a treasure trove of intelligence."

"Roger that, Black Hawk leader, it is all yours now. We will stay on station until you have completed your mission."

At that, the Black Hawk rolled in to approach the bunker from the rear. The BDA team was out before the Black Hawk's skids hit the ground, and they were on their way to the target. Serf threw in two concussion grenades, and the team stormed the compound. They did see one person alive but bleeding profusely, but not to where he wasn't able to get a shot off, hitting Serf in the side. Serf immediately subdued him, although he really wanted to kill him. Surf called for Steve to tend to the prisoner and continued to look for items of interest.

"Serf!" Tommy called, "Get in here, I think I hit the jackpot."

Serf located Tommy, and he was right. Sitting in front of Tommy was what appeared to be a 'Suitcase Nuke' from the USSR days. It had been rumored that when the USSR split up they lost control of several of them. Well, we have just confirmed that story, thought Serf, and there was little doubt as to where it was headed.

Gunny called out. He had located a safe in one of the other rooms. It was small enough that a couple of men could carry it.

All available documents were recovered from the bodies, and the safe and suitcase nuke, as well as the now shackled prisoner, were up where the Black Hawk was going to come in.

As soon as Larry realized what they had, he put in a call to the Apache Leader.

"Apache Chief, we have a change of mission of the utmost urgency. This Black Hawk is flying direct to Langley. The Apache you have with the most ordnance remaining needs to accompany us for the sake of National Security."

"Roger that, Black Hawk leader, I will get an ammo count from my others and get right back with you.

"Black Hawk leader, you will be accompanied by Apache 12. You have a safe trip. We are going repeater and relay hunting. Have a good day, gentlemen."

Steve glanced over at Serf and realized he was bleeding like a stuck pig. He looked at him and decided it was through and through, but he felt Serf still needed to go to a hospital.

Larry asked him if he could make it to Langley, as he really didn't want to stop anywhere except for a mandatory fuel stop based on the cargo they had on board.

"I don't see any problem with that," Steve said, "but he has lost a lot of blood, and I don't know what else has been hit. I will maintain a constant monitor on his vitals; Wilson is hanging a bag on him now to help. If there is any change I will notify you."

The prisoner, while showing signs of external blast damage, appeared to be ok, but there was always a chance of internal bleeding due to blast overpressure. Wilson hung a bag on him, too. At the same time, Larry put a black hood over his head to disorient him.

The 'suitcase nuke' looked like anything but a suitcase. It was about a three foot cube painted Olive Drab and had D ring handles all around it. It weighed approximately eighty pounds, making it a cumbersome carry for one man. Both Ron and Larry had seen this particular model in a briefing on Warsaw Pact weapons put on by the European JUWTFEUR (joint unconventional warfare task force Europe) back in the early 70s.

"Ron, you know no one can ever mention this operation again. It just did not happen; you have to make sure your warriors understand that. This is way beyond our pay grade. Don't expect to hear of it in the media either. As I said, it did not happen."

"I fully understand. You won't get any flak from this end, of that you can be sure."

The Black Hawk landed on the pad at Langley, an ambulance whisked Serf away, and the door to the Black Hawk closed. Shortly, two vans drove up, one filled with agents carrying .40 cal. Uzis. From the other van, two men got out and entered the Black Hawk, covered the Nuke in a black shroud and loaded it into the van, then they came back and retrieved the safe and finally the prisoner. Larry thanked everybody and left with the sedans.

The Black Hawk pilot said they were going to land and get a room and get some rest, as did the Apache pilot. Not only was it needed, it was required by regulation; they had been flying nearly 20 hours straight. There was no argument from the warriors as they, too, were exhausted.

The Apache and Black Hawk were grounded for periodic maintenance. The maintenance team had to be flown in. Larry got the warriors the same jet he, Steve, and Ron flew to Deming in to take the crew back to Deming Municipal. There was no way they could have boarded a commercial flight armed the way they were.

Larry also sent a packet of cash to Ron, to distribute to the warriors as a bonus. Each warrior received $7,500 in cash. Not bad, Ron thought as he wondered how Larry was going to account for that cash.

They rented two vehicles at Deming Municipal in order to carry everyone and their equipment. As soon as they arrived at the safe house, Ron called a meeting.

"Gentlemen, I want to take this opportunity to congratulate you on a job well done. It was executed so well that Larry gave me a stipend of $7,500 per participant as his way of saying thanks. Realize that is the only recognition we will ever receive for what we do.

"This brings me to the next topic. Erase everything you have seen or done from your mind. This can never be brought up again, even amongst ourselves. I think Larry said it as well as it can be said; what you did and what you saw did not happen!

"This is beyond debate; the last three days did not exist as far as any of us are concerned. I can't make it any clearer than that, case closed!

"As soon as I get a status on Serf's situation I will contact you. Steve and I will be heading out tomorrow for Boston. We will return the rentals in the process.

"Gunny, I am proud to say you worked well with us. You did a great job. I am sure I speak for the rest of the team when I say we are looking forward to working with you again in the near future."

After the meeting was finished Gunny approached the Deacon and asked him about the Academy he ran. Ron gave him a quick briefing on it and questioned why he asked.

"Well, as you know, I have two sons, one sixteen and the other seventeen, that I have been bringing up as close as I can in the ways of my people. As a parent, there is only so much you can do. I was wondering if, during the summer break from school, they could possibly be enrolled in your Academy to learn what it is to be a man."

"I see several problems: first, they are civilians; second, they are very young; and third, I doubt they could handle the physical strain of the training, and if they were there they would be expected to do everything the other students do. On top of that, all the instruction is given in Spanish."

"I can do nothing about the fact that they are civilians. They may be young, but they are old for their age; I have been working with them for years. They are likely in as good physical condition as any student you get, and being from New Mexico the language is not an issue, they are fluent.

"In return, I would be willing to teach a class in advanced tracking to your students. I am sure that is something they could benefit from."

"Gunny, I have to give you credit, you make a good case for making this happen, if for no other reason than your class in tracking. I am going to run this by Larry and get his take on it. I will get back with you.

"Tommy, you and Wilson lay low for a while. I am sure we stirred some shit up across the border the other night. Give them a chance to cool off a bit. The Apaches were going to target the cartel as well as the Arabic relays, since they had the ability and were there anyway."

"Guys, I am going to head home now," Ray said. "It was an honor and a privilege working with you. Hopefully, we can work together again soon."

After everybody said their goodbyes to Gunny, the Deacon announced that he was going to bed as he and Steve had an early flight in the morning.

Prior to going to bed, he did give Mary Jane a call to let her know everything went well. "I will be coming into Logan at 1550, if you would care to come and pick us up."

"Oh damn," Mary Jane said. "I have a hair appointment, can you wait? Of course I will be there, dummy. It's good to know you didn't learn any more about women while you were gone. I swear, men! See you tomorrow, babe. I love you. Send me your flight number and gate number. Bye, hon."

Chapter 13

After Mary Jane, the second order of business for Ron was to call Larry, to get an update on Serf.

"Hell, Top, he is doing great, it went through and through, nothing vital hit, just a couple of bleeders. They plan to discharge him in a couple of days, as soon as his blood count gets a bit better. I will take care of getting him back to Deming.

"Five of the passports retrieved from the bodies in the bunker were Iranian, so I guess that just put teeth in that rumor. Our guest is singing his ass off; I'll tell you about it someday, maybe on that fishing trip. So what's going on in Wolfeboro, did Joe ever return?"

"Yes, Mary Jane said he got back the day after I left. He hasn't been by yet, probably avoiding me as long as he can.

"By the way, Gunny came up with an interesting proposition; he offered to teach advanced tracking for us this summer if his sons were allowed to attend the training in the Academy."

"Top, you do realize we aren't running a boys' camp, don't you?"

"Well, some of our students in this class are the same age as his boys. I told him that the instructors wouldn't even know who they were, no favorites.

"It sure would be a boost to our curriculum if we could offer advanced tracking by a genuine Indian tracker. He could

Ron Dahle

also cover stealth movement, as Tommy tells me he glides through the forest like a cougar."

"Ok, Top, you can stop sniveling. Go ahead, but I don't want to hear of any problems with this idea.

"I hope you don't have anything tied up in the Stock Market. Operation Bankrupt has leaked out and the market is in a nosedive. A couple of banks have closed their doors due to insolvency. It looks like you created the monetary crisis you wanted."

"I haven't checked with Bob yet; he is next on my list. So, you have anything in mind for our immediate future?"

"Not a thing, Top, but you know how this business goes. Hell, we may be invading Canada by the end of the week. Who knows in this crazy world?"

"I hear you, Larry. Ok, I have to run, it's time to call Bob. You take it easy, friend. Tell Serf I was asking for him. Later."

"Good afternoon, Robert. How are things going in Monterey?"

"Probably better than they were going in Mexico, unless things have changed a hell of a lot since I was last there. I am sure you called about my week and not yours. Joe did great; he came up with a total of 177 accounts, so that opened the matrix up just a tad.

"Things are starting to slow down now, with some of the cash settling in. I have it set to build the remaining accounts incrementally, to provide a bit of security. Not that it matters, as the final banks are all numbered accounts and they don't really give a rat's ass.

"The Cayman Island accounts will be filled first, then Asia, followed by Europe. A cursory amount, ten million dollars, will be deposited in Monterey and Boston. I am counting on Larry's people to catch those flags."

"No problem, Bob, they are waiting for it. So do you have a rough estimate where we stand overall?"

"The best I can determine, until everything stops, is somewhere in the neighborhood of nine hundred and seventy two billion dollars. Give or take several billion dollars. A goodly amount any way you look at it."

"I would like to be a fly on one of a thousand walls when they find out they are broke. The ripple effect of this will continue for at least the rest of the year. Starting with high-end real estate foreclosures and going right on down. We have cramped a lot of motherfuckers' life styles. The big fish will survive, they always do, but it will take them a while to climb out of this.

"Ok, Bob, I've got to run and track Joe down and see where he is right now. We put him through the wringer for three weeks. I don't think he ever really stopped. I'll talk to you later, friend."

Finally, Ron tracked Joe down at the rappelling tower in the training area. "Hey, stranger, I was wondering if you were coming home or not," Ron said to Joe.

"You, of all people, should understand. Damned if I didn't wind up on the wrong plane at the end of the mission, and landed in Bangkok by mistake. Of course, it was all downhill from there," Joe said smiling.

"You could have called. Hell, I may have joined you. You know I can't find it in my heart to give anyone shit about going to Bangkok, so I guess you skated on this one… Welcome back, and congratulations on exceeding our wildest expectations. Ya done good, lad!

"When you finish here come on up to the lodge. I've got a ton of shit to catch you up on."

"Will do, Top, and by the way… Thai pussy is as good as it ever was!"

"Fuck you, Joe!"

Mary Jane nudged Ron, to tell him he had a phone ringing. He slowly awoke and said whoever it was would leave a message. "Can't you think of a better reason to wake me up?" he asked.

"Now that you mention it, I do believe I can," she said as she started nibbling at his neck.

An hour later Ron surveyed his secure phone and saw Larry had called. Surprised to hear from him so soon, Ron immediately returned his call.

"Top, glad you got back to me so promptly. Ok, this is for our ears only. The device we retrieved in Mexico was indeed a SADM (Special Atomic Demolition Munitions) device. Similar to our old W-54. The Russian nomenclature for them is the RA-115. The experts estimate it has a potential yield of up to 5 or 6 kilotons. The Russians lost control of up to 150 of these weapons as reported by the former Russian Security Advisor Alexander Lebed back in 1967. Of course, the Russians have denied this, but here, 45 years later, we have one show up on our doorstep, and according to our experts it is still fully operational. Needless to say, it is now in an undisclosed location in the south west.

"Need I go into what the implications of this really are? God knows who has the rest of them, or even if any have already made it across the border.

"Your Mexican contingent has just become a high priority operation for the Agency. Tell Serf to put feelers out for more volunteers.

"The Academy is also taking on a higher precedence than it has in the past. This train is picking up speed and I don't see any relief in sight."

"So tell me, Larry, do I need to start planning to expand our billeting capacity? The training facilities can absorb a lot more, but the billeting and messing is getting tight."

"I almost think you need to double your capacity, the sooner the better. We are having all the security in the Academy in Columbia beefed up based on what happened to you guys this spring."

"Ok, I will get John on it as soon as he is available. We need to widen and lengthen the runway to handle the extra traffic. I expect that shortly you will be coming in here with C-130s instead of the Buffalos."

"You're probably right, Top. When do you think you can get started on the project?"

"I can have a local paving company take care of the runway immediately. I will have to check with John and his schedule for the billeting and messing facility. If need be, I can start with locals clearing and setting the forms and possibly even pouring the foundations. We'll get it done, Boss."

"By the way, Serf was released today, and is already on his way back to Deming. I haven't mentioned any of this to him."

"I will brief him on what he needs to know once he gets his feet back on the ground. Have you given any more thought to Gunny's kids?"

"Yes, I have, as a matter of fact. If he can get them to the transfer point in Nicaragua on the 10th of May, they will be integrated onto the next class coming your way on the 13th. It is imperative that no one knows who they are. As far as the other inductees know, they are just regular students."

"Damn it, Deacon, I spend as much time in Wolfeboro as I do in Pigeon Forge," John babbled. You get the pads poured and I will send you a list of materials to have on site when I get there and we will make this happen."

"Great, I was hoping you could work me into your schedule. One other thing: I am having the face, door, and locking mechanism of a massive walk in safe built as we speak. I am going to start the excavation of the area where it is going. I am betting that you can set it in place for me and pour the outer security containment for it. I will send you the plans. It is going to open into the war room."

"That's just fucking great. Get me those plans ASAP. You need to plan for three foot floor and walls when you do the excavation for it. Don't pour a fucking thing. If everything isn't exactly square your locking mechanism won't work. You get the front mechanism there; I will take care of the engineering to get it in place and to make it work. And please, no more surprises for a while.

"Let me know as soon as the pads are poured for the billets, I will head out then. Just have the materials there."

"John, if you get the urge, bring the balloon with you. The weather will be great for it while you are here."

"We'll see what my schedule looks like, I will give it a try. We need to start flying again anyway, the elections are coming at us fast."

"So they are, seems like we just had them. John, have a good day, get me that list of materials. You know I am out in the boondocks here; everything will need to be ordered ahead of time. Talk to you later, sir."

Ron pondered a moment on John's physical condition, just hoping that he would last until the elections.

"Hey lady, you got your ass out of bed yet?" Ron said to Mary Jane. "I figured we could go to breakfast if you feel like it."

"That's a dumb question, do I want to go to breakfast or do I want to cook breakfast. I'll be ready in about five minutes."

"Timed this just right. We have the whole dining area overlooking the lake to ourselves," Mary Jane said, reaching out to take Ron's hand.

"Did I hear you tell John to bring his balloon with him? And what is this new safe you are installing?"

"You know, I liked you better when you didn't have a security clearance. Yes, John has a balloon, and I figured either John or Dief could take us on a ride in it. As far as the safe, that isn't to be talked about outside of the war room."

"Oh, I'm sorry."

"They are coming to pour the pads for the foundation this week. John will be here next week to do his work. The safe will be in during that period. We should be able to get it all finished within two and a half weeks. John is bringing a large crew with him to make it happen."

"That's good. What do you have on tap for the afternoon, anything in particular?"

"Not really. I do need to call Serf sometime today, though. He was just released from the hospital this morning."

"I didn't know he was in the hospital. Sort of like you on Christmas Eve?"

"Yeah, sort of, just not as bad; it was a clean thru and thru."

"Why didn't I fall in love with a mechanic, or an electrician, or someone normal instead of whatever in hell you are?"

"They would be too boring for you and you know it. Plus, I'm a good lay."

"Screw you, Ron."

———

"Serf, how are you doing, my friend?"

"Hey, Batman, I'm doing pretty good, now that I am out of the hospital. Why did you let them take me anyway? I had Wilson to tend to me."

"Hey, dude, I just did what Steve recommended. He makes those kinds of calls. Anyway, the break probably did you some good.

"Based on the other night, we want to beef up your

operation, so that means you have to try to recruit two or three more trusted souls. We think there are more devices where that one came from."

"That's just what the fuck we need! Can one of them be Gunny? He has already been tested."

"Not really, we have other plans for Gunny this summer. You can have him in the winter, unless he wants to go play in the Forest. I'm thinking that now we have whet his appetite he may be looking for a little more action than the Forest has to offer. You know, Semper Fi, De Oppresso Liber, and all that rah rah bullshit.

"Serf, I have to run, Larry is calling in on the other line. I'll talk to you later, dude."

There's times I feel like a frigging telephone operator, Ron thought, as he hung up one phone and picked up the next.

"Yeah, Larry, what's up?"

"Ron, can both you and Joe be available tomorrow around noon?"

"Sure, what's going on?"

"I'll tell you when I get there. Have you briefed Joe on the package we picked up the other night?"

"Hell, no. It didn't happen, remember?"

"Ok, ok, I know… brief him on it. I'll be up by noon tomorrow."

Surprisingly, Larry came up in a Black Hawk. When the pilot got out Ron recognized him as the pilot he had in Mexico.

"You got a new ride, or just styling for the day?"

"Just styling, Top. The twin Beech I normally use is out today, and I really needed to get here."

"Hell, let the pilot come in and chill, we've got a TV."

"He won't come in; they have a different protocol when they fly for the Agency. I know, it's fucked up but that's how it is. We are going to need to talk in the war room anyway."

"Ok. I briefed Joe on all I know. I guess you have the floor."

"This asshole we picked up is singing like a canary. He doesn't know the target for the device, but he does know who he was supposed to deliver the device to. He is Achmed Al Karim from Philly. I have his address and some preliminary photos of his house and car as well as him.

"If we take him, the DOJ will take control of him and tie our hands; we will never find out anything from him. On the other hand, if he were to disappear and wind up in a bunker in Deming, we could probably get a lot out of him. Joe, are you up to something like that? "

"Why did you even bother to ask? That's what I do for a living. I would like the Dief to assist me on it, as a lookout and a driver. What transportation assets will I have to move him?"

"I figure, if you can get him back here, I will have the Black Hawk on station to take the two of you to Deming. I understand that Serf is a great host. Once you get all you can from him, feed him to the coyotes and buzzards, unless he can be of greater value alive. Just realize he will never see the outside of that bunker again, regardless of what he knows. We don't need him to come back and haunt us."

"Top, have you talked to Gunny about his kids?"

"Yes, I did. He is going to have them in Nicaragua for their flight. At that time, he will fly here commercial and get added to the staff. I already have Ronnie Mac blocking out the time he said he needed in the training schedule."

"Ok, guys, that about wraps it up. I will have the Black Hawk back here the day after tomorrow; he's yours as long as you need him."

"That's a good thing; it will take that long to get the Dief here. Then, a couple days for surveillance. It may be a week before we can exfiltrate (exfil) him. You may want to hold off on the Blackbird."

"No, if he is around the flagpole someone may grab him. Up here he is on an official mission."

"Got it, Boss," Ron said. "See you later."

As soon as Larry departed, Joe and the Deacon went out on the porch. "Top, instead of Dief, why don't I take Steve? He is right here, plus he has some great drugs available to subdue this dude for transport and also to loosen his tongue. And if you really wanted to help you could lend us your Touareg to carry out the mission."

"That sounds like a better idea. I've already thrown one curve ball at John today. I don't want to turn around and steal the Dief, too, which would be akin to pouring salt in the wound. I want to get up there as soon as we can, as there is a chance he may get spooked and run when his contact fails to show up with the device."

"I will brief Steve tonight; we should be ready to roll first thing in the morning. By this time tomorrow we will be on a stakeout."

"I will brief Larry on the change in the morning. By the way, try to be quiet when you leave."

"Screw you, Top."

Chapter 14...A New Guest

Al Karim lived in a very seedy part of town. We have all seen them, the neighborhood where you were constantly looking over your shoulder as you walked through the streets; always with a high degree of trepidation. No ethnic group seemed to dominate; rather, it was a mixing pot of the worst humanity had to offer.

It was the third full day of monitoring Al Karim, and frankly he didn't appear to have much of a life at all. The apparent highlight of his day seemed to be his trek to the local Mosque to attend the 1700 hour prayer session, and his subsequent return home. Joe and Steve were confident that he could be gang raped in the middle of the street and no one would notice, so they were very comfortable in abducting him off the street. Steve was standing against a building, which he knew Al Karim would have to pass on his way home from his prayer session. Joe was adjacent to Steve in the Touareg, just waiting for Steve to subdue Al Karim with his drug cocktail. The tempo built, as Al Karim rounded the corner and headed toward Steve's location. Immediately upon reaching Steve, Steve had him in a headlock, and just as quickly had a hypodermic in his neck, which put Karim out instantly. Joe already had the trunk compartment opened, and Al Karim was stuffed into the trunk. Once Karim was covered with a blanket, the trio were on their way back to Wolfeboro.

It was dawn when Joe drove up to the lodge. The roosters were crowing, but then again, they always crowed. The main evidence of dawn was the sound of the students singing cadence on their morning run. Additionally, the Deacon was visible through the window brewing a pot of coffee; that was surer sign than the rise of the sun that dawn was here.

Ron had already poured Steve and Joe a cup by the time they got in the door of the Lodge. "I am assuming that since you returned you got the bastard," the Deacon said.

"Ya, we got him," Joe said. "We need to put him on ice somewhere until tonight when I can fly him to Deming. I need some rest before the flight."

"Steve, can you keep him knocked out from now until then?" the Deacon asked. "If so, we can just store him in the Blackbird. Cuff and bind him, just in case. He can wake up in the bunker in Deming."

"I don't see any problem with that. Just realize he will feel like shit when he finally comes to."

"And I should give a shit how he feels...why?" the Deacon asked.

"Good point."

"Joe, go to bed, get some rest, you have a long night ahead of you. Spend a day or so in Deming to get caught up on your rest."

Joe was preparing for take-off at 0500, as he knew he had a 12-hour flight ahead of him. Joe decided to release the Blackbird and take the prisoner in the Otter. Even with the upgraded turbine 1000 hp engines, he could just barely squeak 200 mph out of the Otter. He coordinated with Bert and arranged for Bert to do the last leg of the flight in his twin otter. That would allow Peter to service Joe's Otter, which was overdue. And if the truth were known, Joe would much rather spend a couple days off in San Antonio than he would Deming.

It was close to 1400 when Serf heard the Twin Otter buzz the safe house. He was surprised as the Deacon had called and told him that Joe would be bringing the prisoner in with his Otter.

Serf and Wilson were prepared for the arrival of the Iranian. With his head still bagged, the Iranian was taken to an underground bunker, where he was locked away. The sole furnishings of his new home consisted of a bamboo mat to sleep on, a blanket, a bucket for body waste and, last but not least, Rodney, a six-foot rattlesnake.

Al Karim was starting to get an appreciation for the gravity of his situation. He was locked up with a sandwich, a bottle of water and his newfound friend, Rodney, who had laid claim to the bamboo mat.

"What's with the rattlesnake?" Bert asked.

"Can't think of a better way to keep that bastard awake, unless we take turns on him, and that concept sucks," Serf said. "This way we can wear him out without doing anything. What he doesn't realize is that it is an Eastern Diamondback, a fairly docile rattler. It won't screw with that Iranian unless he is screwed with first."

"Serf, I hate to hit and run, but we have to get our asses back in the air. I just finished four days of surveillance and a 12 hour flight; I need to get some rest." Joe said, finally, looking forward to a couple of days in San Antonio. "Keep us posted on what you get out of this bastard. Hopefully, he knows the intended target as well as some other shit."

Ron Dahle

"Good morning, Larry. Just thought you would want an update on Al Karim. Thanks to Rodney, the rattler, Karim hasn't slept in four nights," Ron said. "According to Serf, he just cowers in the corner, sitting on the cement floor, while Rodney sleeps on his bamboo mat. He has been water boarded half a dozen times, beaten, staked out in a bed of ants. Believe me, this mother fucker knows nothing. He was waiting for a package that he was to hold until a man with a face but no name came to pick it up. I believe him. He was a cutout, just another middleman. We may never know the intended target."

"Unfortunately, I think you are correct about this, Top. All this really means is that we need to be even more vigilant, for as you know these bastards aren't going to stop, they have been fighting this war since the seventh century!

"We are keeping the ASA units on station searching for the resumption of the radio broadcasts. You know it's coming, it's just a matter of time.

"Whoever your magic mapmaker is, stress this concept to him. We may need to extend our range into Arizona; they have been getting their ass kicked in New Mexico thanks to Serf and company. This is something to ponder."

"You realize, if we do that we will have to confine our operations to south of the border, as Arizona is a lot more active when it comes to policing their border."

"That is a good point. I will have to look into what air assets are available in that area, but it is still worth considering.

"Have you determined what you are going to do with Al Karim yet?"

"We can't release him for obvious reasons. I am sure he is willing to die, based on what he has to look forward to in the bunker. He will be a lot happier as coyote food than snake bait. I will have Serf take care of him tomorrow."

"Okay, Top, let's keep our ears to the ground and see what we can come up with. It's damn sure no one else is doing anything. If it is going to happen, it's up to us to do it. Talk to you later, friend."

Chapter 15...The New Class

The graduating class was standing by their equipment, waiting for the Buffalo to land. Inside the buffalo was a new batch of troops who had no idea where in hell they were or what was in store for them.

The cadre was all standing by in their pressed, starched uniforms, with one exception, "Light Shadow". He was dressed in Indian garb that included a loincloth, a longbow, a spear, and a homemade stag horn handled knife. He looked every bit the Apache warrior he was. He projected a towering, foreboding presence to all. There was an aura about him, almost nimbus-like, which suggested the presence of warriors from generations past watching over him.

The new arrivals carried their bags off the plane and put them in a pile. At that time, half the cadre took them for a run down to the compound. The other half loaded the graduating class into the Buffalo and sent them on their way. They then loaded the baggage from the new class, took it to the cantonment area, and dumped it in the middle of the Company street. "Welcome to hell week, boys!"

The class was just entering its second week of training when the eldest of Light Shadow's sons, Jonathan, went on sick call. That was a prearranged signal to denote a problem. The boys knew the only way they could have any contact with their father or anyone who knew their identity was through Steve in the aid station, as that was the only place a person had privacy.

Jonathan told a chilling tale. There was a group of four students stealing C-4 from the training sites. The younger son, Benjamin, had overheard them say they were going to use it to blow up the Apple Cabin and the Lodge, as instructed. Jonathan had no idea when this was going to happen, but he did have the suspect students' names, and stated the C-4 was hidden in their wall lockers.

Steve put a sling on Jonathan and told him to take the day off, and to keep his eyes and ears open.

Steve went over to the Lodge, where Ron was having lunch with Mary Jane. Steve said he needed to talk to Ron, but the Deacon informed him that Mary Jane was cleared for about anything Steve could come up with. Upon relating Jonathan's story to Ron and Mary Jane, Mary Jane's face went ashen. The Deacon, seeing this, reached out to her and told her to worry not, as all was ok.

"We all knew this day was coming, I just didn't think it would be this soon. The question is how to handle it now that it is here. My gut tells me to go in tonight about 0100 hours and have a shakedown inspection. If we do that, then what is our next move? We can't turn them over to the authorities, remember. We don't exist in most eyes. Homeland security would have a field day with this. The bottom line is we have to send them back to Nicaragua and hope they handle it properly. Anyone have any better idea?"

"If we bust them on an inspection, the only thing we will have on them is possession of an explosive material. Not likely a major offense in Nicaragua," Dewey said. "They'll be back within two classes."

"There is a degree of risk involved, but I would guess they are going to try to take us out with satchel charges. If we catch them in the process of moving the satchels into place, we have charges that will stick," Ronnie Mac said. "We just have no room for error."

"Guys, we are avoiding the issue," Joe offered, "and that is that no matter which one of those solutions we go with, they get a ride and their Bosses will try again. We need to confirm they have the C-4 while they are in training, and if they do, we need to send a message; they need to have a major mishap on the range tomorrow. The four of them need to be teamed up and sent to the mock truss bridge to place charges on it. Once they start working, I will take it from there. All I have to do is go place charges tonight and command detonate them tomorrow. Everyone will chalk it up to a training accident, minimal paperwork, and most important their Bosses will know! No one outside of this room needs to know this."

"Best plan I have heard tonight. Ronnie, Dewey, what's your take on it?"

"Christ, Deacon, when you interviewed me for this job you said it would be exciting, you just didn't qualify that comment. Hell yeah, I'm in."

"I wish I could come up with a better solution to the problem, but I have to admit Joe's plan has merit. Count me in," Dewey said with conviction.

"Ronnie Mac, Dewey, you arrange for the teaming and assignment of the boys in the morning. Joe, you have your work cut out for the night.

"Now, if you will excuse me, gentlemen, I am going to call it a night."

Mary Jane came out of the bedroom, and said "Four boys' lives, just like that? Isn't there another way?"

"Babe, if there was a better solution we would go with it. Remember these four boys were getting ready to put satchel charges of C-4 in the Lodge while we slept, and the same in the Apple Cabin. They would have killed over thirty people. What would you suggest?"

"I suggest we go to bed. I never looked at it like that."

"If you remember, I told you on day one this was a possibility. The men we are at war with don't play. Neither can we. Now, let's go to bed."

From a distance, Dewey and Ronnie Mac were observing the four students placing the charges on the truss bridge, when they stopped for a minute, divided the C-4, and put some in one of their rucksacks, before they finished priming the charge. As soon as they started to prime the charge all hell broke loose. The entire bridge exploded. The boys were scattered over a one hundred yard area. The alarm immediately went through the Academy, but everyone was helpless. The Deacon told Steve to pack up the bodies as well as he could for shipment back to Nicaragua. He then told Dewey to have someone collect their belongings and, as soon as they found the explosives, to conduct a complete shakedown of the barracks.

Now to call Larry. "Hey, Top, what's up? Been wondering when I would hear from you."

"Well, not sure you want this call. We had an accident on the demo range this morning. It killed four Nicaraguans. A subsequent search of their wall lockers revealed they all had a stash of C-4 and blasting caps. They were observed segregating more C-4 at the target site, when it blew. Steve is packing their body bags as we speak. We need the Buffalo to come pick them and their belongings up."

"It will be there this afternoon, as will I. This issue needs to be handled right or it will come down around our heads. I'll see you about 1530, Top."

Ron was comfortable that the stories would match, as everyone who knew the truth was complicit in the murders. That is everyone except Mary Jane.

―――――――

"Damn it, Top, do you have any idea the paperwork this is going to generate? I will be up here next week with a legal officer to take sworn statements from all involved. I am sure that will be no problem," Larry said with a smirk. "I assume this is another one of those issues we will talk about on that boat ride?"

"That's pretty much an accurate assessment, Boss. Sometimes things just happen, ya know?"

"Don't put that in your statement, Top," Larry said smiling.

"What we are going to have to do is be extremely careful vetting recruits in the future. Think about it, twenty-five percent of this class arrived here with the intention of totally demolishing the compound, cadre, and God knows what else they may have had in mind. They could have blown their way into the bunkers and been able to arm a small army.

"We have to tighten up on control of all of our explosives, and run a lot tighter control over it. Accountability is going to have to become paramount on everything that leaves the bunker. That is do-able; it will just place higher demands on the instructors. They are going to have to maintain constant supervision during all phases of demolitions training."

"Other than that, Top, how is everything working out? How is Gunny doing?"

"Shit, they think he is a shaman. If we were in Chicago, they would call him 'Bad Bad Leroy Brown'. He has them two hours a day. We can check out his class in the morning. At the end of the course they are all going to The White Mountains.

He is going to send half of them out on their own, and an hour later he is going to send the other half out looking for them. For the sake of safety, everyone will have a strobe and an IR beacon. As far as his boys go, they are hanging in there with the best of them. They are the ones who tipped us to this whole ploy."

"That's good, I am glad it worked out so well. Do you suppose he would be willing to stay on?"

"I'm not sure about that, as he has strong ties to his local region; it's that Indian thing, ya know. I need to talk to him in the next couple of days; I will run staying on by him, and see what he thinks."

"Give me a read on his decision. I feel he could benefit the program based on what you have told me. On that note, I am going to make an early night out of it, as I have to get back to Langley and work on this goatfuck. I will call you with the exact date the legal team will be here."

———

"Tell me, Light Shadow, are you allowed to drink coffee when you are dressed in your battle garb?" Ron said smiling.

"Only if there is no one watching me," he said with a pseudo-stoic expression.

"Well, in that case, you can have a cup, for as we have recently found out no one is watching anything. Are you aware of the role your sons played in the discovery of the infiltrators last week?"

"No, I wasn't. I have had no contact with them outside the class, as we decided. I trust they were in no way complicit."

"On the contrary, Gunny, we wouldn't be here if it had not been for their paying attention. Obviously, you have taught them well."

The Deacon went on to explain the entire scenario, as it played out, to Gunny, and the role his sons played in what was in all probability the only thing that saved the camp. Ron could see Gunny's chest swell with pride as he listened intently to the tale. "Now, none of what you heard can be repeated, as the manner in which we decided to handle this issue would be considered, by some, to be rather unorthodox. After a lengthy discussion, the course of action we took was the only one that made any sense in the end."

"Worry not, Deacon, as I am a warrior and warriors know what must be done. And for my sons, I can now call them Indian Scouts, for they have earned the title."

"That they have, Gunny, that they have. Now let us move on to you. I realize that you came on board for the class as your sons were attending. What I didn't expect was the level of professionalism you brought to the Academy and your demonstrated value to our curriculum. Our graduating students will be better prepared for their tasks at hand, and will have a better likelihood of mission accomplishment and survival because of your training. You surpassed all our expectations. Not from a personal/professional point of view, but in what you brought to the class in knowledge. I have discussed this matter with Larry, and we would both like to extend an offer to you to consider staying on for the summer classes at the Academy on a recurring basis."

"I have to consider that, Deacon, as you know I also have a mission in my ancestral lands. I need to give it some thought, as well as confer with my wife. I will get back to you in a couple of days. I must add that I am indeed honored to be offered this opportunity. Now sir, I need to leave, as I have a class in twenty minutes. See you in a couple of days."

Chapter 16

Ron kissed Mary Jane as she departed for Maine, to tend to her daughter who had just had a baby. She didn't especially want or need to go, but Ron insisted she leave. Deep down inside, he was not sure how she would fair with the possible grilling from the legal team due in tomorrow.

It was quiet at the Academy, as this was the week when the final training was being conducted in The White Mountains. Tomorrow the students had the final tracking test for Light Shadow, which promised to go through the day and into the night. The rest of the week was fast rope insertion, drills, and land navigation. Overall it would be a very grueling week.

Larry and his entourage showed up about 1130 hours on Tuesday. Ron took them downtown to the Inn where he had rooms reserved for them. While they were there, they all went in the private dining room to have lunch and to break the ice, so to speak. Ron received a briefing on the scope of the investigation, and whom they would need to interview based on the preliminary information Larry had given them.

Ron gave them a briefing as to what he knew about the entire situation, including the roles played by Gunny's sons, and the decision to monitor the actions of the four suspects the following day. Their intentions were to have a shakedown inspection that night as the boys came off the range, looking for explosives. The mishap preempted that action. There was, however, a shakedown of all wall lockers in the barracks and 10 to 15 pounds of C-4 was found in the lockers of each of the four boys, which conformed the cadres' suspicions.

Back at the Academy, while waiting for Dewey, Joe and Gunny's sons, to be brought back by chopper, Ron provided the team with copies of the new Range rules, and the new logistics control measures and SOP that the Academy put in place to control all demolitions and ammunitions. This included the new requirement mandating constant supervision any time students were on the demo range.

The second day they interviewed Ron and Joe, as well as twelve cadre guards that had been positioned near the Lodge and Apple Cabin the night the issue was discovered. The guards were armed and given orders to shoot to kill. They received no additional information pertaining to the mission.

The team went through all of the past inventories and accountability procedures that had been in effect prior to the incident, and found no other discrepancies. The head of the inspection team scheduled a debriefing for select cadre members, including Gunny's sons.

"In essence, while we question the unsupervised use of demolitions, we find little to fault the Academy with. It is apparent, to us, that these four victims were on a clandestine mission to cause grievous harm to the Academy and the Cadre within it. Had it not been for the attention to detail displayed by these two young men we may well be conducting a more solemn investigation, on what was the site of this Academy.

"Jonathan and Benjamin, I want to take this opportunity to express the gratitude of the entire CIA for your actions. I also want to present you with this certificate of appreciation for each of you signed by the Director of the CIA.

"Gentlemen, the fact that this incident occurred is ample proof of the need for this Academy. It happened in Columbia, and now it has almost happened here. I am recommending additional funding for around the clock security throughout the entire grounds. Top, get with Larry once you have drafted up a plan and have a cost estimate. Last week proved how important this Academy is in our fight against terror.

"We have made reservations for all of us at the Inn for dinner tonight. Our plane will be picking us up at the Wolfeboro airfield in the morning. I want to thank you for your cooperation over the last week."

This was all a tid bit Larry threw at the inspection team, as they came directly under him. He wanted them to take center stage on this one, as the news was all good.

During cocktails before dinner, Larry looked at Ron and said, "Top, you can let Mary Jane come back now." He winked at Ron as he spoke.

Chapter 17

Mary Jane was back at the Lodge, and after talking to Ron was grateful that she was absent during the inquest. "I'm not sure how I would have held up if pushed."

"Hell, babe, you would have done great. I just wanted to spare you the anguish of putting up with those assholes. And, had it all gone to shit, I would have married you so you wouldn't be able to testify against me."

"You asshole!"

"Hey girl, you've got the ring, we just haven't picked a date yet. There are legal benefits to not being married to me. In the event this all comes apart, you are shielded. Otherwise, we would have been married ages ago."

"You son of a bitch, I don't know what to believe, damn it. Why can't you be a frigging baker?"

"Simple, my love. Bakers keep terrible hours," Ron said as he took Mary Jane in his arms, where she promptly melted. Moreover, Ron realized he had just dodged a bullet fired by his own mouth.

Upon completion of the land navigation phase of the training, Gunny showed up at the Lodge and asked the Deacon if he had time to talk to him.

"Of course I do, Gunny. Come in, allow me to get you a cup of coffee. I trust you have had time to consider the options we have discussed?"

"Yes, I have, and I have also talked to my wife about it in great detail. My wife and I are both Indians. She is one hundred percent. My bloodlines were broken, but I am still an Indian. We realize that in today's society it is nearly impossible to live the life of an Indian. There is little way to pass our heritage on to our children.

"We are Plains Indians and that is how we were brought up, but as I told my wife, when I was in Afghanistan and Iraq, I was still an Indian. No matter where we are, we will always be Indians.

"The northern Indian, primarily of the Algonquin tribe, including the Mickmacs, were mostly woodland Indians. For the most part, they lived in Wigwams, as the traditional Tee Pees were inadequate due to the weather.

"I pride myself in being capable and adaptable. With your grace I will build a Wigwam for my family in your wooded land by the stream, providing my wife and children can accompany me. This is the only way I will be able to instill in my children what it means to be an Indian. I will keep it neat; I will build a shelter for a chemical toilet in keeping with your regulations. Granted, they will not learn the same skills of a Plains Indian, but as I said, an Indian will always be an Indian. If we were to move to Alaska, and the situation warranted, I would build an Igloo and hunt polar bear. That is the way of a true Indian!

"As much as possible, we will live off the land. There is plenty of game here; anything taken will be by spear or arrow. The ground is fertile, so we can have a garden. It will be a tough life, but it will be our life. In the fall and winter we will return to New Mexico and I will continue my mission in the Forest. I will be available to work with Serf if he needs my help on specific missions.

　　　　　　　　　　　　　　　　　　　　　　Ron Dahle

"I realize this may sound a little crazy to you, but this may well be the only chance to live as my ancestors lived, and that is important to me at this point in my life."

It was not the plains, or the desert, or the coast, or the woodlands the Indian loved; it was the 'Earth' which he so loved, revered, and held above everything else.

"Gunny, I have to take my hat off to you. Anyone else saying that, I would figure that they were just blowing smoke. There is no doubt in my mind that you are serious. Pick your spot and make your Wigwam a home of which your family can be proud and enjoy their heritage."

"Thank you, Top. First I need to fashion three tomahawks to allow us to cut the brush, and start stripping bark for the wigwam in our spare time. I will keep my boys here for the rest of this season to work on it. By the time the season is over, we should have a first class wigwam for my family to occupy next spring."

"You have our full support on this endeavor, Gunny. If you need anything, don't hesitate to speak up. I wish you well on the task ahead of you."

Chapter 18

"Vince, I was beginning to think you had forgotten me. It seems like it has been ages since we last talked," Ron said.

"That's because it has been ages, Sergeant Major. I heard through the grapevine that you had a bit of difficulty at the Academy, and I did not want to pester you until it was over, which I understand it is. So…I'm back!" Vince laughed. "I am getting ready to Nat Exp some maps up for your perusal. They are from the ex-Marine's Forest. I will let you study them and then you can get back to me with what you think. They are date stamped, and were taken every other day for a period of four weeks; we also have night coverage with thermal imaging. Not sure I know what to make of them. Check them out and give me a call. Compare them to previous maps of the same area."

"Can you send Serf a copy, also; he can send Tommy in there to see what's going on."

"Sergeant Major, you may want to hold off on that until you get these images. You'll have them in the morning."

"Ok Vince. You realize, of course, that you have really piqued my curiosity."

"That's a good thing at times, you know. I'll be talking to you soon. Have a great day."

Mary Jane entered the study. "My God, was that Vince you were just talking to? He hasn't called in ages."

"I know. Somehow, he got wind of the crisis we had here with the infiltrators and elected to let that go away before he called. Probably for the best, as we can only handle one crisis at a time around here.

"By the way, babe, have you been down to check out Gunny's wigwam yet? Christ, he is living better than I did as a kid."

"No, I haven't. I wouldn't go down there without you; you know that, dummy. Do you realize that is the first time you have ever mentioned your childhood?"

"Probably be the last, too. I don't go there unless I have to, or slip up like I just did.

"Shit, hon, don't forget to remind me I have to brief the new security company tomorrow. They are sending their big wigs in for the briefing. This will be tough; I need to tell them everything without telling them anything. I have to impress the level of security we need without telling them we killed four terrorists last month, as no one knows that. It was listed as a training accident, and even at that it wasn't reported locally. We had a problem getting a firm that would take the contract giving us the option to fire anyone on the spot if they were derelict in their duties. Fortunately, the contract was lucrative enough to get some takers."

"Who do you think I am, your private secretary or something? I quit that shit when I started giving you pussy on a regular basis," Mary Jane said laughing.

"Well, shit, we need to switch that around. I can get pussy anywhere; good secretaries are hard to come by."

"Screw you, Ron!" Mary Jane said as she gave Ron the finger.

This exchange of banter and the debate of good pussy vs. good secretaries continued all the way over to the rug in front of the fireplace, where they spent the rest of the day evaluating that hypothesis.

The briefing with the security company executives seemed to drag on for hours. Actually, it only lasted a little more than an hour, but the Deacon saw the Nat Exp truck drive up just as he went into the Apple Cabin where the briefing was being held, and he would much rather had been studying the maps than briefing a group of pompous asses, as he referred to them.

Ron was just getting to the maps Vince sent up when Bob called him.

"Good afternoon, Ron. Have you checked the news today?"

"Bob, I know you are going to find this hard to believe but it has been so busy here for the last several weeks, I don't even remember where the remote is."

"When you find it you may want to check out the news. Three more banks have gone under. They have finally mentioned the operation we pulled off. They are trying to pin it on a bunch of hackers in the Mideast. When you have a chance run it by Larry and see what he is hearing on it. The money is finally parked. Our access accounts have all been loaded at the rate of one million dollars in the stateside accounts, ten billion in each of the Cayman Island accounts and twenty billion in our other access accounts. The balance has been divided up among fifty holding accounts. We netted $924,000,000,000, after all fees were subtracted. That's a tidy sum for three months' work."

"That it is. Bob, you realize one of these days I need to know how the system works, in the event I outlive you."

"I will order you a mainframe and come out and set you up a parallel system."

"Then why did you need four mainframes, may I ask?

"Simple. The work has been done, the crunching is over; everything is on autopilot, so to speak. I have turned one of my mainframes into a backup system in the event of a problem. Two of them are finally able to work on crunching our prospective warriors. I would like to do this as soon as possible, to provide an off-site backup system for safety."

"You order the mainframe, and I will notify you when it's here."

"That sounds like a plan, my friend. We'll talk soon."

Ron was finally able to get to the maps that Vince shipped to him. A close inspection revealed a trail on the current maps that didn't appear on earlier versions of the same area. The trail appeared to stop in the middle of the forest, by a cliff. The trail, showing signs of heavy use, was in a different region of the forest than that which Gunny patrolled.

A close inspection of the thermal imagery showed many traces of life forms. The magnified versions confirmed that they were humans. There were twelve persons dispersed in a semicircular pattern along the face of the cliff—about one hundred fifty yards out from the face. They were obviously sentinels; the question was, what were they guarding?

Ron paged Joe and Gunny to come and check out the map; there was a good possibility that Gunny was familiar with this area.

"I have been here," Gunny said. "There is a massive cavern along that ledge. It goes in for hundreds of feet. You could hide a battalion there. Notice there are heat traces emanating from what appears to be the cliff. That is likely from a large number of people inside the cavern."

"It is not likely they are Mexicans," Joe said. "They would not be inclined to gather in these numbers, they would be more inclined to disappear among the Mexican populations in the towns and villages.

"Boys, I think we have a massive terror cell here. The area is off limits, so they feel secure, they have room to train, and based on what Gunny said there is ample room inside the cavern to handle a major force. This may well be beyond our capabilities."

"Joe, I don't believe what I just heard came from your mouth! Did you learn anything while you worked for Larry and me? Nothing is impossible, damn it! Some things are just a bit more difficult than others. I need to talk to Vince and we will need to get Larry involved in this, too. I think it is time for Vince and Larry to meet."

"Do you think that is a good idea, Top? You always said you wanted to shield Vince from the CIA and others we deal with."

"Damn it, Joe, I know it, but this operation will call for extensive sharing of both of their assets. It would be a lot easier if we could work together on this project, and we could share information more freely. They are both in this deep enough to go before the firing squad with us; damn it, it's time for a little trust and cooperation to smooth out our operation. I will leave the final decision up to Vince, as he is the one with the reservations. I just hope he can see through the forest and find the trees.

"Ok guys, I appreciate your input. I have to sit and ponder this whole situation and figure out the best way to approach it. We will have another meeting soon."

Chapter 19

"Vince, I'm glad I caught you in. We went over the photos you sent and compared them to earlier ones, and we think we have a major problem."

"That's what I was afraid of. What can we do about it?"

"It's bigger than it appears. We located a dozen guard posts protecting what all indications suggest is the mouth of a cavern. Gunny has been in that cavern years ago, and says it is massive. The level of traffic leading to it suggests that there is a lot going on there. Is this something Homeland Security would react on?"

"Are you shitting me? Homeland security has turned into a Presidential protection force, and it will likely stay that way till after the election."

"Ok Vince, it is time for you to come out of the closet and work with the team."

"Bullshit. We agreed when we started out that there would be no other agency involvement. What part of no don't you understand, Sergeant Major?"

"Vince. Damn it, you have to quit being the Captain of the ship and become a team player. How in hell do you think we have been able to pull off the shit we have? Not by being a bunch of prima-donnas, and that you can take to the bank. I am asking you to work with my CIA contact, Larry Neider. I have known him for over forty years, I would trust him with my life and he would do the same with me.

"Hell, he put out the hit on Senator Roach. He is part of the team. Damn it, so are you. You have made the majority of my operations possible. Without you on the team, we would still be doing nickel and dime gigs. This one operation needs all of us to work together.

"You for imagery, Larry for radio direction finding (RDF) and air support, if we need it. It needs to be an integrated effort. He should be able to communicate possible coordinates directly to you based on RDF findings. This thing is hot. The more layers of bureaucratic bullshit we have to wade through, the longer it will take to address the problem, and that may just be too frigging late.

"To kick this off I am going to have to commit every warrior I have, and I am willing to do that, as I believe it is that big."

"If I were to agree to meet him, where would that happen?"

"I would suggest here; it is neutral territory, I have secure areas or we have hundreds of acres where you could meet. The call is yours."

"Can he be at your place tomorrow at noon?"

"I will have to call him and find out; I will get back to you as soon as I know."

"Damn you, Sergeant Major, I don't like this one bit, and I want you to know that. Call me when you find out. Tell him to bring sneakers and a brief jogging outfit!"

Vince and Larry had been gone over two hours when the Deacon saw them running up the hill. He couldn't help but wonder if they had been jogging the whole time. Mary Jane commented that they looked like a couple of 60-year-old kids out for a run.

Ron greeted both of them with a large glass of ice water. "Damn, Sergeant Major, I wondered what you did around here. Now I know," Vince said.

"Well, were you two able to sort out your differences on your jog?"

"It was never a matter of differences," Vince said. "However, it is safe to say that we worked out a perfectly amenable set of conditions to which we can work in harmony on a wide range of mutually agreeable projects."

"Halla-fucking-lujah brother. May miracles never cease," the Deacon said. "Do you conduct all your negotiations on the running field?"

"No, but have you ever seen anyone able to conceal a wire in a running outfit?"

"No, I guess I have to give that one to you, Vince. Larry, you have been quiet."

"That's because I am still catching my breath from that fucking hill. All is cool; I think we are going to make a good team."

"Well, shit, in that case we need to get to work. Larry, do you have your ASA vans in place yet?"

"They deployed this morning. As soon as I get something I will contact Vince and he will be able to capture it and get you the maps."

"What I haven't told you, Sergeant Major," Vince said," is that I am planting a blimp over that area. They have the same capabilities as the drones, and then some. They can stay on station for extended periods and cover an extremely large area. This is the right tool for this job. This particular crew is sort of like Larry's accountants, they are loyal to me. A lot of the imagery you have received from me is from this crew."

"Well, then Joe, Gunny, and myself will start to establish a plan; as soon as we put it together we will brief you two, and see if it passes the smell test."

"Top, what about the oversight of the Academy if you pull Joe out?" Larry asked.

"Not a problem. Dewey is good, Ronnie Mac is great, plus he has a historical loyalty to me. The Academy will be in good hands.

"Vince, if you brought anything to wear other than those silly shorts, we can all go out to dinner in a bit, as I know you aren't going to fly in the dark."

"So, Top, what happened between Vince and Larry yesterday?"

"No fucking idea Joe. They left here barely speaking, and returned in a couple hours acting like old friends. I will find out when one of them decides to tell me, or…maybe not. Doesn't really matter, it all worked out for the best. They are now communicating directly, speeding the whole process by a couple of days per exchange. It takes a lot of shit off us, too. Just maybe Vince is becoming a team player."

Ron called Serf next. "Surprised you're still up and about. What's happening in your area?"

"Hey Batman, glad to hear from you, it's been a while. Tommy and Wilson are deep in Mexico, following up a couple of leads. It appears that Hezbollah and Hamas agents are getting hard to find lately."

"That's because they have abandoned Mexico and are holding up in a cavern in Gunny's forest. You need to get Tommy and Wilson back; we've got a big one on the burner."

"I will have to set up an exfiltration with Bert. They are in too far to walk out in a reasonable amount of time."

"You do what you've got to do. Just get them and stand by."

"On it, Batman. Keep me posted."

"WILCO, talk soon."

Ron dialed one more number for the night. "John, how's it going, old man?"

"Old man, my ass! You finally call to thank me for the new mess hall, barracks, and your safe I installed that you were conveniently out of town for? Or do you want something else pulled out of my ass?"

"I know I have been remiss on that. You can't believe what has been going on here since then, it has been a madhouse! And damn it, it isn't slowing down at all. I know that isn't an excuse but it's the best I can offer.

"Got a couple of things to run by you. First, I need you to send the Dief here for a bit; we've got some hot shit cooking, and I could really use him.

"Next, I want you to train a ground crew for the balloon; it is too much for just the two of you to set up alone any longer. Don't brief them on anything except how to set it up and act as a chase vehicle. A three-man crew with blowers along with Dief should be able to set it up in a couple of minutes. We won't know until November if it will be needed or not, but it is more important than ever in the event we exercise that option.

"Tell Dief all he needs to bring is his warm body to me asap. Oh…and John, I do appreciate the job you did this spring…really, you make my job possible! We'll talk later, sir."

"Did I just hear you say you wanted Dief's warm body?" Mary Jane asked. "All this time I thought I filled that gap in your life."

"You silly twit, get your ass over here and we will check that out first hand. We'll let you be the judge when we finish.

"Babe, you know that you are the apple of my eye, the light on my path, the Love of my Life, and the reason I do everything I do. However, the occasional young boy is refreshing."

This elicited a battering about the head and shoulders from Mary Jane, which set Ron off into a fit of sidesplitting laughter that almost made him piss his pants. The harder he laughed, the more Mary Jane beat on him, until she finally collapsed into his arms. "I guess I ought to reconsider that concept, huh." Ron uttered, which, of course, elicited another round of pummeling from Mary Jane.

Thoroughly exhausted, Mary Jane determined that her energy would be much better spent making love to this fool than beating on him, which they proceeded to do, but only after having Ron throw a couple more logs on the fireplace. Not for the sake of the warmth, but for the ambience created by the crackling flickering glow and the aroma of burning oak which spread throughout the Lodge.

Thoroughly spent, they fell asleep in front of the fireplace, Mary Jane thinking of the evening they'd just shared, while Ron was deeply engrossed in thinking of the task at hand in the Forest as they dozed off.

———

Chapter 20

Ron was just finishing his morning shower when he heard the sound of Vince's secure fax printing out documents. He smiled to himself, in a triumphant sort of way, as he knew that he was receiving images sent by Vince that were based on data Vince received directly from Larry. Finally, the two of them have an open channel of communications, Ron thought.

Ron grabbed the images and copied the data onto a thumb drive, to download them in the war room.

Ron glanced over at the rug and saw Mary Jane had dozed back off. That's ok, she'll wake up when I start the coffee, he thought, which he was already in the process of doing.

Sitting at the table, Ron studied the fax images, which left enough to be desired that he knew he couldn't glean anything worthwhile until they were downloaded.

Sure enough, the coffee was no sooner finished than Mary Jane had slithered over to the table sans clothing with the exception of Ron's t-shirt. Ron looked at her and realized that never in his life had he seen a woman just crawling off a rug where she had spent the night that was as stunningly beautiful as Mary Jane was. Most women had to labor for hours to approach this level of natural beauty.

Damn it! A knock on the door sent Mary Jane scurrying into the bedroom. It was Joe, wondering if Ron had heard anything from the prospective AO yet.

"Just got these images in. We need to take them to the war room, to download, and see what we have.

"They are more of the same, as well as a handful from coordinates sent in by Larry from the RDF teams. We are finally functioning efficiently.

"I am going to put Bert on notice that we will need to rendezvous in his hangar to plan this operation. He will have to come get us, as I envision a shitload of weaponry needed to pull this off, more than the Otter or my trailer can handle."

"You really think this is going to be that big, Top?"

"Well, let's just say that based on our last couple of encounters we are going to initiate the assault in full MOPP Gear (mission oriented protective postures, which includes protective clothing and masks for contaminated sites). Our last three assaults involved chemical weapons and in one case a nuclear risk. We don't know what we're going up against or how long we will be on the objective. It is a risk I am not willing to take on this one. Realize our entire force is going to be deployed on this operation. I have already arranged with Vince for the suits. Homeland Security has warehouses full of them."

"I really hate wearing that shit," Joe said, "but nothing else does its job, I suppose."

———

Brought up on the big screen, the data confirmed some of the Deacon's beliefs. The radio sites the ASA picked up were relay sites, much the same as the series they just encountered in Mexico. Basically, they were unattended repeaters laid out in a pattern to extend communications from the Mexican border to the area in the vicinity of the expected cavern deep within the Forest. There was a very low level of traffic on these repeaters, most likely to maintain a degree of communications discipline and avoid being picked up.

"Unfortunately the density of the woods precludes getting an oblique view of the entrance to the cavern, and that is the shot we really need," Ron said. "We are going to have to put eyes in there to see what we're really up against."

"Who do you have in mind? Gunny?"

"Don't want to send in one person alone; I think I will send Gunny and Tommy. They are both excellent in the woods. People tend to exercise more care when someone is with them. It is a quirk of human nature. Joe, you know I've told you a thousand times, humans are inherently flawed."

"Yeah, Top, I've heard the spiel, and I am starting to buy into the theory myself. Shit, do you suppose that means I am getting like you? Oh, fuck."

"Fuck you, Joe! When you are finished here, drop down to Gunny's wigwam and ask him to come up. I will brief him on what I want, and send him to Deming. Tommy is still in Mexico. This will give Gunny a couple of days with his wife."

Tommy and Gunny were going over the imagery the Deacon printed up for them. It was apparent that the twelve OPs were relatively stationary permanent positions. They provided full coverage of the face of the cliff. If there were also fallback positions, this could be one "bad assed mother", to quote Surf.

The mission for Tommy and Gunny was to get photos of the front of the cliff and the entrance to the cavern. Additionally, they needed to locate a MSS location that would facilitate extraction by Black Hawks. Hopefully by landing, if not with jungle penetrators, as a worst case scenario.

Serf was going to insert them by vehicle approximately twelve miles from the OA. A long trek, but determined to be the safest route.

Both wore Ghillie suits. They moved through the forest virtually invisible. Tommy followed Gunny, emulating his every move. Tommy was damn good at silent movement but he deferred to Gunny, who he knew was much better. Tommy thought it had to be the Indian in Gunny, as it damn sure wasn't the Marine training.

Approximately two miles from the objective Gunny signaled Tommy to stop and get down. A couple of minutes later a four-man patrol crossed a path about ten yards to their right front. This was the first sign that there were roving patrols out on security watch. This suggested that their progress was going to become much slower and more tedious.

"Ok, Top, tell me. Why didn't you send me on that recon mission? Damn it, you know I'm the best you've got!" Joe said, obviously upset.

"Well, Joe, it is like this. We have no idea what is in those woods. While I place a high premium on every one of my warriors' lives, there are some people who are more expendable than others. I place a higher premium on your safety than either Gunny or Tommy. You would be a lot harder to replace than either one of them. In addition, when I am finished, I plan to hand the reins over to you. I can't do that if you are dead."

Fortunately, Mary Jane entered the room with a sandwich platter, which served to break the silence that set in after the Deacon last spoke.

"Bert is flying in tomorrow to pick up you, Steve, Dief and me, as well as a shit load of equipment. At the same time, Peter is going to Deming to pick up Serf, Gunny, Tommy, and Wilson."

"Do you have a plan yet, or are we pulling this out of our ass?" Joe asked.

"Until last night it was coming out of my ass. I received some photos Tommy sent to me that cleared up many questions

I had. I plan to brief you and Steve this afternoon, and see what you think of it. Why don't you drop by about 1600 and I will have it all laid out for you."

"Sounds good, Top. I will go put a bug in Steve's ear. We'll see you around 1600 hours."

"Mary Jane, let's have a cup of coffee and talk a bit,' Ron said.

Mary Jane questioned what was coming, as Ron sounded more serious than he usually did.

"Here you go. What's up, babe? You leaving me for that young boy?" she asked. "Something is eating at you."

"No, it is nothing like that. Here, take this," Ron said, sliding her a folded piece of paper. This is the number of an account in Boston. All you need is the number and the password and you can make withdrawals. To be safe, don't exceed $4999.00 a day. There is a million dollars in that account. This other slip has an account in the Cayman Islands; it has two billion dollars in it. If anything ever happens to me they are yours, just don't flaunt it. I probably shouldn't tell you this, you being a woman and all, but both funds are self-filling, meaning that when you withdraw funds, they are automatically replaced. They will never run dry."

"What's going on here? Are you getting ready to do something stupid? Tell me, is it that frigging operation you are going on tomorrow? Where did all this money come from anyway?"

"Hey, hey, slow down. Sorry, but it's none of the above. The accounts have just been set up, a result of some wise investing I have done. And no, I don't plan for anything to happen to me. This is just something I have been wanting to do for ages and just got around to it, so just shut up and kiss me, you foolish woman."

"I'll kiss you, but remember I have been handling your finances over 12 years now, and I'm here to tell you have never been wise when it came to money. That dog doesn't race."

Bert's hangar was at near capacity. In addition to the entire team and all of its equipment, Larry and Vince were also in attendance for the mission briefing. This was the first time the team had seen the two of them together.

Gunny and Tommy were presently giving a briefing on what they encountered and saw while they were in the Forest.

"The first points of interest are the guard positions. They are constructed by a half moon of adobe, providing a degree of protection. It also makes them easy to locate, as they stand out among the greenery." Gunny continued on. "The most significant issue is that there is a wooden door covering the entrance to the cavern. The good news is that there is about a two or three-inch gap at the bottom of the door that will provide a basis for an aiming point. The night we observed them, they changed the guard at 1800 hours and 0200 hours. The level of awareness on the part of the guards was very low, with a couple of them dozing on and off. They did not have any night vision goggles that we saw."

Steve was next, discussing the steps to take in the event of contamination with chemical agents. "There is a low likelihood of a problem, as Top will explain later, but you do need to keep the points covered in mind."

———

"Ok guys, this is the big one!" said Ron. "We have no idea what we are up against, and we will leave here not knowing. We do know the security contingent alone outnumbers any force we have encountered to date. Stealth will be the key to success on this operation. Originally, I intended to go in with full MOPP Gear, but MOPP Gear and Stealth are antithetical. The oxygen gathering and sucking of the Thermobaric warheads we are using should keep all gas within the cavern, at least until you are in your MOPP Gear that is coming from the C&C bird via a jungle penetrator.

"As soon as the operation is completed, I will lower your MOPP Gear with the jungle penetrator. You will don it, go in, and conduct a search of the area. You will need oxygen as the area may well be depleted due to the Thermobaric rounds. If you find anything good, retrieve it. Look for anything that may be considered to be of intelligence value. Particularly identification papers, maps, documents, and get me a body count. Bring in a Chemical Agent Detector Kit so you can evaluate the scene.

"This should prove to be a great target for Thermobaric warheads, due to the conical shape of the interior of the cavern. It should provide a text book scenario for the weapon.

"After taking out the security, the next obstacle will be the doors on the cavern. We will engage them with an RPG-29 with HE warheads. A barrage of six Thermobaric rounds will immediately follow this. I guarantee you that everyone in that cavern will be dead, or in the process of dying when the smoke clears."

Ron continued issuing individual task assignments and their exfiltration plan and location, which included two Black Hawks with an Apache flying covey. When he was finishing up he reminded everyone to replace all the batteries in their strobes, beacons, and squad radios. As soon as the Deacon identified the individuals on the silent kill team, he turned them over to Steve for a factual briefing.

"Ok guys, what is the most silent quick kill technique with a knife? Any takers?"

"The throat and carotid artery." Dief, who was a quick kill trained warrior offered.

"Sorry, Dief, I hate to break your bubble but that has the possibility of being one of the noisiest of all means due to the gurgling and the possibility of a bungled first cut allowing the victim to scream. The only true "silent kill" is a deep thrusting and twisting into the kidney with a large knife, which is why we issued SOG Stilettos for this mission. The properly executed kidney thrust is so incredibly painful that it completely paralyzes the victim while he rapidly dies. I want to take a couple of minutes rehearsing locating the kidney. One other thing, when you execute the maneuver be prepared to catch your subject and carefully lower him to the ground. Otherwise, he will drop like a load of bricks, and probably sound like it, too."

———

At 0800 hours, everyone loaded into the Albatross and took off for Deming. They would rendezvous with the chopper support there at 1500 hours.

The warriors broke down into three groups. The first component to deploy would be the silent kill component, consisting of the Dief, Gunny, Joe, and Tommy, the four best Ron had at stealth and silent kill. They would all be armed with garrotes, SOG stiletto, M-4 carbines and, of course, silenced .22 cal. Ruger pistols with laser sights.

Next came the assault element made up of Wilson, Steve, and Serf. The Dief would join the assault element once they reach the objective. The assault element will be bringing in the RPG-29s and the ammo for them. Upon infiltration, the RPGs will be loaded with the HE round for the doors. In addition, each team member would carry in three Thermobaric rounds as well as an M-4 carbine.

The third group would be the Command and Control element, consisting of Ron, Larry, two UH-60 Black Hawks equipped with jungle penetrators, and one Apache flying covey. Ron jokingly stated that he was armed with mini-guns, chain guns and hellfire missiles, as well as his .40 cal Springfield.

The first element was to leave the line of departure (LD) at 1945 hours. The assault element was to depart the LD at 2100 hours, giving the silent kill component ample time to do their job. Stealth was the reason they divided into two components.

You cannot move that quietly carrying an RPG with ammo in addition to an M-4 carbine.

Ron and Larry drove the elements to the selected RP, which was near the LD, and wished them luck. The walk in was only five miles, a much shorter route than Gunny and Tommy took initially. Upon dropping the team off, they headed back to the safehouse in Deming where they would re-unite with the chopper pilots, who were taking a nap.

The silent kill element elected to take out the sentinels closest to the cliff first and work their way around the arc towards the middle, in two teams of two, one of which would keep the sentinel in the sights of his silenced .22 cal Ruger until his partner killed him. This would provide an absolute minimum likelihood of being observed by the other sentries. When they completed the mission, they would be right in the center, where they needed to be to link up with the assault element. From there they would proceed within 150 yards from the door, at which time they would tear down the gates of hell, and commence to create a major demand for virgins in paradise, Allah Akbar!

Gunny and Tommy had just reached the first sentinel. They were waiting for Joe and the Dief to reach theirs on the far side of the arc. Gunny was going to take out the prey with his stiletto while Tommy kept him in the sights of his pistol as a backup.

Joe and the Dief were now in location, with the Dief being the triggerman on their team.

Gunny made the first strike, totally amazed by the effect of the kidney plunge. He grabbed the victim and slowly lowered him to the ground.

Joe was next, but without the amazement that Gunny had experienced, as the kidney thrust was nothing new to Joe. Joe was cursing under his breath due to the volume of blood.

And so it went along the arc of sentinels, one at a time being dispatched to a different plane.

It took two hours to work their way to the last two sentinels. These two were undoubtedly the most dangerous, due to their proximity to each other.

Gunny approached his first and decided to knock him unconscious, which he did. In the process of lowering him to the ground, the guard's rifle fell to the ground. This caused the one remaining guard to turn to see what the noise was. He caught a quick red flash in his eye as he turned his head. The red flash immediately preceded two .22 caliber holes appearing in his head. To Joe and Dief the reports sounded like cannons going off, but they were the only ones who heard them.

Everyone remained momentarily silent and still to determine if they had been heard. Gunny then bound and gagged the unconscious sentinel. They then joined up and waited for the assault crew to arrive. Joe called them on the squad radio; they were ten minutes out.

Upon the arrival of the assault team, the Dief joined them and Steve gave Dief his RPG. At this time Steve took one of the additional rounds off each gunner to make their travel lighter.

They proceeded toward the light at the base of the wall when, suddenly, about one hundred seventy five yards from the doors, one of them opened and there was a man silhouetted by the light inside. He came out apparently to have a cigarette. An RPG HE round is not the weapon of choice for a single human target but it sure as hell is effective. Wilson fired off the second HE round into the other door. By the time Serf got the first Thermobaric round into the cavern both the Dief and Wilson had the second and third Thermobaric rounds on the way and Serf was reloading. It was over as fast as it started. It was obvious this was not going to be a prisoner recovery mission, thought Joe with a smile.

Ron Dahle

The crashing sound in the trees to their left startled the entire crew, and then they felt the downdraft.

The Command ship was a Stealth version of the Black Hawk. The jungle penetrator coming through the trees to deliver the MOPP Gear made more noise than did the Black Hawk.

The team all donned their MOPP Gear, put on their oxygen tanks and took off towards the cavern in two groups. The first group consisted of Steve, who had the Chemical Agent Detector Kit, with Gunny and Tommy as security, not that they would be needed, as it was highly unlikely anyone could have survived that attack.

The second team was to go in when they got the all clear from Steve. In the event there were chemical or biological agents present, the search would be conducted by Steve, Gunny, and Tommy. The Black Hawk would lower a portable decontamination station to the three to decontaminate themselves prior to exfiltration.

Steve came out after a thorough scan of the different parts of the cavern and gave the all clear sign, at which time the remainder of the team went in to assist in the search. There were several people lying on the floor, moaning. Poor bastards, thought Steve, they don't realize they are already dead. The overpressure caused by the Thermobaric warheads is sufficient to rupture all internal organs; it is just a matter of time. Out of compassion Steve shot every 'living dead' in the head to end their misery.

An hour later, the Warriors exited the cavern with two large bags of paperwork, some burned, some charred, and they were dragging a small safe that had obvious blast damage to it. It was being dragged by rope as it was still too hot to handle with bare hands. Gunny got the surviving guard on his feet, and they all headed to the exfil LZ, where the Black Hawks were waiting.

Upon arrival at the safe house in Deming, Larry took all the documents and the safe with him to Langley. With his head in a bag, the guard was led down into the bunker by Serf, where he joined Rodney, the rattler.

In less than ten minutes, the hollering started from the bunker. Serf went down to see what was going on, and discovered the guard spoke perfect English. He should; his original name was Jason Schmidt, he was a third generation German from Milwaukee. He currently went by Jamaat al Zuhdi. Serf assumed that was the name he elected to go to Paradise with.

The first thing he demanded was a lawyer, which elicited a round of laughter from Surf that was heard all the way upstairs.

"You don't get it at all, do you, dude? You'll never see a lawyer, in fact you may likely never see the outside of this fucking bunker again. Basically, you fuck with me and you'll never see tomorrow!" Serf said as he knocked him down. Rodney was coiled and rattling as Jason landed beside him.

"Now, if you get the urge to talk intelligently give us a holler. Otherwise, your best hope is that Rodney isn't too hungry.

Jason looked around the room, and all there was in it was a bamboo mat that Rodney claimed, an old army blanket and a five-gallon pail.

-

"Good morning, Bert. Any time you are up to it you can come and get us. We picked up a portable decontamination station on this trip and I want it at the Lodge for future use, plus we have ten sets of MOPP Gear to go back."

"Peter is flying jumpers all day. We can come up tonight and head to Wolfeboro tomorrow. You can fill me in on the operation during the flight."

"Sounds good to me, see you tonight, Bert. Have a safe flight."

Ron hung up and addressed Serf, who'd just come back into the safe house. "Damn it, Serf, don't you fuckers drink coffee around here? Or is it a make your own proposition?"

"Well, Batman, that is the surest way to get a cup. Do you want to come down while I sweat this asshole in the basement?"

"I don't think so. The fewer of us he sees, the better. Although I don't really suppose it makes a rat's ass when he becomes coyote food. You start out being the bad guy and I will come down and be the worse guy. We need to break him; he has to know something, and I want it. I don't care if we have to reach up his ass and pull it out!"

"Top, let me have him after Serf, save yourself the trouble. You know I have a way with people," Joe said with an evil grin.

"Ok, you got him. Let's see what you can do with him."

Serf worked on him an hour and Joe went down and asked Schmidt what he had against growing old. At this point Joe shot him in the foot with his 22 cal. "Now you realize, asshole, I have nowhere to go but up. How high I go is up to you. I won't stop until I put a round in your fucking eyeball, you need to know that," Joe said as he shot him in the knee. "Remember, this is all up to you," Joe said as he aimed at his groin.

"Stop, stop, I'll tell you everything I know."

"Finally, you are displaying a bit of common sense. I am going to record everything you say, to make sure I get it all clearly."

Joe spent three hours with him. When he came up he suggested Steve go patch him up.

"Well, how much success did you have?" the Deacon asked.

"They are/were the beginning of a nationwide network. Their mission is to carry out selected acts of terror across the country. He claims this fall they are smuggling in a nuclear warhead on a medium range rocket, probably a SCUD. He thinks it is coming into Oakland on a Chinese container ship. He doesn't have any idea where it's destined to go. He claims it is destined for an airburst at maximum altitude in a large metropolitan area. Sounds like an EMP attack to me. According to him, several of the people that died in the cavern were technicians that were going to help in setting it up. Ultimately, that could kill over two hundred million Americans, by the time it is over. That is well over half of our population. We will wind up in the stone ages and no way to recover. Life in America will have to start over. A spattering of Shakers and survivalists are all that are likely to thrive, due to their already Spartan lifestyle."

Ron called Larry and briefed him on what they found out from Schmidt. "Unfortunately, I had Joe interrogate him, so you know we can't do anything else with him. Do you want us to keep him here?"

"Damn it, Top, wring what you think you can out of him and then do what you have to do. Life would be so much easier if the DOJ would let us do our job. I haven't received any feedback yet on the information we retrieved. The rate they move, it will likely be a while.

"Oh, before I forget it, pass on to Joe that Jimmy Paxon hung himself in his cell yesterday while we were out playing Rambo. I picked it up on the daily inter-agency sitrep. Just thought you'd like to know. Have to run, Top. Frigging meetings. Later, Top, great job last night, pass that on to your guys."

The four turboprops on the Albatross belched their characteristic blue-grey smoke cloud as each one started. As soon as all four had smoothed out, Bert taxied to the far end of Serf's dirt runway and started his takeoff roll. Even at that, the Albatross did not go wheels up for at least a hundred yards beyond the end of the runway.

The Warriors on board were all busy exchanging tales of the operation they had just completed, noting in particular the lack of the large amounts of weapons they had encountered in prior operations, leading them to wonder why, and to speculate if there may be another cache in the area. Little did they know how soon they would be returning to the Forest.

Mary Jane was waiting on the edge of the runway as the Albatross rolled up and stopped adjacent to the Lodge, anxiously awaiting Ron's return, as the last time he went on a major operation he had been shot. Relief swept over her body and a smile crept across her face as Ron deplaned. She couldn't help but notice how they all looked mentally and physically exhausted. Totally understandable for a bunch of old men fighting a young man's battle, she thought.

Knowing this crew, Mary Jane had a fresh pot of coffee and pastries waiting for them as they all came in.

Hey, Lady, I am going to have to gulp down a quick cup, as Dief, Peter and I are heading back to San Antonio shortly. I just wanted to get out of that cockpit for a minute," Bert said.

The Deacon asked Bert to grab his coffee and join him in the war room for a minute.

"What's up, Boss, rough ride home?"

"Hell, no. I realize that I am putting a strain on your business. While you have never complained, I know that I drain a lot of your time away from your company. Why don't you consider hiring two more pilots to assist in your regular scheduled work to offset the time you spend with my venture? I will pick up the tab on their salaries."

"Well, I've never complained because I really believe in what we're doing, plus deep inside it is fun. But you are right about my business taking a hit due to my being gone so much."

"Tell you what I'll do. Get yourself an office manager, two pilots and a new twin engine whatever you want, and bill me. That's the least I can do for having my own private Air Force," Ron said as he smiled.

"You know damn well I would be a fool to decline, but are you sure you can handle all that?"

"Bert, if I couldn't handle it I wouldn't have made the offer, and yes, I expect you to accept it. Case closed. You have to get back to San Antonio."

Serf was walking down into the bunker, not sure what he was going to do. He looked in through the port and saw Jason curled up in the corner, probably wondering what the day would bring to him.

Serf sat in the opposite corner with his .22 pistol in his hand. Finally Serf spoke. "Jason, did you wonder why Joe shot you with a .22 caliber pistol instead of a .45 caliber?"

"No, it never dawned on me; all I knew was that I had been shot."

"It is an act of mercy on our part. Nothing would make me happier than to release you without the massive amounts of damage that a larger round would inflict. That is, if you are released.

"And that, my friend, is entirely up to you. You see, I don't believe for one minute you told us everything you know. I have a suspicion that you told Joe just enough to save your life. I bet there is a whole lot more that you could tell us, if you decided to. I am going upstairs now; I will come back down just one more time. You need to do some soul-searching between now and then. You need to tell me everything you know the next time we talk. I think you know the price tag attached to not talking. You think it over," Serf said as he was leaving the bunker.

A while later, Wilson, the team medic, brought Jason several sandwiches and a half-gallon of water. He also turned a couple of rats loose for Rodney.

"I understand Serf talked to you today," Wilson said. "You need to seriously consider what he told you. Serf, if nothing else, is a man of his word."

"I sort of figured that out on my own," Jason said as Wilson left.

Ron Dahle

Jason heard two sets of steps coming down the stairway to the bunker. Serf entered first, carrying a chair. Wilson followed, carrying a folding table and a field first aid kit. However, the first thing Jason noticed, was the .45 caliber auto on Serf's hip.

"Ok, dude, it is time to fish or cut bait," Serf said, while Wilson was taking a syringe and a bottle out of the first aid kit.

"Here is how it is going down: you are going to tell me everything you know about Hezbollah, Hamas, Iranian activities in the area and you get to walk up those stairs. Wilson has sodium pentothal to keep you singing for a week, if need be. The choice is yours! What do you know?"

Mary Jane and Ron were just getting up when the phone rang. Ron saw who it was and ignored it. "That wasn't very nice, " Mary Jane said.

"I don't think it was very nice of him to call before my feet hit the floor, either, to say nothing of calling before my first cup of coffee."

"And how many times have you done that to me?"

"None, my love, you're not Serf. I don't want the first thing I am called in the morning to be 'Batman'. I would much prefer 'hon', coming from your lips."

"What a crock of BS!" Mary Jane said laughing. "You're as full of shit now as you were the day we met."

The Deacon finally had his morning coffee and a quick dose of the news when he decided to return Serf's call.

"Hey, Batman, glad you finally called back. When are they going to put answering machines on these damn secure phones?"

"Somehow, I think that defeats their purpose. You didn't call me to complain about the phone service. What's up?"

"Well, I gave our Kraut another opportunity to tell us what he really knows. He talked till 0300 hours, then Wilson hit him with sodium pentothal and he talked another two hours. I feel it is safe to say we need to go back into the Forest.

"There is another cavern on the other side of the mountain, where all the equipment is stashed. Weapons, ammo, RPGs, and according to him at least two more suitcase nukes. It does not have the number of personnel this one did, but the ones that are there are heavy hitters. They are there as they feel it is safer. Not the level of human traffic as the one we just hit. The one we hit was a shuttling point for new infiltrates. They would go there from Mexico and then be moved all over. The new cavern is the backbone of the operation."

"Do you have a definitive location of the new target?"

"Yeah, the guy spilled his guts. I am confident we got everything he knows."

"Is he still alive?"

"Oh yeah, he is still keeping Rodney company."

"Listen, get his ass back to the original target site. No one has been there yet, according to the blimp reports. Bring him back to his guard post and kill him there. In case they are checked out, I want all personnel accounted for. Otherwise, they may figure they have been compromised and get to fuck out of Dodge. In the meantime, I am going to alert Larry and Vince. By the way, how is Rodney doing?"

"Shit, he has never had it so good. Private room most of the time, a steady diet of squirrels and rats. Hell, he's happy."

"That's good; I will have to report that to John. Rodney was his favorite rattler. You guys get some rest; I have a feeling we're going right back in."

Ron called Larry with the news first. "When you contact Serf for the areas so you can move the ASA vans, have him send Tommy in to see what he can find out. Make sure you coordinate with Vince first thing. I've got to go, Boss. Keep me posted."

Vince was next on the list. "Vince, you need to contact Serf for new coordinates for your blimp to monitor closely. We may be into some real deep shit on this one. Call me when you have something."

Ron then alerted Bert to the fact that they would likely do a replay very shortly.

Chapter 21

Ron was surprised to hear from Larry so soon, but he was even more surprised to find out that Larry was flying in later that morning.

Mary Jane just looked at Ron and said, "It's never going to stop, is it, babe?"

"The base problem will likely exist for years. With a good functioning government they can contain it, which is what my main goal is: to install a government that has the interest of America first and foremost in their hearts and minds. I have already notified Joe that he needs to start taking on more of the leadership role here, as I intend for him to replace me."

"Right, as if you are going to relinquish any control! That's your middle name, or have you forgotten? You would be unbearable if you weren't waging war. Don't worry, I may gripe but I have accepted it. I love you, you miserable old bastard."

Larry landed at 1115 hours. "Let's go downstairs," he said. "There is some serious shit going on. I have been given a green light, but they want it to be a prisoner snatch operation, due to the nukes. All of Delta Force and the Seals are currently deployed in Afghanistan, as the roof is coming off over there. Is this something you feel comfortable trying to pull off with the Warriors?"

"In recent years the Russians have been known to use a fentanyl derivative to incapacitate large numbers of people. There is no doubt in my mind that something similar exists in our inventory, likely on your side of the house. If we could get our hands on enough of that gas, there is a good likelihood that we could pull this off. And after all, we can use gas because we don't exist, remember?"

"I was afraid that was going to be your answer. OK, but not a word of this can leak out. I will provide ample gas when we get ready to go in. Make sure your people have serviceable gas masks."

"What about your interrogators? They're bound to find out. What then?" Ron asked.

"I will hand pick the interrogators. When we are done with the prisoners, I will infiltrate them back to Deming a couple at a time. We'll let Serf fatten up the coyote population. We have no option; we need to find out what they know and where those nukes were destined. There is no way we can get approval on this from the top. My boss will ignore the whole thing, just proving that ignorance really is…bliss."

"I can live with that, and I am sure Serf can, too. Ya know, it isn't like we have any real options. There is a price tag attached to messing with the bull.

"I have put everyone on alert, I will have Bert fly up as soon as he can and we will do all the planning from his hangar again, and stage out of Deming. We are going to have to beef up the chopper support from you to transport the prisoners back to Langley. I know it's difficult to call, as we have no idea what kind of numbers we are looking at.

"Tommy is in the area now, trying to get a feel for what's going on. I am just waiting for imagery from Vince, if the blimp can get a fix on anything. Were your ASA units of any help to him?"

"They picked up a couple of rough coordinates; they weren't transmitting long enough to get a good triangulation plot on them. I gave Vince what I had. The ASA interpreters are working on what they were saying. I should have something for you as soon as I return to Langley. Talking about Langley, it's time for me to head back as I have a lot of coordinating to do, and some of it isn't going to be easy. I will keep you posted."

Tommy was high on the hillside across from where it was believed the Iranian insurgents were holding up. He was scanning the opposite hill mass with a spotter scope looking for the tiniest thing out of the ordinary. He had moved three times already, and he was getting ready to settle for the night.

Three hours into the darkness using his night vision goggles, he scored. He picked up the flicker of a match or cigarette lighter on the opposite hill mass about two hundred yards to his right oblique. He then focused the spotting scope on the area until he saw the glow of a cigarette. He zoomed in to 60 power and even in the dark the 80 MM lens on the spotting scope was able to clearly resolve the image of a man smoking a cigarette. He was much better camouflaged than the guards at the canyon were. Tommy spent the rest of the night scanning the far side, alternating between the night vision goggles and the spotting scope. The net result of his efforts was the definite location of four more manned positions and six additional positions that were unoccupied.

Tommy covered his entire body with his poncho, set up his satellite link, and sent a digital text of the coordinates of the positions on the other side, to the Deacon, hoping the ping would wake him up.

Tommy knew that he would have to move tomorrow to get a better view of what was really going on over there. With any luck at all, he would be able to get some photos to send back to the Deacon.

The ping sat Ron straight up in his bed. He knew immediately what it was. This was one call he didn't mind being woken up for. He wrote the coordinates down and sent them directly to Vince and Larry. This was confirmation of the presence of the enemy, solid actionable intelligence, not just the babblings of a terrified prisoner trying to stay alive. Now, the blimp would know exactly where to focus.

Ron went back to bed, only to find that Mary Jane was awake. "This one is going to be bad, isn't it?" she asked.

"I prefer to say it is going to be different. In my heart, I don't believe it is going to be any more dangerous than the last operation was.

"You have to remember, babe, that yes, we are all old farts, but along with that comes experience and wisdom. Within the Warriors, we have a combined total of over 400 years' experience of fighting wars all over the world. That has to count for something, ya think?"

"I know, hon, but still…"

———

As it had so many times in the past, the Albatross taxied in on Ron's runway. Ron, Joe, Gunny and Steve were awaiting its arrival. All the equipment they were taking was palletized and ready to load.

Mary Jane watched the plane take off without even shutting down. She didn't know what, but there was something very different about this mission; she could sense it on the part of Ron, Joe, and Steve. She also couldn't help but notice Steve was carrying in two aid kits and an additional box of medical supplies.

———

To look at the Warriors riding in their cargo seats, one would assume they were all sleeping. Nothing could be further from the truth. Each one of them was playing different scenarios through their heads. This one was different, and had a potential for danger the other operations they pulled off didn't have. If the intelligence (intel) was right, there were two nukes on site, and an unknown number of guards. Their mission was to retrieve the nukes and take as many prisoners as possible. That's what complicated the mission, as it would be so easy to kill everyone on site, grab the nukes and leave, but that was not in the making this time.

Serf, Tommy, Wilson and the Dief were all waiting in Bert's hangar when the Albatross landed. The only player missing was the intel team of Larry and Vince. Vince was flying in from DC, and Larry was already at Cannon air base, coordinating the air support needed for the operation.

"Tommy, while we are waiting, how about briefing us on what you found in the operational area?" the Deacon said.

"Ok, I am sure Vince will go through the actual objective with current imagery when he gets here. I initially discovered five manned and six unmanned well-camouflaged guard positions on the front of a canyon that appeared to be small in size, if you can base anything on the size of the entrance.

"I knew that this was either the dumbest maneuver on their part, or there was an outlet to the canyon. A close investigation revealed that the canyon terminated at a cave. The cave entrance has a half-hearted attempt at camouflaging it. My guess is they are depending on the guard posts to give them ample warning in the event there are signs of activity. The guard changes at 2200 hours, 0600, and 1400 hours. All activity in the cave seemed to cease by 2200 hours; it isn't like they are going to watch Letterman.

"A closer inspection revealed a well-camouflaged outlet to the cave about half a mile from the entrance. From that point there are numerous avenues of escape. I did not observe any security on that end of the cave; apparently they are comfortable with their camouflage, and don't want to tip their hand by having guard posts on that exit. It opens up into a valley that could contain a myriad of escape and hiding options."

During the discussion, a basic plan started to evolve. "The way I see it, based on what we have to go on with now, we are going to have multiple elements involved in this operation. We have three initial tasks.

"First: we have to eliminate the security, a fairly straightforward exercise barring any problems. Next, we have to seal off the exit to the cave and hope there aren't others that Tommy failed to locate. This has to be coordinated with releasing the gas into the cave. It is then a waiting game, and then suck up your balls and go in ready to fight anyone who may still be conscious.

"Our job is to recover the nukes and take as many prisoners as possible. That entire cave full of prisoners isn't worth losing one of us, so if you have a doubt or question, shoot first. The spooks will have to deal with what we bring them.

"I have to give Larry a quick call for 200 pounds of C-5 and detonators to close off the far end of the cave. He will likely have to jump through his ass for that with this short notice. In the meantime, we are going to break down the teams the same as we did before.

"Gunny, because of your age, I want you and Dief to haul that C-5 over the hill to the other side and take care of blowing the entrance. As soon as you are finished, you need to return and join the assault crew. Before I forget it, prior to departing from here I want everyone to pre-fit your gas masks, and check the seals and filters."

Bert came over and told Ron that Vince just radioed in, and he expected to be there within thirty minutes. Ron cleared off the map board, as he knew Vince had some hi-resolution imagery from the balloon of the entire operational area. Ron was thinking to himself that this operation was getting right on down to the nuts and bolts. Depending on Larry's luck with the air support, this operation could kick off as early as tomorrow night, Ron thought.

Vince showed up with the maps. They actually showed little that Tommy hadn't already covered. They did help to ascertain that the rear exit hadn't been used in ages, based on the lack of trails coming from it. It appeared that they only came out periodically, to freshen up the camouflage. The maps did show that the area between the guard positions and the beginning of the canyon would make an excellent LZ pad for the choppers.

"So tell me, Vince, how is it working out with you with Larry in the loop?" Ron asked.

"I hate to admit it, but it seems to be a lot smoother than it was before. The time from when Larry gives me coordinates until I have images is mind boggling, as you would say, especially with the blimp on site. It is real time intel, as good as it gets. I guess you could say Larry and I teamed up pretty well. It is a shame our respective agencies can't do that."

"Now that would make too much sense, and you know it. Everyone wants to showboat and take all the credit for themselves. There are no winners, and the only loser is America. That really pisses me off, but it has been like that ever since I can remember. I really get frustrated; I remember back when the only thing we worried about was the body count and the price of pussy in the ville. I know I spent most of my career watching my leaders for things never to do when I got in the position to make decisions. Best education I received in the military.

"Got a question for you. Vince. During the assault, would it be possible to get real-time updates from your crew in the blimps?"

"Can't happen, Sergeant Major. They can only pass on info to Homeland Security assets, and we disseminate the intel as we see fit. Sorry."

"Ok, how about this, then? You accompany Larry and I in the command chopper, and you can be the intermediary between us and the blimp."

"That is highly irregular, but shit…what about our relationship isn't? Yeah, I suppose we can try it. I agree the real time imagery will be a big help to your guys on the ground. And it will be interesting to watch the Warriors in action. Have all of your operators wear IR beacons for ID."

Chapter 22

L arry, having already briefed Ron, was getting ready to brief the Warriors.

"Seems like we were just here... oh, that's right, we were. If the intel we extracted from Jason is correct, we are getting ready to kick off the largest, most complex and potentially most dangerous mission we have been on since the 1960s in Nam. The potential is all here. Possibility of nuclear weapons, unknown enemy strength, we are using a gas that technically doesn't exist, nor do we really know how effective it will be.

"This chemical agent has been used once that we know of: it was employed by the Russians in a theater. It had a very high mortality rate. We think that was due to the high concentration of the agent and the duration the victims were exposed to it. We believe that, once rendered unconscious, the victim needs to be removed to fresh air as soon as possible. In some cases, they may need to be administered oxygen. Of course, they need to be restrained hand and foot prior to that happening. With luck, we won't lose too many to the gas.

"I have what should be sufficient air resources laid on. We will have two Apaches, one UH-60-C Black Hawk for Command and Control (C&C), and six UH-60-A for troop and prisoner transport. One of the Apaches will accompany me to deliver the nukes, the other will stay with you guys to fly cover for the Black Hawks with the prisoners. We may not need that many, but better to be safe. If in fact we do retrieve nukes, I will use the C&C to transport them to an undisclosed location. That will take me approximately three hours. During that time the prisoners will be transported to, and remain at Deming, as I have to accompany them to their next home, so tomorrow is going to be a long day.

"Any documents you recover will need to accompany me. Anything else in the cave can augment the Warriors' equipment pool. Don't give me that puzzled look, you know damn well what I mean. Realize I'm still the same person who, along with Top, brought most of you up.

"That's about all I've got, guys. If you come up with any questions, don't hesitate to ask. I am going to turn the floor over to Top at this time."

"Hell, it has all been said. Gunny, Dief, I want you to wait five minutes after the assault crew pops the gas. I don't want to risk the explosion waking someone up and having them go out the front or don protective masks. We need to have everything we can going for us on this one. We need to get ready, as Bert is looking at wheels up in two hours. You can all draw straws to see who sleeps with Rodney tonight. Sleep in as long as you can in the morning, our day will not start until it gets dark."

———

The warriors watched the Albatross disappear in the distance, still leaving a trail of blue grey exhaust behind each engine.

They went to the pallets, opened them, and retrieved their equipment for a final check before tonight. Larry gathered the assault team, issued each member six canisters of the Fentanyl, and instructed them on how to deploy it.

"Basically, pull the pin and roll it into the cave. I would say throw it but we don't want to wake anyone up in the process of putting them to sleep. The worst-case scenario is for a couple of them to get to their gasmasks, if they have any, and start firing on us. That will make for a long night."

The Deacon interjected. "In the event that this turns into a total shitstorm for us, Wilson is carrying in an RPG-29 with three Thermobaric rounds. Their deployment is an absolute last case scenario, to save our bacon. If that happens, we will have to use the oxygen we brought for the prisoners to go into the cave with, as the rounds will deplete all the existing oxygen in it. Joe, you are the ground commander, do whatever you feel you need to, just remember we really want those nukes. Also remember that there are two 100 pound rucksacks of C-5 that can be rotated between everyone."

Larry continued. "The choppers should be arriving by 1200 hours. They will be taking a six-hour break; I will conduct their operational briefing at 2000 hours. By that time, you will be well on your way into the forest. I keep telling myself this is going to be a piece of cake. Let's hope it is. Top, Vince, and myself will be flying in the C&C bird. We will have direct real time intel updates from the blimp overhead. Make sure when you hit the ground you turn your IR beacons on. The C&C bird will be airborne at 2100 hours; you should be approaching the AO by then. We will contact you for a SITREP as soon as we get in range."

It was hot and sticky in the middle of the forest. There wasn't an old man in the lot who wasn't dreading his turn to carry the rucksacks. The common thread in all their thoughts was 'how much easier this was 45 years ago' but to the man, everyone here was a volunteer and ready to give his all to the mission at hand. It didn't go unnoted that Steve and Serf were taking the bulk of the time with the rucksacks. They both fell on the younger side of the average for the Warriors, so it was understandable. Gunny and the Dief were being spared, as they had the task of carrying them over the mountain at the cutoff point which was straight ahead.

A recent rain in the forest was a cloaked gift. True, it made it sticky and humid, but on the plus side it made movement much quieter under foot, allowing the team to make better time than they had anticipated. It also allowed for a couple of ten-minute breaks along the way. Joe's primary concern was having everyone reach the target with the energy to fight, if need be.

On one such break Steve approached Joe and said, "Joe, do you realize how fucking long you, Top and I, along with Larry have been doing this shit? Fucking Top has been at it fifty three years."

"I try not to think about it. Sometimes it just doesn't seem like we are making any progress. Every time we beat an organization to its knees, another one rises in its place. If the average American knew how fucked we are right now, they would shit their pants. As for Top, I don't see any signs of him slowing down. Just ask Mary Jane."

"From Castro in 1961 and 1962, to Ahmadinejad in 2012, it has been one firestorm right after another. Unfortunately, with the leadership we have now, across the board, we are in more jeopardy then at any point in our history," Steve offered, as he rose and got ready to start out again.

Gunny and Dief finally took the rucksacks, as their turn off was about fifty yards ahead. It was pretty much an uphill trudge for the rest of the way for them. Fortunately they were fairly fresh for the task ahead.

———

"Stalker Leader, this is Night stalker one, I have a visual on you, just entering my cone. Everything is calm on the AO, the detachment is making better time than we thought, they will be on station early at the rate they are moving, over."

"Roger that, Night stalker one, I will pass that on to their leader. Keep me posted on any activity in the area, over."

"Wilco, Leader, this is Night stalker one, out."

"Sergeant Major, your crew is ahead of schedule according to Night stalker."

"Pure adrenaline. I'll slow them down."

"Ground Leader, the Deacon here, over."

"Good to hear from you, Deacon, what's up?"

"All's quiet in the AO. You are running well ahead of schedule. Don't get too close with time to spare, we don't need anyone to hear you."

"Roger that, Deacon, we are getting ready to hold up for a while. Gunny and the Dief have already split off. You will likely have to act as a relay for us, as I think they will be out of radio range, especially with the mountain between us as soon as they cross the ridge."

"Not a problem, we are holding a pattern away from your AO for security, but we will be able to maintain contact with both sides of the mountain. Keep me updated. The Deacon out."

It was five minutes when Vince's monitor showed the detachment come to a halt. Right after that you could see the two beacons of the Dief and Gunny already at the base of the mountain and heading up. While rugged terrain, it was totally navigable along the copious game trails, especially with night vision goggles.

"Deacon, this is Ground Leader here, in position and ready to take out the guards. Request update on other side of hill, over."

"Gunny, this is the Deacon, request status, over."

"Gunny here, we are on site and ready. Notify us when the detachment eliminates the guards. At that point we are going into the cave and set our charges about twenty feet inside it. With luck we will still be in contact with you so we can know when the team pops gas. We will set the charges to go five minutes after that, over."

"Roger that, Gunny. We will be on your side of the mountain to insure commo isn't a problem, Deacon out."

"Ground Leader, Deacon here, the other side of the hill is ready to roll. Let us know when the guards are eliminated and when you pop gas."

"WILCO, we are starting on the guards in ten minutes, we are moving into position now. I am going to radio silence until they are eliminated. Ground Leader out."

"Vince, how does the monitor look? Is it going as smooth as Joe says it is?"

"Here, take a look for yourself. It looks like they are on top of everything to me."

Ron marveled at being able to watch the action unfold on the ground in real time. He watched the guards drop one at a time, without a hitch.

The Deacon radioed Gunny that the guards were dead before Joe had called him. Gunny said they were ready to proceed as soon as he got word that the gas was deployed. At this time, Gunny and Dief disappeared into the mouth of the cave to set charges.

———

Mousa al Mazrui was in a semi lucid state when he smelled the aroma of freshly mown grass and he realized that something was wrong. He sat up and saw a fog throughout the cave. He panicked, grabbed his gun and started running to the emergency exit. Suddenly, he saw two people dressed in Ghillie suits working on something between him and the exit. He was still only partially in control of his facilities, but he knew he had to shoot them to get out. He set his weapon on full automatic and opened fire hitting the Dief immediately, and then the Gunny, but not before

Gunny killed him. Gunny checked the Dief. He was hit bad. Gunny was wounded twice but neither one was critical. Gunny set the timer for three minutes, scooped the Dief up like a ragdoll and limped for the door.

Joe heard the gunfire and wondered what in hell was going on. No one had exited through the front yet, nor was there any noise from within. Joe heard the massive explosion of the 200-pound charge of C-5 going off in the other end of the cave.

———

Gunny scrambled out of the cave with Dief in his arms and stumbled to the right of the opening of the cave just as the charge exploded. The blast, although indirect, threw Gunny and the Dief over twenty feet. Once Gunny's head cleared, he went to Dief to see if he was still alive. He was, but just barely.

Gunny appraised the Deacon of the situation on the ground there.

"Gunny, can you get him to the clearing fifty yards to your west."

"I think so, Top. I'll try."

"Ground leader, this is the Deacon, send Steve to the LZ where we were going to pick up the prisoners. Both the Dief and Gunny are wounded bad. I am going in to get them right now. We should be right over."

The C&C bird landed and the Deacon and Larry jumped out to go help Gunny and the Dief get to the chopper. As soon as they were in, they went directly to the LZ where Steve was waiting. The rest of the team were in the cave binding prisoners and searching the cave.

"Top, we've got to get in the air, so I can contact the other choppers, and have them get their ass here. As soon as one gets here, we will transfer me to one of the others and you and Steve get Gunny and Dief to the University Center Hospital in Tucson.

I will have a special agent there who will grease the way for them and handle the BS."

"Steve, how is it looking for them?" asked the Deacon.

"No problem with Gunny; he's shot up, but nothing critical. Not sure about the Dief, he took a couple bad ones. He took two in the gut, and one in the left lung. Gunny sealed the chest wound before he moved him or he would be dead now. It all depends how fast we can get him to a hospital, and how good the emergency staff is."

They managed to save twenty-two of the insurgents. They were a duke's mixture of Iranians, Pakistanis, Libyans, Syrians, Somalians, not one from a country sympathetic to America's cause. Moving them in their drugged state was akin to herding cats. Several of them still remained on oxygen.

The salvage team located the suitcase nukes, a large cache of weapons and ammunition, and two large bags of U. S. currency. Two nukes went in one pile, along with a batch of documents, and the weapons and cash went into another. All of the ID documentation the insurgents possessed was taken from them and packaged to go with Larry.

Joe saw the C&C ship land, and then it took right off after someone got out of it. It was Larry.

"What's going on, Boss?" Joe asked Larry.

"The other birds are due in in ten minutes. The C&C bird is taking Dief and Gunny to the hospital in Tucson. They couldn't afford to wait around."

"What shape are they in? It doesn't sound too good."

"They were both shot up pretty good; the Dief is touch and go right now. Gunny will pull through ok. Top said for you to take it from here, he will be back in Deming in a day or so.

"How did we make out in the cave?"

"We scored on the nukes—two of them. A bag of documents plus their IDs. We policed up some weapons and ammo, as well as some cash for the team fund."

"That's great. That means you need to hold the prisoners at Deming until I drop off the nukes. I am going to swing down and check on Dief and Gunny on my way back. I may grab Top and Vince and bring them back to Deming when I come to collect the prisoners."

Vince spoke up, "I would rather stay at Deming; I don't want to be seen by too many CIA types, if you know what I mean."

"That's totally understandable," Larry said. "Hell, you may be able to sleep with Rodney."

"That sounds like a plan boss. When you take off don't be surprised if you hear an explosion. We are going to dump a Thermobaric round or two into the cave, so no one will ever figure what happened there."

"How do you plan to handle the prisoners till I pick them up?"

"They are still so fucked up, they won't be a problem. I'm going to put two guards in each chopper to make sure they stay settled down. Any problem on the trip, we'll shoot them. When they get to the safehouse, they will be shackled outside and guarded till you come and get them."

"That sounds good. I have two loads of guards flying in tomorrow to escort them the rest of the way. That is my bird landing now. Have a couple of the guys load the nukes up, and we'll see you tomorrow. You guys did a great job."

The ambulance and two gurneys were waiting by the edge of the helipad when the Black Hawk touched down. Steve and the Deacon assisted the hospital personnel getting Gunny and Dief on the gurneys.

Steve had been giving updates to the trauma unit in the hospital by radio since they departed. They already had an operating suite fully staffed and scrubbed waiting for the Dief. All they had to do was x-ray him on the way into the operating room. Gunny was taken to another operating room for the same treatment.

While Ron was waiting, he saw what was either a mobster Boss or a CIA agent approach him. Under the circumstances, Ron figured he was the CIA agent Larry said would meet him and arrange with the hospital and authorities. He was correct.

"The Deacon, I assume, the agent said. "Agent Thibodaux. Pleased to meet you, sir. Agent Neider said I was to render any assistance you needed."

"What I really need right now is a cup of coffee."

"Well, the hospital cafeteria is closed but there is an all-night café just around the corner. I'm sure they could satisfy that craving."

Steve came out from the x-ray room and joined the Deacon and agent Thibodaux. They all went to the café in agent Thibodaux's sedan.

"Well, what do you think, Steve?" the Deacon asked.

"Gunny is no problem. He will likely be discharged tomorrow or the next day. I don't know why Dief is still alive. He has a lot of internal damage, based on the x-rays. The duct tape patch Gunny sealed the Dief's sucking chest wound with, likely saved his life. Of course, the oxygen and saline drip didn't hurt, either. I laced his saline with morphine, to help with the pain. Nothing we can do now but wait and see. I expect him to be in surgery three to four hours at least. There is a lot of internal repair work to be done to fix up the Dief."

It was breakfast time when the doctor finally came out of surgery. "He had a lot of internal damage, as we expected, but there was nothing ruined except his spleen, and that is no major problem. I feel reasonably confident in saying that he will make a full recovery. From what the other surgeon just told me your other man, the one called Gunny, will be on his feet today; he is in the recovery room now, you can drop in and see him anytime. They were both lucky; apparently, they were shot with military ball ammo, as it was through and through, no mushrooming and tearing. We are expecting the one I operated on to be in the recovery room within an hour. He will be groggy, but you can go in and see him for a couple of minutes when he regains consciousness."

———

"Gunny insists on leaving here with me, typical bull-headed Marine. It will give him some time with his family, so I see no harm in it. I need to find out what's going on, get things under control and get my ass back to Wolfeboro."

Steve looked at the Deacon sheepishly and said, Deacon, when you unload the booty from the last raid, you will find a suitcase nuke. There were three and Larry only thought there were two, and we figured we could use at least one, as like you say with grenades, you never know when."

The Deacon looked over his glasses at Steve when he got a phone call and all he said was "See you in a bit."

"That was Larry; he is inbound. Steve, I want you to stay with the Dief. Update me daily on his condition. When he's ready for discharge, the two of you come to the Lodge."

———

"Well, what were in the cases? Nukes, again?"

"Yeah, they were the same as the other one. It's scary, Deacon. Strategically placed, one of them could take out a small city, and we have turned up three already."

"Do you suppose that will kick up the security on the border?"

"I'd like to think so, but I doubt it. Nothing is going to get in the way of the status quo or the upcoming election."

They looked out the window when they heard the change in pitch of the rotor and saw the safehouse coming up in the distance. "Jesus Christ, it looks like a frigging airfield down there. The runway is littered with choppers," the Deacon said.

"Hey, when you run with the big dogs…"

"Yeah, Larry, I know. Did you say big dogs or big dorks?"

Larry, Ron, and Gunny no sooner got out of the chopper and Serf was on his way to meet them. "Hey, Batman, I hope to fuck you are here to take some of these goat fuckers off my hands."

"Well, good day to you too, Serf. Having a rough time, are you?"

"As soon as the pilots are ready, we are going to take all of them off your hands," Larry said. "I trust they have all been behaving?"

"Shit, yeah, half of them are still groggy from the gas. We had one more die on us, put him out for the coyotes last night, by this morning there wasn't a trace of him."

"How is Jason doing? Is he still keeping Rodney company?" the Deacon asked.

"Oh, yes. He never made it back to the forest as we discussed; we got overcome by events. Poor bastard just sits there and stares at Rodney all day and night. What are our plans for him, anyway?"

"Hell, I guess we're done with him. We can't let him go; he knows too much. Technically, he is American. That complicates matters, as his DNA may be on file in some frigging database. Fuck it, feed him to the coyotes south of the border; let it be a Mexican problem. Use an AK-47 to shoot him, that will muddy the waters; they'll think it was cartel related."

There was a flurry of activity by the chopper crews getting their birds ready to depart. The additional guards they flew in started to load the prisoners into the Black Hawks. The lone Apache escort was off to the side, already cranking up for the flight.

"Where are you taking these assholes?" Serf asked Larry.

"Sorry, can't tell you that, but rest assured that when we are done with them you will probably be seeing them again a couple at a time, to take care of for us. We're not really sure on their disposition, as no one knows we have them. We need to extract as much info about the nukes as we can out of them, and see what they know about the missile that is supposed to be coming in on a frigging container ship. That's all the fuck we need right now. Ok, guys, I've got to head out. You all did a great job, too bad no one will ever realize that. See you for the next crisis," Larry said as he headed to the C&C bird.

"What now, Batman? When are you and Joe heading out?"

"I suppose I need to get Bert here tomorrow and start the flight home. Sort of dread getting there and telling Mary Jane about Gunny and Dief. I am going to have to listen to that sermon of hers about how it is time for me to hang it up. What the woman doesn't realize is that I don't want to hang it up! I'm doing exactly what I want to right now and have no plans on changing, at least in the near future, anyway."

———

Ron and Joe were waiting on the runway for Bert, who radioed in that he was ten minutes out. In the distance, they could see an aircraft that they didn't recognize as one of Bert's.

As it landed and Bert got out of the cockpit, Ron realized Bert had taken him up on his offer. Bert had a new refurbished Twin Commander. It was a used model 1000, reconfigured to allow jumping, while it still offered all the luxury originally designed into it for corporate travel.

Bert was obviously proud of his new acquisition as he showed it off to Joe and Ron. "Not only does it enhance my jump operation, it is fully adequate for business charters. The good news is its range. Now we can keep the Albatross on the ground unless we need her twin cannons. The good news is I don't need to pull Peter off line to assist me flying the Albatross when we have a long trip. This thing has a range in excess of 2000 miles on it. Major drawback is it prefers paved or at least improved dirt runways.

"Worry not, Ron, I bought it right. I had a friend in the business in Dallas whose operation just went tits up. I bought this before the bankruptcy courts got involved. A little up front, a little under the table, we all won."

"Well, shit, stop talking us to death and show us what this fucker will do," the Deacon said. "I still think it would be better with mini-guns, or at least a couple of rocket pods on it."

———

Mary Jane watched the new plane land from the porch, and got a sick feeling in the pit of her stomach when Steve, Gunny, and the Dief didn't get off. She wanted to ask, but knew Ron would tell her when he was ready.

It was early in the evening and Ron suggested they all go to the Inn for dinner, just to make things easier all the way around. Bert seconded that, as he needed to get an early start in the morning.

———

"You seem to be missing some people," Mary Jane said while lying in bed with Ron that night.

"Yeah. Gunny is spending a couple of days with his wife, Dief got banged up a little, and Steve is with him till he gets released. Had a minor problem, but everyone is going to be ok, nothing to worry about, babe."

"Why does your air of nonchalance make me question the truthfulness of what you just said?"

"Well, maybe the Dief got a little more than banged up, but he is definitely going to make it and will be as good as ever. And yes, Gunny also got shot a couple of times, but they were thru and thru flesh wounds; he is doing good. Other than that it was pretty quiet, just a routine operation."

"You fucking call two people shot up, with one still in the hospital a 'pretty quiet routine operation'! Tell me, whose definition of quiet and routine is screwed up, yours or mine?"

Ron knew he wasn't going to get any pussy till they put this matter to sleep. "You're right, babe. I just hate to worry you. I know how much you fret every time we deploy, but you have to admit we've actually got a pretty good average overall. Yes, hon, there is a degree of risk involved in what we do, but we do it for you, your daughters, and millions of others. If not us, who else will do what we do?"

"I know, babe, but I still worry about you," Mary Jane said as she snuggled up next to Ron.

Ron was up early cooking breakfast for Bert. Their conversation over breakfast took them from Wildflecken, Germany, in the early 60s, to the engagement last week. "It has been a while, that's for sure," Bert said. "Hell, it's been over fifty-two years we have been at this, and still plugging along. Do you suppose it will ever end?"

"Actually, I don't, Bert. I don't think America has the will and resolve to stand up, recognize the problem, and fight for our freedom. We have several generations who have been programmed to expect handouts and someone to take care of them. Look at today's kids. How much true 'love of country' do you see? We have a frigging President telling us how wrong we have been since the beginning. The progressives and the frigging media are in lock step with him. So you ask why fight it. It's in my blood. I intend to take as many of these sorry bastards as I can out with me when I go. What we need is a change of the entire government, and I am working on that. I should have done it two years ago, when I first intended to. This election cycle, I definitely plan to, unless we make some major changes in both sides of Congress and the Oval office. Can you imagine up to four more handpicked Supreme Court Justices selected by this asshole? It is all over, Katie bar the door, the US Constitution, and all it stands for will be totally negated.

"We have our work cut out for us; we need to start working on some of the people that need to be taken care of on this side of the border, too. Like Senator Roach, more need to follow in his footsteps."

"Christ, Ron, I guess we have covered the gamut from the Fulda Gap to Valley Forge. And you're right, you know? We'll be fighting this shit till the day we die. On that, I have to get my ass in the air and head home. Till the next battle, my friend."

———

"Hey, Top, Steve here. I want to give you an update on the Dief. His wounds are doing ok, the prognosis for a full recovery is excellent. Now, the good news: they decided to do an MRI of his brain based on his history and they are willing to attempt to try to radiate that specific spot in his brain to minimize the effect of the tumor. As you know, this is a teaching medical center, and they stay right on the cutting edge of technology. Well, they have a new machine that is supposed to be the cat's ass when it comes to pinpoint radiation. They are not saying that they can eliminate it, but feel certain they can give him a couple of years that he otherwise wouldn't have had."

"That sounds great!" the Deacon said while wondering if that would cause the Dief to have second thoughts about "We the People". "What does the Dief say about the whole idea?"

"He is obviously excited about the concept, but doesn't know where the money for it will come from; since the process is in the experimental stage, Medicare won't pick up the tab."

"You tell Dief to worry about the sky falling, and not about the money. Inform him, if he wants it, to go for it. I will pick up the tab. That's the least I can do for you, guys. I will check in with Larry and see if the Agency can kick in a bit on it, also; maybe his room during the treatment, as he is recovering from a line of duty (LOD) injury. With a little luck and a white lie or two we can blur the lines and split the cost. Either way, it will happen if the Dief wants it to.

"How much longer are you planning on staying there? Since you never did come up with an assistant, you're the only medic on site."

"Shit, Top, I meant to tell you. Ray Maggi has agreed to come on. He is damn good, and is cool with how we operate, and the things we do. I interviewed him here two days ago and he is due at the Lodge by the end of the week. Frankly, I would like to stay with the Dief throughout his treatment. If for nothing else, just for moral support."

"I've worked with Ray at Devens and have no problem with him coming aboard. In light of this, by all means, stay with the Dief."

"I was hoping you would say that. We've been together so long it's as if he is a brother. Remember, I cured his first case of clap in England back in the 70s."

Ron Dahle

"If my memory serves me right, that was your primary function on the team back then. Got to run, Steve, Joe is on his way in through the door. Give Dief my best."

Joe entered the Lodge and proceeded straight to the coffee pot.

"You're up and at it early, Joe, so tell me what's been going on at the Academy?"

"According to Dewey, all is going well. I guess they almost had a crisis in the grenade pit, but everyone involved escaped unscathed. They are missing Gunny and his tracking course. Have we heard anything on him?"

"No, not yet. I just got off the phone with Steve, the Dief is doing ok. They are talking about radiating his tumor. I will give Gunny a call today after I go down and check on his boys to see how they are doing. This separation was a test for them on making it off the land. Gunny is a tough old bird; he has proven to be a hell of an asset.

"Ray Maggi is due in at the end of the week as Steve's assistant. When he gets here get him set up with a room downtown with you and Steve. Hell, at this point we may be better off to lease a four or five bedroom house for you guys, it would be a lot more comfortable. Why don't you look in on that? In fact, I will have Mary Jane look into it for you, she'll do a better job anyway. She knows what to look for in a house beyond a refrigerator, a TV, and a shitter."

"Do you have any irons in the fire yet, Top, or are you taking a break?

"I am giving Serf and his crew a couple of days off, then I want them back on the border operation; there are still a shitload of real bad guys south of the border who speak Arabic. We need to find them and take them out. As for the rest of the operation, I am down to you until I get Gunny, Steve, and the Dief back. I've got the components of two mainframes sitting on the porch. I guess I could get Bob up here to set them up and put them on line for me. I need to do that while the temperatures are up, as Bob doesn't do cold at all."

Chapter 23

Joe, Ray, and soon Steve all moved into a beautiful six bedroom 19th Century Victorian home right off Main Street in Wolfeboro. Mary Jane did well on her task.

Bob was about halfway through installing the mainframes. He came alone as his wife, Rae, was off visiting with their daughter. The Dief was over half way through his radiation treatments, and all was going well there. Gunny was due in tomorrow, and finally things were slowly getting back to normal.

This last series of events made Ron realize how fragile his operation really was. He pondered beefing it up, as if "We the People" took place he would again be shorthanded. Ron decided to talk to Ronnie Mac, as he just left Ft Bragg and had a good handle on potential personnel resources. Like the Marines, Ron was just looking for 'a few good men'.

"What's the occasion that warrants my being invited to the Lodge on the hill?" Ronnie Mac asked.

"You asshole, you know you are welcome here any time you damn well please. I'm looking for input from you. As you know, we lost a couple of guys on our recent operations, the Dief is still hospitalized, and Steve is with him. I need a couple of operators who can get the job done, and not question orders.

As you know, half of what we do is sanctioned, but we also do a lot of freelancing, only because the government doesn't have the inclination or the balls to.

"I know you have tons of contacts at Bragg. I'm looking for people in our age range; we remember what America was and can be. These kids coming up are good, but they don't have a frigging clue."

"The first name that jumps into my mind is Cognac Blue. I was talking to him before I came here and he really wants to get back in the game. He didn't try out for the Academy as he doesn't speak Spanish. If you'd have him, I bet I could get him here in a week."

"Shit, Bu-Dop Blue? (Bu Dop was the name of a Special Forces camp in III Corps in Vietnam. It was an extremely active camp with more than its share of enemy activity.) I almost forgot the name. Hell, yes. He brings a lot of baggage with him, but a couple of those bags are filled with Whoop Ass. He carries his balls in a wheel barrow.

"I remember in the late 60s being on operation with him when we came under heavy fire. I heard Blue moan, I called out to him to see if he was ok. He replied that he had been hit.

"How bad did they get you, Blue?"

"Bad, Deacon, worse than I ever imagined," Blue said.

"Where did they get you?" the Deacon hollered.

"Cocksuckers got a direct hit on my bottle of Cognac. It's running down my leg and back. That's the only bottle I brought with me too, the rotten bastards!"

"Damn it, Blue, did any bullets hit your body?"

"Fuck, no. They got my Cognac, damn it!"

"Ronnie, I can tell you Cognac Blue stories till the cows come home. I would love to have him aboard. He is one crazy motherfucker. He's just as deadly as he is crazy, too."

"If you two battle-worn warriors are ready for a break, I could use a hand getting the rest of the modules downstairs. We should be up and running by tomorrow," Bob said as he emerged from the guest bedroom.

"Ok. What do you need and where? You just point and I will get it. Ronnie, you can go back to what you were doing. Try to think of a couple more recruits. Let me know what Blue says.

"Let's get to it, Bob, what do you want first?"

"Try breakfast, and then we will take it from there."

"Make that two," hollered Mary Jane from the bedroom.

"Shit, breakfast was served two hours ago; I guess round two is coming up." The happiest beings in the Lodge were Zeus and Molly, Ron's dogs, for they knew they had another round of leftovers coming at them.

Suddenly, it was quiet at the Lodge again. Bob had left yesterday for Pacific Grove. The students were spending this week in the White Mountains for the final phase of training. They would graduate and ship out Sunday, only to be replaced with a fresh batch. Gunny was due in with the rest of his family on Friday, as he wanted to be here, to meet the new class. This was his way of intimidating them from the beginning.

The Dief was about half way through his radiation treatment. When he returned, Ron was going to put him in charge of the arms room until he got back on his feet and then he was off to Pigeon Forge with John. They really needed to get up to speed on their balloon training, Ron thought. The team will have to be on top of its game right after the elections, as if the election results fared poorly, the team would need to react shortly after the results of the election were announced.

Ron called Larry and Vince to see if he could set up a meeting between the three of them, as his concerns about the situation in the nation were really starting to bother him. A new plan was needed to keep the wolves at bay. The angle of the downward spiral the nation is in was increasing much faster than anyone could ever have imagined.

Larry and Vince landed within a half hour of each other. They were having a cup of coffee over small talk, when the Deacon stated that "if something drastic doesn't happen soon, we are going to be stuck with the same Administration for another four years, and that is all it will take for America to slide so far to the left that we will never be able to recover. The Constitution or at least what remains of it will become a historic document in the archives alongside the Bill of Rights. America is doomed unless there is a change of Administration to try to right our badly listing nation."

"Tell me, Ron, how you intend to stop this. They have a very well-oiled machine cranking along," Larry said.

"Neither of you has denied what I have just said, therefore I am assuming that you know I am right. Conversely, I don't expect either one of you to like my cure. Before you shoot it down, come up with a better one.

"We already hit them hard in the fundraising department with our banking raid. They are less than half way where they expected to be. Now it is time to start killing some motherfuckers! The whole re-election apparatus is working out of Chicago. We need to take them out.

"That is just the beginning. The DOJ is running rampant over America, and no one is stopping them at all. We need to disrupt their chain of command. The Secretary of State needs a funeral. If not, she will be our President in 2016, and she is every bit the socialist ideologue the President is. We have to stop it before it happens, otherwise it will take a fucking revolution to turn things around for the best. The way the Administration is fucking with the military, they may well be able to be turned on the government. Remember, I have over 960 billion dollars with which to fund a revolution. Bob has two mainframes going full bore distilling the personnel lists I got from Ed before he was killed. We should be able to come up with a cadre of trained willing volunteers.

"There are hundreds of militias out there that will jump in at the first sign of earnest rebellion. I dare not contact them, as for the most part they have been infiltrated by the government. We can't afford any link with them. They will act when the time is right.

"All this can be prevented if we can prevail at the voting booth, but we have to take out his Chicago crew. Vince, you've been quiet. What are your thoughts on this?"

"I don't like it at all, but I don't have a better solution either. And, yes, Sergeant Major, you are right about our situation. I also realize we have to deal with it or America is doomed. I just wish there was another way."

"So do I," Ron said. "I have searched my soul for months trying to come up with a better solution, and I can't."

"Do you have a plan, Top, or is this a typical pull it out of your ass from the ground up operation?"

"Larry, I am sending Joe in tomorrow to put eyes on the ground, and see what he can come up with. I am going in to meet him in about a week and we will see what we can work up for a plan. As you know, this is time sensitive, so once the train starts rolling, it will be full steam ahead. I may wind up bringing Serf in on this operation since we are shorthanded right now. So yes, I guess you could say we are pulling this out of our ass."

"Ok, Top, I have been holding out on you. We have an ex-agent, Tracy Nebel, that lives within 40 miles from here. She was the top assassin the agency had until she told us to shove it up our ass. Her major complaint was that we had become a bunch of pussies, and had become too frigging politically correct, and of course we all know this is true.

"We have been keeping an eye on her in case she turned and started working for the other side. Deacon, she is one bad assed bitch; I'm not sure even you could handle her. Don't let her looks fool you, many men have died because of those looks. She is drop dead gorgeous, 40 years old, and deadly as a fucking Cobra. In fact, we used to call her Cobra Lady, for once an adversary thought he had charmed her she would strike. Rumors have it that she also shared the traits of a Black Widow spider on occasion. We never questioned her how she got her job done; we just knew she always came through for us."

"Ok, Larry, you've got my attention," the Deacon said (thinking that she only had ten years left). "Do tell me more."

"She lives in a house outside of Concord, deep in the woods, with her two children. She breeds Dobermans, and they are always on guard. She has a large fenced-in yard, topped off with a row of concertina wire. The property borders an active Railroad track and a stream. She runs her dogs twice daily, but I wouldn't approach her then, as if her dogs don't get you her .45 automatic will.

"She is the person to go to for effective clean assassinations. The KGB made her once, and she took out the whole cell just to be sure her anonymity was assured. I feel she would welcome the opportunity to get active, as you well know, once it is in the blood, it's there forever.

"If you are interested, I will make an initial contact with her and see about you meeting her. Just realize you may be getting more than you bargained for."

"We'll see who can handle whom. Sure, if she is as good as you say, which I question. Remember, like me, you tend to think with your dick occasionally. I would love to check her out and see for myself. I am planning several high priority individual hits that call for a top-level operator. Go ahead and make the meeting arrangements."

Ron Dahle

Ron was intently following his GPS to get to the location of Tracy's house. He finally got to the clearing. The entire house was fenced in. There was a parking pad just off to the right of the only gate he saw. He parked and approached the gate only to have two massive Dobermans appear from out of nowhere and take a stance on the other side of the fence, letting it be known that no one was entering. Just as suddenly, the dogs withdrew and the intercom on the gate announced that it was safe to enter, but to stay on the path straight to the front door.

When the door opened, everything Larry said about Tracy was immediately apparent. She was dressed in a blouse that did nothing to hide her figure and a sheik skirt that had a slit up the side of one leg. "Hello, I'm Ron D," Ron managed to say before he was cut off by the goddess that stood in the doorway. "I know who you are. I'm Tracy, come in."

Tracy had a fresh pot of coffee waiting, so apparently Larry had briefed her. The house had a homey feel to it, unlike the Lodge which in all its splendor was a house, not a home. while This was Tracy's home.

When she sat, Ron caught a glimpse of her thigh pistol, which accounted for the slit skirt, or did it? Tracy broke the ice. "Larry said that you may have some work that falls within my specialty. Would you like to discuss it?"

"Frankly, I would rather you explain your specialty and capabilities before I brief you."

"That sounds fair," Tracy said, and then went on to describe her past ventures to Ron, when suddenly she stopped in the middle of it.

"Is something wrong? Ron asked.

"Not really, but it has been my experience that you can determine the validity of what one is saying a lot better by watching their eyes and facial expressions, than by ogling their tits!"

"Actually, Tracy, it is my job to evaluate the whole package when it comes to covert operatives. And that is precisely what I was doing."

"At the risk of not getting hired, I have to say that is a bunch of bullshit and you know it as well as I do."

"Ok, I'm busted. Would you care to continue? I will try my best to behave, but you don't make it too easy, you know."

Tracy was laughing inside, as Larry had already warned her about Ron's weakness for beautiful black haired, blue eyed, well-endowed women, and yes, she had dressed a bit provocatively for the occasion just to torment him.

The situation lightened up for both of them, and the interview went on well for the next three plus hours. Tracy seemed to show a heightened degree of interest when Ron told her that there were several high risk targets on the list that needed to be taken out soon.

"You need to come up to the lodge to get a feel for what we are doing and where we are doing it. By then I should have a good start on a target list for you."

As Ron drove away, he had to admit that he was more than a little intrigued by Tracy, while Tracy wondered just what in hell an old man like Ron thought he could offer her. Little did they know, both their answers would become clear in time. However, Ron was convinced that he had a new assassin on his team, and wondered where her talents would take her. Due to the Black Op aspect of her job, no one except Larry and Ron would know what she was doing and why she was on board. Ron already anticipated having a problem with Mary Jane over Tracy, for as stunning as Mary Jane was, Tracy came out ahead in that department.

The farm appeared much as she had envisioned, based on what Ron and Larry had told her. What Tracy or no one else saw was what was buried underground here. She was thinking what an awesome place this would be for her Dobermans.

She took a deep breath as she parked by the Lodge, as she had no idea what was in store for her. She knew from talking to Larry that the Deacon was totally dedicated to his mission, very unconventional in his methodologies, and a hard taskmaster when it came to the job at hand. The one glitch in his amour was his weakness for the fair sex, and that was something that Tracy filed away for future use, for there was no doubt in her mind that she could have Ron sitting up and begging within five minutes if she put her mind to it.

Ron came out to meet her, and invited her into the Lodge for coffee. Mary Jane let her presence be known by bringing Ron some papers to sign. And yes, Larry had already briefed Tracy on the Ron/Mary Jane connection.

Ron asked Tracy to join him in the war room. Needless to say Tracy was impressed with Ron's underground fortress, wondering what other surprises this relatively inconspicuous farm was holding.

Ron came right to the point. "Are you ready to pick up where you left off? I have some big names that need to be taken out and whoever does the jobs needs to bring their 'A' game with them."

"Frankly, the only game I have is an 'A' game. You don't succeed at many of the things I have accomplished unless you're firing on all eight cylinders. If they can be got to, 1 can do the job.

"That's good, as all I have is 'A' game operators. I am going to start you off at the top of the heap. I want you to kill the Secretary of State," Ron said watching intently for Tracy's response.

Without batting an eye Tracy replied, "Do you have a plan, or do you want me to handle it from the ground up? She is going to be hard to get to."

Ron noticed her calm demeanor during this exchange and thought to himself that if she isn't the real deal she is one hell of an actress.

"There are meetings and social affairs all next week that she will be attending. Larry has got you passes to all of them. It is strongly rumored that her sexuality may be in question, which is likely the truth, based on the extensive research the Agency has done on her. I can't imagine anyone there who will attract as much attention as you, especially if you tend to brush off male suitors.

"Ideally you would be able to get close enough to her to start a conversation; unless I am mistaken, she will take it from there. If that is the case, your job will be very easy. If not, it will still be doable, just not as easy."

"And do I bring a frigging machine gun with me to the party or do you have a better idea? You know the security is going to be thick as hell there."

"The security will only be tough getting in, as everyone has to be vetted to get in the door. That has been taken care of." Ron walked over to a shelf over the desk, and retrieved a small Cordura pouch. "This, my dear, is your machine gun for this operation." Ron revealed a diabetes test kit within the pouch. "Your vetting has you listed as a diabetic; you will have no problem getting this in the facility. You have 12 lancets in the kit, two of which you will use at different times to check your glucose levels in plain sight. Also in the kit you have three marked lancets that have enough ricin on them to kill a horse.

"If I were to hold you and whisper something to you or kiss you I could pop one of these in your ass and you would never know it. One is all it will take; two would be good insurance. She will appear to be totally normal for several days then she will start dying. That will take a day or so. They may or may not figure out her cause of death. I would expect them to, as important as she is.

"Your identity will be wiped clean from everything associated with the week. We have already modified your image in the facial recognition database, so you will not pop up on that if they were to check. This will likely be the easiest job you will ever have with me. Just remember, whatever the cost, go along with her."

"Just fucking great, my first job and you have me trying to seduce and then kill a lesbian. Not exactly what I had in mind."

"You should be able to accomplish your mission before it gets to that. Shit, who knows, you might like it," Ron said with a grin.

"Like it, my ass," Tracy said.

"Like I said, it probably doesn't have to go that far. Just play it by ear. Are you in?"

"Yes I'm in, but if I have to eat that bitch's pussy, you are going to pay the price."

"Hell, I'll repay the task tenfold," Ron said smiling. "Here, take this and get a wardrobe befitting the occasion."

Ron handed her $50,000 from the safe. This should be enough. Your room reservations as well as your new identity are in the Lodge. I also have volumes of data on her that you need to research before the job.

"OK, if we are done here, I'll show you around the compound and the Academy so you can see the assets that are at your disposal if you need them. We have ranges from 10 yards to 2,000 yards, and weapons to compliment them.

"If you ever need anything to do a job, just holler, and if we don't have it, we will get it. I will be your only point of contact here. The less anyone else knows about you, the better."

While Tracy was driving home her mind was racing at full speed considering the assignment she'd just received from the Deacon. Not what she was hoping for, but she was determined to pull it off, if for no other reason than personal and professional pride.

She had two weeks to digest the reams of data she was given on her target, and that was how she thought of the Secretary of State, as a target, not a name or position. Tracy theorized that no one had bothered to go through the documents, but she was going to learn as much about the target as possible prior to their meeting. Tracy looked back over her past and realized that these principles were the only reason she was still alive. Yep, that's how I roll, there's only one way, and that's my way, she thought as she was pulling into her house, with Zeus there to meet her as she got out of her car. She was anxious to get home to see that Kiki, her daughter, had fed and taken care of Talia, her new baby blue Doberman.

It was 2:00 am when she first discovered it in the piles of paperwork she was trying to digest. There were several references to the target not only being a lesbian, but she was also into S&M, with her preferred role being the submissive. The first thing that went through Tracy's mind was a sigh of relief. Then she thought, and this is what we have leading the nation's foreign relations efforts. No wonder we are so fucked up.

This presented Tracy with a completely new set of challenges; she had to learn the entire S&M scene and only had a bit more than a week to do so. She went directly to her computer and started researching the dark side of sex as she called it.

Over breakfast, Mary Jane looked at Ron and said. "So when are you going to tell me about the woman who spent the day here yesterday?"

"Sorry, babe, but I'm not. None of the warriors will have any contact with her. She falls directly under me and her role within the operation will remain known only to Larry and me. I wish I could tell you more but I can't, that's just how it is. And hon, before you even try, that is non-negotiable."

"Fine," Mary Jane said, "I guess that settles that."

Deep down inside Ron knew this matter was far from settled with Mary Jane. He would just have to fend off the salvos as they came.

Chapter 24

Vince called and said he was flying in that afternoon, and they were going to burn some midnight oil. That was all he would say, so Ron agreed that they would meet shortly.

Ron noticed that Vince had a strange, almost tenuous attitude as he walked into the Lodge. As soon as Ron poured them both a cup of coffee, Vince asked to go downstairs into the war room.

Upon entering the room, Vince closed the massive door behind him. "Sergeant Major, I don't know where to start, but the problems we have in America are more dire than we ever expected, and my agency is involved up to their ass."

"We have always known that Homeland Security had issues. What have you found out, Vince?"

"It is more like what haven't I found out. When I took over the aerial reconnaissance branch, I was given certain areas to avoid totally. I guess too much of you has rubbed off on me over the last couple of years. I have discovered what could only be termed as detention camps, capable of holding hundreds of thousands of people, in several areas. They are minimally staffed now, but they exist. The power is on in them, based on night over flights. FEMA is right in the middle of this shit, too."

"I have heard rumors that these existed; this is the first evidence I can use to place any credibility on that rumor, though."

"Sergeant Major, I haven't scratched the surface yet."

"There's more, I assume."

"Oh, yes. They also have a major training area where they are administering combat training to the attendees. I have done some subtle research and it appears that they have a highly trained assassination component, and they are working throughout the government at different levels. The word has it that each of the trainees has a specific target, just one, to take out on order of the Director. The kill command will be electronically transmitted, probably by text, with a nonsensical message with the kill phrase used in it twice. At that time, the executioner has 24 hours to eliminate his specific target. None of the executioners knows any of the others. I have been told the targets are the President's cabinet members, czars, certain Senators, and department heads. The word is that in the event the President plans to implement his Executive Order that will proclaim Martial Law there are certain people he wants dispensed with ahead of time. This could be the basis for the implementation. The President knows that a lot of his team is on shaky ground, and he intends to eliminate any weak sisters before they become a liability to him. He won't replace any of them, as they know too much."

"And I take it your Boss has bought into this program?"

"Lock, stock, and barrel. She is such a frigging idiot, she will do anything to preserve her position."

"Ok. How do we find out who is on the list, who the assassins are, and their individual code words?" the Deacon asked.

"It is logged away in a completely secure computer in the Director's office."

"Vince, I hate to break this to you but there is no such thing as a completely secure computer; if you don't believe that, check out my bank accounts," the Deacon said with a smile. "Get all the info you can acquire; you, me and Larry are getting ready to take a trip to Monterey, to visit Bob."

One Week Later

Tracy was sitting in her bedroom office familiarizing herself with this mission's weapon of choice, a Diabetes test kit. She had mastered pricking herself with the lancet and drawing the blood to obtain a reading. She figured it had to appear to be second nature to her to any onlookers. Actually, she was taking a break from the tons of S&M porn she had been studying for this mission. She was confident that she could carry the role of a dominatrix off without a hitch. It was then that she questioned if she had not always had the tendencies of a dominatrix; she had major control issues, and her chosen profession led right into that conclusion. She pondered the theory and then she smiled.

Tracy had exactly nine days left, and then she would become Tina Manson, a fitting name for her mission. She was a rich debutante who had an invitation to a fundraiser for the people of Haiti, one of ex-President Clapton's pet projects. His primary pet project being avoiding spending time with his wife. Her position as Secretary of State made that easy for him.

The Deacon had created a bank account with Tracy under her new identity as Tina Manson. Tracy had mastered the skill of writing ambidextrously, so when she presented Hilda the fifty thousand dollar check for her husband's "cause" it would not be able to be traced back to her handwriting. It seems, she thought, that I have about all the bases covered, on this one. And she did, as she wanted to leave a lasting impression of her abilities on the Deacon. She smiled as she thought that would likely be easier to do in the bedroom then on the battleground they were in the middle of.

The only variable was the actually hooking up with Hilda, but Tracy, or Tina, would likely find that an easy task. The check would be the icebreaker. Tracy was fully confident in her own sensuality, and sexuality; she knew that if Hilda thought there was any possibility of scoring with this incredible specimen of womanhood in front of her, she would jump at it.

———

"And to what do I owe this honor?" Bob asked, as he hugged Ron. "The three biggest bad assed good guys in the nation in one place right here, in my driveway. One grenade could get us all, ya know," Bob said as he motioned them inside.

"Every time the Deacon comes to see me he has an impossible project for me. I can just imagine what the three of you have come up with."

After dinner and several hours of talking and studying Vince's material Bob swirled the cognac in his snifter, took a sip and proclaimed, "I can do it! It isn't going to be easy, and I may not know I have it when I get it. I may well need a code man to break it out for me if Bertha (his pet name for his bank of mainframes) can't recognize it."

"That's no problem," Larry said. "I have the best in the business working for me. If he and Bertha can't do it, it can't be done, period. Just tell me when you want him and he is yours for as long as it takes."

———

Tina was duly impressed with the hotel where the gala fundraiser was taking place. Probably the finest Los Angeles had to offer, but then again, she would expect no less considering the guest of honor and the event. This was a chance for all the pretty people to strut their stuff in Ben's presence and try to impress him.

Tina went to her room, put the vials of insulin she was carrying as a cover in the refrigerator, and inspected the test kit to insure everything was where she needed it when the time was right. She also had three packets of Goo, a potent glucose supplement used by endurance athletes as a pick me up. This was her safeguard from having to eat pussy. If Hilda was hot, just maybe, for the cause, Tracy thought, but she is a frigging beast-ain't no way.

The pretty people started trickling in early, in the hopes for a chance encounter with the ex-President. Tina was among the early arrivers, but for a different reason. She wanted to be the first item on the menu for Hilda, as that would make it all so much simpler. Tina still was unsure how this would go down, and realized that there was at least a fifty percent chance against her being able to carry this off successfully. Damn the Deacon! He knew this when he came up with this whole idea, Tina thought. This is basically a test of my capabilities. I'll show that old bastard!

Tina watched Hilda and her entourage come in and sit at their table. There were six of them at the table, all relatively innocuous looking. Tina positioned herself where she could inconspicuously observe Hilda's table to enable her to strike when the iron was hot, so to speak.

Right after the dinner, which was excellent—lobster tails flown in from Maine—Ben got up and started to deliver his pitch. At this time, Tina tested her glucose levels, and of course, they were a bit high, having just eaten. She got mentally prepared, and reassured herself that she was up to the task at hand.

She stood up, and a vision of loveliness she was, a scant six feet plus in heels, wearing a form fitting black dress with a deep scooped neckline. A four strand genuine pearl choker graced her long elegant neck. The trap was getting ready to be set, and she was the bait.

She approached Hilda from the right side, as there was no one sitting there She bent over and asked if she could join her for a second to give her a check for Ben.

Hilda didn't hear a word she said. Her eyes were riveted on the open scoop neckline which, when Tina bent over, revealed her full, ample, voluptuous breasts in all their glory. Hilda broke out in a cold sweat and invited Tracy to have a seat.

Tina introduced herself and said she wanted to donate fifty thousand dollars to the cause.

"That is very generous," Hilda said. "Do you have a special interest in or connection to Haiti, Tina?"

"No, not at all, I just have an interest in spending my husband's money on something besides his frigging hookers. Damn fool had a heart attack while screwing his intern and died mid stroke."

"So, I take it you have a sour taste in your mouth for men at the present time," Hilda asked.

"That puts it mildly," Tina replied. "I couldn't care less if I never see another man, unless it is to take advantage of him.

"I hate to barge in on you like this, but I am getting ready to go somewhere else, not that I don't enjoy your husband's talk, but I really have no interest; I had an invitation and just came in cruising."

"Frankly, dear, I haven't paid attention to anything he has said in over twenty years. Would you like to come up to my room for some Champagne? I'm sure you'll love it."

"Well, I don't know... considering who you are and all..."

"Nonsense. Give me twenty minutes to dismiss the security, and then come to the penthouse. Believe me, dear, you don't know who I am. So, are we on?"

"Why not? It will be an honor. I will see you in twenty minutes." Tina returned to her table and Hilda excused herself from her guests and said she was going to turn in for the night.

Tina immediately called Bert, who was on station at a local airfield with his new twin engine Commander. He was on standby to get Tracy back to Wolfeboro asap. He had no idea what she was doing, but he was convinced it had to be a hot operation.

On her way, she went to her room to oil down and put on different clothes, more befitting the occasion she was about to partake in.

Hilda released her security for the evening, and said she would not need them for the rest of the night. This was nothing new to them; they just took it in stride and departed, thankful they could go party. They knowingly turned off the security cameras on the floor. This was standard procedure anytime Hilda dismissed them.

With great trepidation, Tina knocked on the door of the penthouse. As she did, it swung open. Inside, the penthouse was illuminated with candles; the scent of jasmine was prevalent throughout the suite. Tina didn't know what to expect, but she was ready for all conceivable scenarios. Hilda hollered out from a different room and suggested Tina should get dressed in something more comfortable.

That was her cue; she removed her outer garments and stood there clad in a garter belt, black mesh stockings, and hip-high black high-heel boots. She had oiled her body down and she glistened and rippled like a bronze Greek goddess. Her body was as tight as a snare drum, her abs like a washboard. Her shaved pussy appeared to glow from the oil. She was a striking goddess that would render man or woman to jelly, and bring them to their knees just by her mere presence.

Hilda came in and gasped at the sight dominating the center of the room. "Oh, mistress, I have been so bad. Do with me as you will," Hilda said with a hint of a quiver in her voice. She was wearing a jeweled spiked choker collar that had a chain attached to it. She passed the loose end to Tina, and then got on all fours.

Hilda started to lead Tina into the other room when Tina jerked on the chain and said, "Slow down, bitch. There is no hurry."

Hilda climbed on to the bed, handed Tina a candle and said, "Burn me. God, please burn me."

Tina lowered the candle close to Hilda's breasts and started to spill molten wax on her nipples. Hilda squirmed and moaned in ecstasy. Then Tina started dripping hot wax down her body, and filling her navel. "Open your legs wide, slave, I want a mold of your pussy." At that, Tina started letting the hot wax trickle into and around Hilda's pussy until there was a perfect mold.

Hilda was crying from pain and screaming from pleasure simultaneously. Tina spotted a whip, grabbed the collar, and rode Hilda like a horse back to the room where her belongings were, whipping at her all the way.

She dismounted when they got there and said, "Forehead on the floor, dink," and slapped her buttocks first with the whip and then with a bare hand. At this time Tina took the Goos. At the same time she charged the lancet with one of the ricin points and laid another out while whipping Hilda during the entire process.

She then started to whip Hilda's buttocks harder; she spanked her by hand, too, while injecting a ricin lancet in each buttock. Shortly, Tina said she was having a problem. She told Hilda to relax, and she checked her blood glucose level. The level was over 500. Tina said she was on the verge of going into hyperglycemic shock and had to get to her room for an insulin injection, and a possible trip to the hospital.

Hilda said she fully understood. Actually, she was a little relieved because, as good as Tina was, it was a bit more than Hilda had bargained for. She gave Tina one of her private cards, and said if they were ever in the same city again to call.

Tina went to her room, called Bert and told him she was on her way, and then she took a measured dose of insulin to help her glucose levels get back to normal. She changed clothes, packed her one bag, went to the lobby, and grabbed a taxi to the airport.

In the meantime, Hilda spent an inordinate amount of time peeling her pussy, navel, and nipple molds off, to keep them intact, to help her remember this woman from heaven.

At 20,000 feet, heading northeast, Tracy poured a glass of Champagne to celebrate what she knew was a brilliantly planned and executed operation. What a shame she could tell no one about it. That Tina's one badass bitch, Tracy thought with a smile. She then broadened her smile, as she now had a new persona to file in her bag of tricks.

———————

Chapter 25

"Dief, damn it, you look pretty good. How are you feeling overall?" the Deacon asked.

"Shit, Top, I don't really know. It is hard to sort out my overall condition as I am recovering from being shot and receiving radiation. It is going to take me a while to get back on my feet again, but I will make it."

"Don't push yourself, but at the same time don't sit around feeling sorry for yourself either. We need you back up and running as soon as possible. I am going to put you in the arms room. You set your own hours as you feel up to it. Shit, you're lucky to be alive.

"It's good to have the team back together, although both you and Gunny are banged up a bit. Fortunately, we have added a couple of folks to take up the slack, all warriors. You will meet them in due time. In fact, Bert is flying in with one today from an operation in LA; they should be here late this afternoon. Joe is due in from a recon of Chicago in the morning, and it's off to the races again."

Bert landed as scheduled, but he was the only one to exit the Commander.

"So what did you do with Tracy?" Ron asked.

"She insisted on landing in Manchester. Said something about her car was there and she had to go check on her dogs."

"I should have figured she was going to do just as she damn well pleased!" the Deacon said. "Just once, I would like to see a frigging woman that followed orders."

"She said not to worry, everything went as planned in L.A., and she would be up to debrief you in a couple of days. She seems as professional as hell," Bert said.

"Shit, you don't know the half of it. A great asset, but a hell of a price tag attached to it. She definitely has her own mind.

"Dief and Steve flew in today, Gunny is already here, Joe is due in tomorrow. Shit, we're just lacking Serf's crew and we could have a pow-wow."

"Mr. Dakle, please."

"Speaking," the Deacon said to the stranger on the other end of the line.

"Mr Dakle, I am Jonas Bernstein, a court appointed attorney, assigned to represent Tracy Nebel. She asked me to call you and appraise you of her situation. She is currently locked up in the County jail for killing a man, and requested I contact you."

"I will be there in about an hour," the Deacon said. He no sooner hung up when he called his attorney, Benson, in Manchester and requested he meet with Tracy and himself in an hour. Of course, smelling money, Ron's attorney said he would be at the County jail waiting for him.

Ron's mind was racing at full speed on the way to the jail wondering what in hell happened. I just knew that this was too good to be true, thought Ron, a skilled assassin and drop dead gorgeous to boot. Larry said she came with a bit of baggage; I just wonder how much.

The two lawyers were talking to each other when Ron pulled into the jail. "So, what is going on?" Ron queried.

"It seems that Ms. Nebel shot and killed a neighbor of hers while she was out running her dogs yesterday afternoon. The neighbor was also armed and Ms. Nebel has claimed self-defense. Her bail hearing is set for tomorrow, the prosecutor is asking one million dollars," said Ron's attorney.

"Ok, I will post the bond for her, but I want to see her as soon as she walks out of the jail. I don't want to talk to her while she is inside, as the walls have ears. Mr. Bernstein, I appreciate your service on this matter, but we will take over from here. I am sure you will want to confer with Ms. Nebel for her concurrence.

"What is the status of her children in the meantime?" Ron asked.

"Children's services have them under their control, and animal control has the dogs, " Ron's lawyer said.

" Immediately initiate authorization through Tracy to release the children, as well as the dogs, to me and Mary Jane . Benson, you handle that and get right on it; I don't want those kids to spend another night at DHS. We will put them up in the lodge for the time being, until we get this sorted out. Don't take any shit from DHS, just make it happen. We will probably have to cage the dogs initially, until they get comfortable. The kids will go a long way in easing that transition."

"What in hell do you mean, they are moving in here?" Mary Jane asked, obviously outraged.

"It is for her and her family's safety. I talked to the sheriff and he feels it is an open and shut case of self-defense. However, the man she killed was very well liked in the town and there is concern for her safety. Plus, I don't want people sneaking around, as long as she is working for me."

"So just how long do you expect her to live in the Lodge?"

"I have been planning on moving the cadre into the cadre rooms in the cantonment area for a while, I will just expedite that and make it happen. All I will need to do is have a containment fence erected for her dogs."

"Well ain't this just honkey dory," Mary Jane said, her eyes flashing as the green-headed monster stirred within her.

"Damn it, woman, you have to realize that I am running a major clandestine operation out of here and there are some things that just need to happen whether you like it or not.

Ron then lied through his teeth and stated, "I have no sexual interest in that woman what-so-ever. My major concern is that she brings a skill set to this team that no one else has, and no, I am not sharing that with you or anyone else!"

"Whatever!" Mary Jane mumbled as she went into her office.

Larry's secure line rang. The Deacon was full of anticipation as he answered it. "I trust you have some good news for me," Ron inquired.

"Ron, I hate to be the bearer of bad news, but the Secretary of State is hospitalized in India. She went there the day after the fund raiser. She has been hospitalized 2 days now, they don't expect her to pull through. They have their suspicions what the problem is but everyone is being tight lipped. They have managed to keep this from the press so far, but when she dies, they will have some explaining to do. Tell Tracy I am proud of her."

"I will as soon as I see her," the Deacon said and he explained the Tracy situation to Larry. "We will beat this, it is just a pain in the ass."

"Do you want me to intercede on behalf of the CIA?" Larry asked.

"Not yet; I would rather avoid any undue attention directed at her, if at all possible. Her children are due here this evening, as are her dogs. I expect her to be out of the can within two days, depending on what the lawyer can swing. By then I will have the Apple Cabin fenced in and she will be able to move right in. I have already issued the order for the cadre to move into the cantonment area; it's happening as we speak."

"Ok, Top, seems like you have a handle on things. Keep me in the loop on Tracy and let me know if you need my assistance." Larry wondered how long it would take Ron to discover what Larry knew about Tracy. The complete vetting process on Tracy when she came to work for the CIA and was selected to be an assassin turned up some interesting facts about Tracy, that even she wasn't aware of.

———

Tracy hugged her kids as soon as she walked into the Lodge. Her next question was where the dogs were. Ron assured her that they were in good-sized cages, and were doing well. It was at that time when Talia, her baby Dobie, barely two months old, came around the corner with Molly. As soon as she saw Tracy, she pissed on the floor, and ran over to her. Tracy scooped her up and smothered her with kisses.

Ron explained the Apple Cabin situation to her, and said that they needed to have a talk as soon as she got settled in.

"Yes, you're damn right we do," Tracy said with a degree of ire in her tone, which the Deacon didn't really understand.

———

Tracy and Ron both had a fresh cup of coffee as they went down into the war room. "How did you make out in court? I notice I didn't have to post bail; how come?" Ron asked.

"The DA, and prosecutor, as well as the sheriff declined to file charges stating the investigation disclosed that it was a clear cut case of self-defense."

Ron smelled influence and pressure from Larry on this situation, but kept his opinion to himself.

"That's good. Congratulations are in order; Hilda died in the middle of the night, in a hospital in India. The cause of death hasn't been released. So, how did it go down?"

"That topic is not on the table. You gave me a mission, I completed it. That's all you need to know. That, sir, is how I roll, as you would say. Now, let it be known, the next time you need a lesbian killed you need to find someone else for the job. That is where I will put my foot down!"

Ron was a little taken back by the belligerence of this uppity display from someone whose ass he'd just pulled out of the fire, but decided to give her this one and chalk it up to a bad day.

"I will take that under advisement and file it away for future assignment criteria. Joe got in last night from Chicago. I have decided to let him in on who you are, and team you up with him for a multiple hit in Chicago."

"That won't work! I work alone. I am alive today because I am a loner and I don't intend to change that!" she said, almost defiantly.

Ron was starting to get a royal case of the ass when he realized that, in many regards, she was just like him. Ron was always a free agent and basically did things his way, having little regard for authority, much the same as she was displaying. While it pissed him off, he also liked the spirit this woman had. There weren't many men that would stand up to the Deacon, the way this woman was. Pissed, yes, but she definitely earned his respect that day. He pondered; if she was this hard to deal with on routine matters, how in hell was he going to talk her out of some pussy? Definitely a monumental task ahead of him, he thought.

"Ronnie Mac will get a detail and a couple of trucks and go down with you, to get your belongings. Take a couple of days to settle in, and then we will figure where you will fit into this organization. We just got off to a rough start, but it is good having you aboard. I am looking forward to great things from you in the coming months."

"Top, I just called to let you know we are getting ready to fly a load of coyote food down to Serf. We have got all we can from here; if Serf wants to try before he gets rid of them, more power to him."

"Larry, were you able to get anything at all out of them?" Ron asked.

"Not much that we didn't know. They said one of the suitcase nukes was headed for the UN building in NY, one in Chicago, and the last in Los Angeles. Which makes me wonder where the third suitcase is."

"Larry, did ya ever think that maybe it hadn't arrived there yet? We know they are coming across the border; it is unlikely that they would transport all of them at the same time for the sake of security. Hell, it could already be on the way to its target for all we know."

"Yeah, that is a possibility. The bastards also mentioned a nuke warhead with a launcher coming here by cargo ship. They didn't know the port it was coming into but it is probably Oakland; when it was coming, or its target. This is the third time we have heard this story from three different sources. This is the one that worries me."

"Me too, and it isn't an issue the Warriors can do anything about without actionable intelligence. You never know, we may get lucky and get more info on it. Remember, we have received a couple of ref flags on Canton, Ohio, but with no details. Basically the bastards are setting up everywhere, and what burns my ass is they are doing it with the government's blessing."

"I know, Top, but what in hell can we do? What did Joe come up with on the President's team in Chicago?

"There is too much security on the ground there. I was thinking of Tracy and Joe taking them out, but it's too risky. We probably need to pass on that, as much as I hate to, unless we take the whole block out with a car bomb, and that isn't something I want to do."

"Tell me, Top, how is Tracy working out?"

"She is a bullheaded bitch, but she gets the job done. Sort of reminds me of myself when I was younger."

"What the fuck do you mean 'when you were younger'? You're as bullheaded now as you were the day I met you."

"Anyway, I gave her a couple of days to get settled in in the Apple Cabin. It would be good if I could get a debriefing out of her with the Hilda scenario. I have no idea how it went down."

"And you probably never will," Larry said. "She does her own thing and doesn't talk about it. Initially I had problems with that, but she is so frigging good at what she does, I elected to pass on pushing the point. Trust me, Top, you've got a lot to learn about Tracy," Larry said with a grin. "Anyway, I have to hang up, as unlike you, I have a day job."

"Yeah, fuck you, Larry. Before you hang up, are the ASA vans still maintaining a listening watch over the forest area?"

"Yes, 24 hours a day, and haven't heard a peep since the operation. We figure that area has been considered compromised and won't likely be used again."

"I'm hearing the same thing from Vince, they have seen nothing but wildlife. Ok, Boss, going to let you go. Keep me posted."

As Ron hung up Mary Jane came out of her office and asked, "And how is Miss priss doing in her new free home?"

"I am assuming you are talking about Tracy, who, like you, is occupying a space on a government compound. I am not sure, as I haven't talked to her in a couple of days. She is getting settled in."

"It must be nice to have the Boss wrapped around your finger," Mary Jane said.

"Babe, will you knock this bullshit off? She is on board, in the capacity of a professional, and that's all!"

"Yeah, well, remember I do her payroll and couldn't help but notice that she is the highest paid person you have working for you by about two times."

"That may just relate to her skill set and unique qualifications."

"I've seen her qualifications, they're hard to miss. As for her skill sets, I guess that is your call."

"Damn it, Mary Jane, this conversation is over! I don't want to hear any more about it!"

"Whatever," Mary Jane said as she stormed back into her office.

Tracy finally took a break and dialed her mother in Washington state to advise her of her new job and address.

"Hey Tracy, I was beginning to wonder if you had dropped off the edge. What has been going on?"

"Mom, you wouldn't believe it if I told you. It has been a hectic month for me. I have moved and I have a new job."

"Well, you going to tell me or do I have to guess?"

"Ok, I am doing private contracting for the government, sort of. I work for an old fucker that goes by the name of the Deacon. I live in a set of quarters right here, on the compound."

Tracy's mom was quiet for a long time. Finally, she spoke. "Tell me a little more about this Deacon character."

Well, he is close to 70 years old, I would think, although he refuses to acknowledge that. His real name is Ron Dakle. He retired as a Command Sergeant Major. He is widowed, and I get the feeling he would jump my bones in a minute if I ever dropped my guard."

A long silence ensued. "Mom, are you still there?"

"Oh yes, baby, I'm here. Are you sitting down? If not, you need to."

"For Christ's sake, mom, drop the theatrics and tell me what to fuck is going on!"

"Ok, in a nutshell, the Deacon is your biological father. He and I had a fling in the seventies. He and your dad were good friends, your dad went on an extended TDY and, damn it, things just happened. Ron left to go to Monterey before I knew I was pregnant. Your dad knew that he couldn't be your father, so he volunteered to take an unaccompanied tour to Panama, just to clear his head. He was there about ten months and was killed in South America. Right after he was killed I moved back home to Washington. I never told you, as I wanted to spare you thinking ill of me. So there, now you know."

"Holy fucking shit! And I was considering giving him some sympathy pussy. Guess that's out of the question. So what to fuck do I do now? I don't know if I should tell him or not. There's a lot at stake here. I've got a great job."

"Well, if you don't tell him, I will. I know him better than you realize. He is all business when it comes to what he does. He would put you at undue risk for the sake of the mission. Maybe if he knows he's your father he will moderate his stance a bit."

"Damn it, I'm not looking for a free ride, never have and don't plan to start now."

"Ok, babe, but it can't hurt. The Deacon I knew will still throw you to the lions, but if he knows who you are he'll put you in with an old sick lion, to give you a fighting chance. There are no free rides with the Deacon, it doesn't matter who you are."

"Ok, then, but I want you to tell him. The last time he and I talked it didn't go too well."

"And that, my dear, is the streak of him that runs through you. You two have always been of one mind. There was never any doubt in my mind whose daughter you were. You're both bullheaded, stubborn, and capable of being mean as a fucking rattlesnake. That's one of the reasons I would send you off to stay with your grandmother, you reminded me of him too much. I'll call him when we hang up and break the news to him. Keep in touch, baby."

"I will, mom," Tracy said.

———

Ron had just sat down to have a cup of coffee with Mary Jane, when the phone rang. "It never fails," he muttered as he answered it. He didn't recognize the number on the caller ID or the voice on the other end of the phone.

The caller spoke softly, "Ron, I don't believe you can't recognize this voice who repeatedly whispered "fuck me" in your ear so many times in the early 70s."

"Shit, is this Charlene?" Ron said, finally realizing whom he was talking to. "You dropped off the face of the earth, I never did find out where you guys went after I was reassigned to Monterey."

"Bobby was reassigned to Panama. He was killed on a trip to South America. I relocated back home to Washington State, but this has nothing to do with why I called."

"Well, out with it, lady, no reason to be secretive, considering what we shared over the years."

Taking a deep breath, Charlene was able to force out the words. "Ron, I don't know how to say this but you and I had a daughter. I didn't know I was pregnant when you went to Monterey, and after Bobby died I decided to let that die with him, as he is the only other person who knew she wasn't his."

"And you are telling me this now…why? Is there anything I can do for her?" Ron asked.

"As a matter of fact, there is. You can keep her alive! Against all odds, she wound up working for you. Ron, Tracy is your daughter! I know you, and I know Tracy's line of work. I just hope that you will try to keep her safe. I just talked to her, and she doesn't want to give up her job, so the ball is in your court. I hope you will do whatever is in your power to insure she dies of old age, and not on one of your rabbit—assed operations.

"Barring a crisis, this is the last time you will hear from me, as we have both moved on in our lives. I just hope you will do what is right by our daughter," Charlene said as she hung up the phone.

Ron sat almost motionless, staring at his coffee cup for what seemed like an eternity, when Mary Jane finally broke the silence. "Well, are you going to tell me what that was all about or make me guess ?"

"You'll never guess this one, babe. I just found out that an old friend and I had a daughter together and, lo and behold, it is Tracy! I just fucking knew she was too much like me to be a coincidence."

"So what now?" Mary Jane asked.

"I have no frigging idea. I need to talk to her and we need to weigh our options. I could create an administrative position for her, as I really don't want to deploy her in her specialty. Ultimately, the call will be hers," Ron said.

———

Tracy arrived per Ron's request. It was obvious that neither one of them was comfortable with the situation at hand.

Ron broke the silence first. "So, this was quite a surprise that has been sprung on both of us. The major question is how we go forward from here. I am wide open to suggestions. I can create an administrative position here that could keep you busy as hell."

"Obviously, we have a different assessment of the situation. It appears that you see yourself as a protective father. On the other hand, I see you as a sperm donor. Through no fault of your own you were never a part of my life, and I am having a little trouble with the whole concept of your being my father.

"As far as I am concerned, nothing needs to change. I am not an administrative clerk, damn it, I'm a fucking assassin, and I don't have any intentions to change my line of work just because you had a hard-on 42 years ago!"

"Why did I know I was going to get a basic load of shit from you over this matter?

"Ok, assassin it is, but I reserve the right to select your assignments. I promised your mother I would try to keep you alive and I intend to do just that. I know you are secretive, but I would appreciate it if, at your convenience, you could give me some insight on how you work, to enable me to select your targets."

"You know that goes totally against how I work. Under the circumstances, I will work up a briefing on some of my methods and procedures. Realize you won't be getting it all."

"Nor do I expect to. I just need something to go on for targeting data."

"I hate to break your bubble, but no one is safe when I am on them. You need not worry about targeting criteria. Furthermore, get this little girl, daddy thing out of your mind, for it isn't in mine."

What a bullheaded bitch, Ron thought as she left, but at least he realized where she got it from as he smiled to himself. Ron pondered what she said about being able to get to anyone and his mind immediately went back to the President's crew in Chicago. He decided to have Joe brief her on his recon report of the overall situation, and send her to Chicago with a prioritized list of names, just to see how good she really was.

The fact that he had four grandchildren didn't escape the Deacon, but he opted to put that on a back burner and deal with it at a later date.

———

Chapter 26

"**D**amn it, Top, you have no business sending a woman into that mess in Chicago. I told you, there is too much security. She will be dead as soon as her feet hit the ground," Joe said, obviously upset.

"Joe, she is going in with an open-ended ticket. If she thinks she is over her head, she will return. If not, she has free reign to accomplish whatever she thinks she can. I would really like for some of those bastards to meet their demise, plus it would be a great test of Tracy's abilities."

"Then at least let me go with her as a backup," Joe said.

"Not no, but hell no! The last time I suggested that I listened to a twenty-minute dissertation on her being a free agent and a total loner.

"She will be here in a little while. I want you to brief her on what you found, your estimate of the situation, and the reasons for that estimate. I want you to paint as realistic and bleak a picture as you can. I don't want her accepting this mission with any delusions about its complexity or potential danger."

"Ok, then, how about if I take her to Chicago, take out my own target and just wait for her to contact me to bring her back? I was able to track down Jonathan Akers while I was there, and it would be relatively easy to get to him. Granted, he doesn't pop up on the radar now, but as you know, once a "Domestic Terrorist", always one.

"Plus, I can bring an assortment of munitions for each of us in the event they are needed."

"Damn it, Joe, you talked me into it. It is a shame no one took him out in the 60s and 70s, when he was a member of the Weather Underground. If I remember right, his girlfriend and two other friends were killed making their own bomb. What a shame he wasn't there then. I don't think Tracy will have any problem with that."

Joe wrapped up his briefing with Tracy by giving her a dossier on every known power player on the President's team who was in Chicago, to include the security personnel. "As you will notice, they are living high on the hog; most have penthouses in the finest hotels in Chicago. Why not? They are on the taxpayers' dime. You will find maps, drawings, and blueprints, including locations of all security cameras, of the hotels they are in, as well as their favorite restaurants. Hopefully, this information will be beneficial to you on your mission."

It was then Joe told her of his mission in Chicago. "We will be operating in different areas, there isn't any overlap on our mission, except that we are both going to kill someone who needs to die. And I will be there to lend a hand in the event you need it."

"I appreciate the offer, Joe. However, as I told Ron, I tend to be at my best when working alone. Although I do appreciate the work you put into these dossiers; they will save me a lot of time, and make my job a lot easier. Just keep your distance in Chicago; I don't need a babysitter."

"Well, I wish you all the luck, and if you think of anything you need, you will know where to find me. If there is nothing else, I need to go set up a traveling kit for my mission."

"Tracy, I hope you were able to benefit from Joe's briefing. I want you to know this is no cakewalk you are embarking upon.

They have security, and Chicago is notorious for it anyway. I don't want you to feel you have anything to prove. If you get there and decide it is too risky, just call Joe and he will extract you. Joe will fly you to Chicago, as you will be armed, and I don't want any record of you being there even though you will be going there under a different identity. So, have you given any consideration to briefing me on your MO?" Ron queried.

"If I must. There is a basic fact of life that is undeniable. I don't mean to sound conceited, but the fact that I am drop dead gorgeous makes my job a breeze. There are very few men that walk that I can't lead around by the pecker, and you know it, as you were like a dog in heat until you found out you were my father.

"As we recently found out with Hilda, I have the same effect on a lot of women. I guess I have you to thank for that, as you make up half of my gene pool. I am not above using this to my advantage when it comes to targeting a victim.

"Additionally, Larry and his boys trained me well; I am a technician with many different skills. I like to mix up my methods, and if possible make it look like an accident, or as a result of natural causes. I work alone because I am fluid, I may change my plan at any instant, and frankly I haven't found anyone who thinks on their feet as fast as I do. That could compromise them, me, and the mission. That, daddy dear, is all you are going to get out of me. Have Joe file a flight plan into Chicago for the day after tomorrow."

―――

Tracy had just finished bleaching and coloring her hair. She was now a stunning honey blonde. New mission, new look. She'd learned to produce her own ID documents while in the CIA, as it was often required. This saved a lot of hassle. She was traveling under the name of Tina Harrington. Tomorrow she and the Deacon would have to go to Portsmouth to set up an account under her new ID. If push came to shove she still had the Tina Manson account, along with the appropriate ID.

She poured a glass of wine and just sat pondering the paths her life had taken. She wondered how and why she wound up here, working for her father. Tracy was not one to believe things just happen. Everything is caused, she maintained, and everything has a reason, although we may not know what it is. She knew that she was the way she was largely due to the fact she was brought up without a father. She harbored resentment towards men, as she knew her mother had been lying about the situation with her father. She'd spent her whole life believing that her father had deserted her; she still didn't know that her father had been unaware of her existence.

This, along with two failed marriages to abusive losers, resulted in a deep-rooted philosophy of life: men, she believed, were to be used for whatever suited her fancy, and discarded at will. She resented the fact that men found her so attractive, as if it was their fault.

Maybe that is why she found killing so easy, for the vast majority of her victims were men.

———

Joe landed at Schaumburg airport, approximately 20 miles west of Chicago. They rented a car and Joe took Tracy to her hotel, and then he went back to Addison, where he got a room. He called the Deacon to apprise him of the situation, and was surprised that the Deacon sounded relieved. Joe didn't know what, but he felt there was more than met the eye between the Deacon and Tracy.

———

Joe immediately set out to establish surveillance on Akers' residence and set up a plan to affect his demise. It took only three days before Joe realized that one well-placed shot to Akers' heart while he was relaxing on his patio, which he did nightly, would do the job. The fact that the patio abutted a large wooded area played into this decision, as it provided cover and an easy path for egress once the job was complete. Were the truth to be known, Joe had gone through the same process during his initial visit to Chicago.

The fourth day, Joe went to the Caribou and picked up his .308 caliber rifle, complete with scope and silencer. The silencer was massive, but extremely effective.

That evening, a little later than usual, Akers came out to the patio and settled down with a book. Joe was in the prone position on a knoll approximately 300 yards away, that provided a clear view of the patio. He realized that he was losing light rapidly so decided to take the shot as soon as his heart and breathing were back in control from the exertion of having to move to reposition himself for a clear shot.

There is a degree of exhilaration when you line up your cross hairs on a target that is deserving, thought Joe, as he adjusted the parallax on his scope, bringing Akers into sharp focus. Joe went through the familiar process, aiming, three deep breaths and a final sight correction on the exhaling of the last breath and then a slow gentle squeeze on the trigger. This unleashed a 180-grain spitzer partition round travelling at 2700 feet per second packing 2913 ft. pounds of energy. The round smashed into Akers chest before the sound, what little there was, reached the patio. In fact the last recollection Akers had was a searing pain and the muffled sound of the rifle as he passed from this world into the next.

Joe gathered up the poncho he was laying on (to insure a sterile crime scene), and departed to his car which was parked on a dirt road. He returned to the Otter to pack away the rifle.

Chapter 27

Every time Ron watched the news, he was filled with disgust at what was happening in the country. Everything had stopped. The only thing the Democratics had done since they gained control of both houses of the Congress, was strive to defame the previous administration, render the military ineffective, shore up their own political position, and rubberstamp the new President's socialist agenda items. These included taking control of the automobile industry, the banks, health care—the list was never-ending with the steps the President was taking to bring America to its knees. Now, with the House in the hands of the Republicans, it wasn't much better, as the Senate refused to move bills forward. This, compounded with the President ruling by edict in the form of Executive Orders, meant nothing was moving forward in the name of progress, there were massive anti-war demonstrations the likes of which hadn't been seen since Vietnam, and yes, that worthless fucking whore, Hanoi Jane, was right in the middle of it again.

"Somebody needs to cap her communist ass," thought the Deacon, "and most of her Hollywood friends along with her." At this point the Deacon started considering the feasibility of another major event; the Academy Awards ceremony would lend itself favorably to a spectacular statement. Couldn't think of a finer bunch of people to expedite on their passage through life to their own personal Valhallas, he thought. He realized that this was obviously a job for Freddie's expertise, if he could get him on board. This, unknown to Freddie, could be a new lease of life for him, although the Deacon was softening on his stand about taking Freddie out unless absolutely necessary, as he really liked him. The Deacon got excited thinking about getting rid of two such large groups of "worthless mother-fuckers".

The Deacon knew that massive skyscrapers were demolished with miniscule amounts of explosives, the secret being the precise placement of the charges. The literal and figurative object of this operation was to "bring the roof down on them". What more befitting end to a bunch of totally worthless assholes, he thought. For the first time in Oscar history "We the People" would get to cast the deciding votes. While pondering this whole concept, a sobering thought crossed the Deacon's mind. As pathetic and complacent as the American population had become, there was always the likelihood that there was going to be a large segment of the population more upset with losing their favorite movie heroes and heroines than losing the entire Congress the following year.

This venture would have to start soon, as the charges needed to be emplaced as soon as possible, to minimize the chance of being caught leading up to the Oscars. The Deacon saw another trip to Jersey in his near future. He smiled, thinking that with a little luck not only would he get to see Freddie, but if he planned an overnighter, he may get to spend an entire night with the gal with the $40 ass. It dawned on him that he still didn't know her name, but actually that didn't really matter.

Ron pulled into Freddie's parking lot at about 3:30 pm, hoping Freddie would be there, but he didn't see his limousine. The bartender told him that Freddie would be back in an hour or so and had left instructions for them to take good care of the Deacon. Ron wasn't sure what that meant, but as soon as the $40 ass showed up, he got the big picture. Suddenly, he wasn't as upset about Freddie not being there as he had been initially.

After an hour or so he heard Fred's voice booming across the bar downstairs. He sent the girl, Angela, as he finally found out her name was, down and asked her to tell Freddie he was upstairs. Fred came in and cast a dubious eye upon the Deacon.

"So what the fuck brings you here? I am sure that there was more than just Angela to this trip."

"Fred, I've got a proposition for you, and you are one of the few men I know who can pull this off," Ron said.

With that Fred interrupted, "Oh shit, wait a minute while I go get the Vaseline; I feel this fucking coming already."

"Damn it, Freddie, I'm serious. I want you to figure out how to blow the Kodak Theatre during the Academy Awards next year. I want the roof to come down and crush every communist left wing mother fucker in there! Don't even start to get negative on me, damn it; it can be done. We've just got to figure out how. We've got damn near a year to do it."

The blood drained out of Fred's face because he knew the Deacon was dead serious. "You're fucking insane, you asshole. You have finally gone off the deep end," Fred said, and then he looked at the Deacon and asked, "What's in it for me?"

"That's the Freddie I fucking love, damn it. Never mind what the fucking task is, what's the damned price tag? That's all that really counts. Admit it, you prick! Damn it, Freddie, I'm not a bank robber. I'm going fucking broke. We need to do this for the country, not for me. Not for the money, but for our kids and our grand kids, as well as for everything America can and should be. For once in this miserable, fucking existence you call a life, do something because it is the right thing to do, not just to stuff your frigging pockets! No one is paying me to save America, and I damn sure can't pay you. It is something we need to do, asshole."

The Deacon was on a roll, definitely in rare form, and he could tell he was getting across to Freddie. "Half these assholes in Hollywood are borderline illiterate peckerheads, damn it, and because of their frigging money and celebrity status they can buy politicians, manipulate national policy, and mainstream America's attitudes. You can take your Fondas, Streisands, Penns, Clooneys, Glovers, Jacksons, and the rest of these sick self-righteous communist assholes, and they wouldn't make a pimple on a real Americans ass. Freddie, we've got to do it and you know damn well I'm right. Sure, there will be some good ones dying along with them, but count them up; the dregs of society will outnumber the good fifteen to one. Freddie, with those odds you can win any war you fight, and you damn well know it."

Fred paused for a moment. "Frankly, it is probably beyond my abilities, Deacon, but I know someone who can do it and he owes me big time. He used to do all of the major construction demo jobs in the city until he crossed the mob. They contracted me to take him out, and to this day they think I did, thanks to forged dental records, which, by the way, is where Angela really enters the picture. By day she is an office manager in a large dental office. She creates records and identities for us at will. She only does the stage stripping gig because she likes to watch horny mother-fuckers like you get all hot and bothered, and drool all over the place." They both laughed.

"Anyway, he supposedly went up in an accident during a skyscraper demolition. In reality we knocked out an illegal that we had taken to the dentist a week earlier as part of the company benefits package and blew that cocksucker back to Juarez. The dental records confirmed it was the kid," Fred said smiling. "I set the kid up with another identity and life. I like the kid, and figured I may be able to use him some day. It shouldn't be a problem; he thinks like us and has no scruples at all."

Chapter 28

Ron and Larry flew out to see how Bob was coming with his latest project. He had succeeded in isolating the computer in Homeland Security where all the names of the assassins and their victims were stored. While he was able to isolate the data, he was having trouble correlating it into a useable matrix. Larry looked at what Bob had and told Bob that he would send his code man out there, and that he felt sure that it would not be a problem to break; especially with the amount of computer power Bob had.

They adjourned to the den, where they partook of several snifters of an incredible Cognac. "Bob, I see your taste in Cognac has improved!" Ron said. "Larry has to return to Langley tomorrow, but I will be around for a couple of days. I am meeting some friends in Los Angeles this weekend, so it looks like you are stuck with me for a bit."

Ron was scheduled to rendezvous with Fred in Los Angeles this weekend, to allow them to work on the plan for the Kodak Theatre Event, (KTE, as Ron called it).

Freddie's man was already there, and was part of the theater maintenance staff. There was an advantage to being hardwired in the mob, Fred said. Unions run everything and the mob still exercises a lot of influence over them. Placing one man in a position as a supervisor was an easy task. With luck, he would have a workable plan by the time Ron and Fred got there, and would just give Fred a list of explosives needed to do the job.

Fred had a room in the LA Marriot, about seven miles from the theatre, where they all met Sunday evening.

Nick Jamison, the demo man, was smaller than Ron had expected, but he was rugged. Ron had never gotten over sizing people up and judging them on the spot. He contended he had a knack for this, and the fact that he was still alive was testimony that he was pretty damn good at it. Nick passed the test.

There was a total agreement on the part of the three of them that this was one task that was going to challenge every creative bone in their collective bodies. Looking at the physical character of the theatre and considering that anything done to prepare for the event would have to be done while the theater was conducting business as usual, they ruled out conventional explosives, as the amount required to accomplish the desired effect would be next to impossible to emplace and conceal.

They kicked a dozen or so options around and found a major flaw in each approach. It was well after midnight, and they were no closer to a solution than they had been when they started. They made the decision to break for now, and to get back together at 10:00 am the next day. Ron challenged everyone to think outside the box on this one, as it obviously was a unique problem and called for a unique solution.

Ron tossed and turned all night, thinking of how to accomplish this mission, when he thought of Henry Roach and the operation that took him down. Suddenly, Ron smiled, rolled over and went to sleep.

The next morning the Deacon arrived at Freddie's room with a plan. Nick showed up, and they all went downstairs for breakfast. Small talk over breakfast indicated that neither Fred nor Nick had come up with anything meaningful. This pleased the Deacon, as he enjoyed being in the creative driver seat. It affirmed his role as being fully in control.

"Is it safe to assume we have not made any progress since last night?" Ron asked.

Both Fred and Nick indicated that this was an accurate albeit undesirable appraisal of where they were.

The Deacon started off, "Before you stop me, hear me out. Propane in its purest form is totally colorless, tasteless, and odorless. It isn't until the industry adds an odorant such as ethanethiol to it, for the sake of safety, that it acquires its trademark aroma. Additionally, it isn't especially noxious when inhaled. The major problem when breathing high quantities of it are oxygen deprivation. Other than that, there are no immediately obvious effects of the gas. You would never realize you were in a propane-rich environment without the odorant mixed in with it."

Fred interrupted, "So, how does this help us, Deacon? All the propane sold is laced with the odorant. It is the law."

"Freddie, have faith. Bear with me. This is going to be a lot like a sixth grade science class, but in the end it will all come together. Propane has several other unique characteristics, other than those I have already mentioned," the Deacon continued. "It is heavier than air by a factor of 1.5, which means, when released in an area, like water, it will sink to the floor or the lowest level. In addition to the uses we normally associate it with, propane in its purest form is becoming widely used as a refrigerant. It averages a 10%-20% increase in efficiency over other commonly used refrigerants. It takes the name of R-290, in refrigeration applications. It is marketed under several different names when used as a refrigerant or coolant, and it is available in small quantities or by the tanker load.

"Think about this, guys: it is ridiculously simple. Nick, you are the building maintenance third in command. That means you can do about anything you want, as those above you are totally disconnected from day to day activities of building/facility maintenance. First, we need a new 500 gallon tank installed in the theater's propane storage area. One more tank will never be noticed. It needs to be tagged at the valve "Do not fill". It will need to be hard-plumbed into the building, and ultimately spliced into the air conditioning and heating ductwork.

"You need to insure you use valves suitable for high pressure gasses. The splices need to be central enough to allow the gas to warm up, to preclude a visible frost vapor within the theater. The ducts are at floor level and that works in our favor.

"I see very few potential problems with this approach. The first is in getting the R-290 in sufficient quantity. That is doable. We just need to figure out how and from whom. We may even need to create a dummy refrigeration company to make the purchase. Freddie, get one of your Jersey pretty boys out here to take care of that end of it. Start a refrigeration company, buy a used tanker if you have to, just do whatever you need to make it happen.

"Next, we need to come up with a positive method of ignition. I think we need to come up with a propane detector much like those used in campers, with the audible alarm disabled and redesigned instead to produce an open arcing. I would think four of these at the stage level and above would insure an adequate concentration and dispersion of the gas to bring down the house, so to speak.

"Lastly, Freddie, you are going to have to create another identity and look for Nick, for as soon as he turns the propane valve on, he will be a marked man. If we can pull it off from across country with Angela and the dental record scam, we might let his teeth die a second time." With that they all laughed.

"Gentlemen, I think we have our plan. Nick, you know your job, Freddie will arrange for the tanker, and we should be set to send the stars to the stars, so to speak.

"We have plenty of time to kick this off, so there is no reason to draw suspicion on the operation by trying to race through it. Just keep me posted on your progress."

———

Chapter 29

It was the morning of Ron's third day back at the Lodge, in the middle of his first cup of coffee, when he received a call from Larry stating that he was going to fly up that afternoon.

"We are getting ready to deliver the last batch of prisoners to Serf as soon as he is ready for them. We have extracted all we can out of them. There were additional reports that there was a third suitcase nuke in the cavern they were captured in.

"And still more about a missile coming in on a container ship. Supposedly, it is a North Korean made SCUD missile with a nuclear warhead on it. They were talking about it coming in through Bremerton or Oakland as far as they knew, but no time frame on its arrival or target.

"It is more than likely a Scud D Hwasong 7 system. It can be fitted with chemical, high explosives, or a nuclear warhead. Its range is 700 km, or slightly less than 500 miles. The good news is, its accuracy isn't all that great—only within a three km radius. That is also the bad news, as they would likely target the center of a city and use either a chemical or a nuclear warhead. The Koreans exported them to Syria, who is now believed to be building them in a facility that was originally designed to produce the Scud C variant."

"So basically, we think a Korean SCUD D missile is destined for our shores, but we don't really know where the fuck it is coming from, it could be coming in from either North Korea or Syria. That is a lot of ground to cover," Ron said. "Syria is ripe right now, with the internal strife they are going through. I will see if Serf can get more out of the prisoners. He uses some enhanced interrogation techniques that I am sure wouldn't pass muster even with your most trusted interrogators."

"I have no doubt about that," Larry said. "My people think they are being released in Mexico by Serf, they have no idea his safe house is in reality a restaurant for wayward coyotes," Larry said with a grin.

"A man's got to do what a man's got to do," Ron said with a grin.

"I assume you and your pilot are spending the night. I will have Bu Dop Blue take your pilot downtown for dinner. That should fuck his mind up royally; Blue has that effect on most civilized people. You and I can grab Mary Jane and hit the Inn for dinner."

"Ok, Top, I will get the prisoners off to Serf as soon as I can. Have him put them through the wringer and get rid of them. It would be great to know where this suspected missile is going to originate from, as that could give us a rough idea where its point of arrival would be. As it is, I am going to publish a general security upgrade to all ports. Not much, but unless we get more to go on that's all I can really do. I thank you and Mary Jane for your hospitality. I am not sure I want to thank Bu Dop Blue or not; my pilot looks like shit today. Good to see Blue hasn't changed much. It's comforting to know that some things in this world are sacred, and Bu Dop Blue is living proof of that."

Chapter 30

Tina (Tracy) was sitting across the table from Dane Apfelbaum, the head of the President's reelection committee. This was their third date, after an accident in the lobby of the hotel they were both staying in, which resulted in Tina tripping and spilling coffee all over Dane.

"So tell me, Tina, what do you want to do for the weekend? I have cancelled all work, and am devoting all my time to you."

"I would dearly love for just the two of us to rent a small yacht, something with a cabin, and cruise the lakes a bit. I would love to spend the night anchored in the middle of a lake sipping wine, while doing some stargazing. I promise not to spill my wine on you."

Dane immediately saw this as an opportunity to score with this gorgeous creature who had so far maintained a degree of decorum and acted like a lady. This was almost an offer to get laid. All he had to do was say yes, which he did.

"That is settled, then. I will make the arrangements for a yacht and we can make a weekend out of it. I will pick it up Friday afternoon so we can get an early start on Saturday."

"That sounds great, and I promise to make this a weekend you will remember as long as you live, " Tina said, almost purring.

"Hello, Joe. Did you think I got lost?"

"Frankly, I was getting a little worried, but didn't want to call as I wasn't sure what you were up to."

"OK, take notes: Friday you need to rent a small yacht out of the marina in Milwaukee, rent it through Sunday. Saturday night I plan to be anchored with a guest about twelve to fifteen miles due east of Doctors Point. You wait for my call and come and get me, it will probably be around midnight. We will be taking off as soon as we can get back to the plane."

"So that's it? I don't get to play?" Joe asked.

"That's it, and no…you don't get to play."

Dane went first thing Friday morning to pick up the yacht he had rented. Actually, he went early, to become familiar with the yacht, as he didn't want to appear inept in front of Tina. This was his big chance, he thought, and he didn't want to blow it.

He also stocked the refrigerator with munchies and several bottles of Riesling, a wine he knew Tina had demonstrated a fondness for. He went to great measures to insure that everything was as proper as he could make it. His excitement over the upcoming weekend was evident. There was no doubt in his mind that Tina would be one of the most exotic women he had ever had. Deep in his heart, he knew this was destined to be a memorable weekend.

Tina was also going through her preparation phases. She packed her bag. In it was an incredibly sexy two-piece bathing suit, several sexy tops and pairs of shorts, in addition to the rest of her belongings. She then packed a gallon of chlorine bleach, several jasmine scented candles, a container of a sensual body massage lotion, and a long rigid pin/blade affixed to a hair barrette; she also packed her .22cal Ruger and her .40 cal XMD automatic in the event everything went to shit.

She determined that she was going to enjoy the weekend in spite of the task at hand. She got a twinkle in her eye when she thought of the smile Dane would have on his face just before he died. There was a reason some had likened her to a Black Widow spider. Her last task of the night was to shower and exfoliate as much of her body as possible.

Joe, in the meantime, was topping off the fuel in the Otter, and making sure all systems were a go on it. He then planned to drive to the marina in Milwaukee, where he had rented a yacht under an alias from his worldwide tour, different from the one he had used to rent the car, which was also different from the one for the hotel. He was going to "pre-flight" the yacht in the same fashion he had just used to pre-flight the Otter. He then packed a small duffle of munitions to take with him when Tracy called.

He couldn't help but wonder what was getting ready to go down, as this had been the first that he had heard from Tracy in almost two weeks. Likewise, he hadn't been in contact with the Deacon since they left the Lodge. Whatever was about to occur would be a surprise to everyone. Joe didn't appreciate being left out of the loop on the operation like this, as usually he was calling the shots on the ground. The Deacon had made it perfectly clear what each of their roles would be, but that didn't assuage Joe's feelings at all.

What a delightful day to spend on a lake, Tina thought as her taxi drove up to the marina at noon. The weather was ideal for the outing. She was really excited to be going on this trip.

She couldn't help but notice that Dane was already there, waiting. He's probably been here since sunrise, she thought.

Dane spotted her and came down to help her with her bag. "Damn, it feels like you packed enough for a week," he said smiling.

"Never question a girl's luggage or age," Tina said, "as you won't get a truthful answer from either question." Little did Dane realize that all of her belongings were in that bag, and she had checked out of her hotel. Have you plotted out our course for the trip yet?"

"Not really; I figured we would take it as it comes. I live a structured existence almost all of the time; I just want to go with the flow this weekend."

The entire time Dane was talking, Tina was looking around the cabin, to figure where she could conceal the pistols so she could get to them in an emergency. "And now, sir, if you will get this boat underway, I will slip into something more comfortable."

That was an offer Dane couldn't refuse, as he was waiting to see what 'more comfortable' really was. As the boat got underway, Tina latched the door on the cabin and changed into a halter-top and a pair of short shorts. She took care not to step on the deck of the cabin. She put on a pair of deck shoes to prevent leaving footprints or epithelia behind. She wanted to make the clean-up task as easy as possible prior to leaving the yacht.

Dane liked what he saw as Tina came out of the cabin. He immediately poured them a glass of wine. Tina recognized this as an attempt to get her to relax and drop her guard. Little did Dane realize that he was going to have a degree of luck tonight, both good and bad. Mostly bad, though.

After four glasses of wine, most of which was poured overboard when Dane wasn't looking, Tina excused herself to again change clothes. While Tina was changing, she placed both pistols in strategic locations where they would be out of sight but readily accessible if needed. When she came out this time she was wearing a very sexy bikini. She handed Dane a bottle of suntan lotion and asked him to do her back.

It was all Dane could do to refrain from getting lewd while applying the lotion to Tina; as he didn't want to chance ruining the weekend.

When Dane was done, Tina completed the rest of the task while lying on the bow of the boat. When she removed her bikini top and applied lotion to her ample breasts, Dane almost hit a marker buoy. He could barely take his eyes off her the rest of the afternoon.

They pulled into the Marina at Manistee Lake, on the east side of the lake, to grab dinner, a task which required another change of clothes for Tina.

"I now see why all the luggage," Dane said smiling.

"I'm glad you said luggage, and not baggage, as I come without baggage," Tina said while giving Dane a "cum in your pants" expression and blew him a kiss.

After dinner and a few drinks they returned to the yacht. Tina asked if she could take the helm, and Dane, wanting to please, turned control of the wheel over to her. She knew she had about 65-70 miles to cover before it got dark. That should be no problem, as this little tug topped out at 50 MPH, she thought.

According to the GPS and Loran, she throttled back an hour and a quarter after she started. She looked at Dane, who was almost shit-faced drunk by now, and asked him to lower the anchor. She was lucky, she thought, as it was starting to get darker than she felt comfortable with, bouncing along at 50 MPH on a lake that was starting to pick up a little chop, from a westerly wind.

Tina was now in mission mode, her senses heightened and her latent desire to kill this puss-gutted cocksucker started to kick into overdrive. She approached him, embraced him, and suggested they go to the cabin. She watched as he stumbled down the stairs.

Once in the cabin, Tina turned on some soft music which she slowly started to strip to. Dane started to drool, and got undressed himself. Tina had to stifle a laugh when he was naked, as she wasn't sure she would be able to find his dick. I knew the government had no balls, it appears that they are dick-less also, she thought.

Dane reached out and pulled her toward the bed. She told him to be patient and to lay down. "I am going to give you the works," Tina said as she straddled him and applied oil to his body. She then began a slow sensual massage starting at the neck and working her way down. As soon as she touched his scrotum and penis, he came instantly. "Don't worry," she said, "we have only just begun." She turned him over and started massaging his neck. At this point she reached into her hair, and grabbed the barrette. With one hand massaging his neck, determining the precise location of the 2nd and 3rd cervical vertebrae, the second hand slipped the steel blade attached to the barrette between the two vertebra, killing him instantly. As soon as this was done she got dressed, retrieved the two pistols, strapping the .40 cal to her belt and started a methodical cleaning of the body and everything she had been in contact with using the bleach.

She then called Joe to come get her. "No problem, lady, I am about half a mile south of you. Be right there."

Joe pulled alongside the yacht and tied off to it fore and aft. Tina was cleaning the wheel. "I will be done in a little while, I need to insure this is sterile.'

"Save your energy," said Joe as he grabbed his duffle bag. "I have an ideal sterilizer here," and he pulled out two 2½ pound blocks of C-4, a roll of Det Cord, and one of the Russian timers/detonators he had. He set his charges and attached them to the Russian timer, which he set. He also wired a burn phone attached to an electrical detonator into the circuit. He located one block of C-4 under Dane's body, and the other block in the engine compartment. They were connected with a double strand of Det Cord.

———

Joe checked the time as he docked in the yacht's slip in the marina where it was rented. He was pleased as he was right on schedule.

Joe was dilly-dallying around at the airport, and Tracy commented on that. "Relax," Joe said, "we have a schedule we have to go by. If the Russian timer fails, I will have to detonate it by phone. Go ahead and get in." Joe took off and circled around to the west side of the lake. Half way up the lake he looked at his watch and headed east. They were just about over the middle of the lake when the yacht below and to the south exploded. Joe looked at Tracy and commented, "A job well done, lady," as they continued on an easterly course heading back to Wolfeboro.

———

Chapter 31

Larry had just had the first batch of four prisoners dropped off at Serf's safe house. Serf and Tommy led them into the underground bunkers. One was put in the bunker with Rodney, the other three were chained to the wall in an adjoining bunker.

Serf had brought Tommy and Wilson back from Mexico as Tommy was an ex-Special Forces linguist fluent in Arabic. He would serve as Serf's interpreter. Wilson, being a medic, would be able to administer sodium pentothal. Serf had already made the decision to interrogate these prisoners aggressively, to see if they had been holding anything back. Serf had already made up his mind that he was going to brutalize the first prisoner, to set the tone for the other three.

They had spent two days in their cells with no nourishment beyond bread and water when Serf and Tommy came down to the cell that the single prisoner shared with Rodney. With Serf interrogating and Tommy interpreting, it was obvious that the prisoner was not going to speak.

Serf drew his .22 caliber pistol and shot him in both knees. Again, he refused to divulge anything. Serf had Tommy help him get the prisoner on his feet, which were useless, and then threw Rodney, who commenced to bit him three times in rapid succession.

Serf and Tommy then retrieved one of the other three prisoners and put him in the bunker with his dying friend and

Rodney. Again, they left the prisoners alone for two days.

Periodically, the prisoner who had been bitten by Rodney could be heard screaming in pain as he was going through the throngs of dying. "I wonder if this will have any impact on the other three when it comes time to interrogate them," Serf said.

"If they don't talk after this, they obviously don't know anything. However, if one should talk, we will have to take him out to kill him, just to give the others hope," Wilson said.

"Take a couple of Rodney's rats down and release them in the cell. They will dine on our dead guest until Rodney gets hungry. That should really fuck up the other one's mind," Serf said.

"Remember," Tommy said, "that bastard is going to start stinking soon. We need to get rid of him before it gets bad, or we'll never get the stink out. The fucking coyotes are getting fat and lazy. If we moved out they'd die of starvation."

Ron was debriefing Joe and Tracy on their recent venture. He was perfectly happy with the events that took place in Chicago. "In addition to what you two accomplished, one of Dane's assistants dropped dead for no apparent reason. I would say that, overall, America had a good week, due in no small part to your actions.

"That's the good news, the bad news is we haven't scratched the surface on the problems America is faced with. We have precious little time to salvage the elections. I have Larry working on coming up with the names of the officials in each state who have been instrumental in instituting voter fraud. We need to take them out before they get their apparatus in high gear. Unfortunately the FBI keeps most of that data, and Larry no longer trusts them, with the exception of a couple of close friends.

"As soon as I get some names you two will be spending a lot of time traveling, so be ready to pack and scoot at a moment's notice."

"Hell, Top, just like being on alert in the army again," Joe said. "Keep your "A" and "B" bag packed to enable you to move out at a moment's notice."

"When we kick this off, how are we going to execute it?" Tracy asked.

"Well, I hope to be smart and pick targets that you can fly out together on. I envision Joe dropping you off at a location and continuing on to his location. At that rate we should be able to hopscotch all over the country if we come up with the intelligence to support this operation."

"That sounds like it would work out well for all," Joe said, "and on that, if you don't have anything else for me, I am going to check with the Dief and see how he is doing."

Tracy sat there for a while after Joe left, and she finally asked. "Ok, what do you want me to call you?"

"Shit, I don't care. You can call me Top, Deacon, or even asshole, just don't call me sir, damn it."

"So tell me, how did you come up with the nickname? 'The Deacon' seems a little out of place, considering what you do."

"Actually, the Dief pinned it on me in Vietnam, back in 1965." The Deacon got quiet as he thought back to that period.

It was early in November and Ron was on a ten man search and destroy mission (S&D patrol). They made contact right at dusk with a much larger Viet Cong force. When the smoke cleared, there were 2 dead ARVN soldiers. Additionally, one ARVN soldier and one American, the team medic, Ray, were missing. The remnants of the patrol knew they couldn't move far due to not having any idea where the enemy had gone, compounded by the fact that the night was pitch black. The six remaining patrol members—Ron, the interpreter, and four ARVN privates—sat upright in a circle, back to back in head high elephant grass to wait out the night. Ron had taken a round in his radio, which probably saved his life. Unfortunately, they couldn't call in a situation report or a request for exfiltration.

About midnight, they started hearing blood-curdling screams that appeared to be coming from a couple of hundred yards to their east. One of the ARVN privates started to freak out at the sound of the screaming, and Ron knocked him out with his rifle butt to the head, to prevent him from compromising their location. Apparently Ron had hit him harder than he realized, as the soldier dropped dead the next day. But another face on the many masks of death, thought Ron.

First thing in the morning, a Regional Force Company, a force similar in concept to our National Guard, showed up with Daiwi (Vietnamese term for Captain) Merrill Woley on the point. Ron apprised him of the situation, and they set out to locate the source of the screams of the previous night. It wasn't long before their fears were confirmed. Ray and the ARVN Sgt were staked out, and had been skinned alive. That was one of the major defining moments in the making of who Ron ultimately became, as at that moment he was forever changed. He suddenly felt an intense hatred, a totally new emotion he had never really experienced, but it was on board and fully involved, and would fester for years. Many of these feelings of disdain and bitterness towards the human race continue to this very day.

Two weeks later on another S&D operation they made contact with a VC squad, and this time they had the upper hand. Two Viet Cong soldiers were killed, and one was wounded. Ron approached the wounded Viet Cong soldier to make sure he was unarmed. When he saw the wounded VC had Ray's lucky scarf around his neck, Ron approached him and put a foot in his chest to keep him in place. He looked at the terrified VC, and said lovingly "Bless you my son, for you have sinned. Ye shall reap that which ye have sewn!" Upon finishing the sentence Ron put a three round burst into the man's head. It's amazing what a .30 cal round will do to a brain, he thought. (Ron carried a 30 caliber M-2 carbine, as it was more reliable than the M-16, and for the actual contact ranges involved in Nam it was more than adequate.)

He bent over and took the scarf back to mail to Ray's family. At that time the Dief loudly proclaimed, "Goddamn, we've got a fucking DEACON with us, and he's a baaad mother fucker." The nickname "the Deacon" has stuck to this day, although most people are totally unaware of its origin.

"That seems like it was just yesterday at times, and at others it seems as if it was several lifetimes ago. A lot of water has passed over the dam since then."

The phone rang. It was Bob. This gave Tracy an excellent opportunity to excuse herself.

"Hey, old man, how are you and your code man coming with that program? Are you having any luck breaking it?"

"Yes, we broke it this afternoon. Actually, it is fairly simple. I am building a program to break it for us in the future, so it won't be a problem next time. You need to see this data as soon as possible. As soon as I am finished, I plan to download everything and export it to your mainframes. I may have to come to the Lodge to accomplish that."

"Hell, Bob, you are always welcome. With luck, Rae will be able to accompany you.

"Well, shit, this is good, as I have to call Larry today to update him on some intelligence matters. This will be the only good news he will get today."

"Ok, Ron. I just wanted to update you on our progress. I will check with Rae on the trip, which will likely happen next week. I will talk to you as soon as I know something for sure, old friend."

———

"Good morning, Larry, got a couple of minutes?"

"Hell, Top, I always have time for you."

"Well, Larry, you may not like this call. The prisoners are all disposed of. Two days of watching his friend, who was killed by Rodney, being devoured by a pack of rats turned one of them into a talking machine. I think Serf's suggestion that they were hauling him off to be fed to the pigs was the last straw.

"Anyway, according to him, there are two containers coming in by ship. One will be carrying the vehicle/launcher, the other will contain three SCUD D variant missiles. He didn't know the type warhead they were carrying. It could be anything from HE, chemical, biological, or nuke. He believed that they were coming into the east coast, and not the west coast. That means if they are coming from Korea they will be going through the Panama Canal."

"I will put the word out to all the eastern seaboard docks to be extra vigilant," Larry said. "If it is coming in from Libya God only knows what will be in them. They are going through a meltdown now, and I wouldn't put it past them to unload as much as they can of their WMD stockpile. That's the last frigging thing we need."

"On a lighter note, I just talked to Bob, and your man broke the code. Bob was rather adamant that I see what he has. He is planning on coming up next week to download all of it into my mainframe, to include a program he is building to enable us to crack any additions or changes."

"So tell me, Top, are Serf and his crew making any progress across the border?"

"Not really. I think we scared them off on our cavern raids. I will have Vince check to the west and see if he can hit on anything. If you could relocate some of your RDF equipment, we may be able to get a fix on them that way. If you guys come up with anything, it would be good to get some air support for infiltration and extraction; I don't want Serf and crew idle too long."

"I will see what I can work out, that shouldn't present a major problem. Ok, Top. I have to run. Keep me posted."

"Later, Larry. Check on that air support if you would."

———

"You know," Mary Jane said, "if you could leave that phone alone for a while, I could occupy your dick for an hour or so, that is unless you're too busy."

"That is the best offer I have had all day," Ron hung up the phone.

———

Chapter 32

Bob and Rae had just driven in from Manchester, where they had flown in. They were talking about the old days, and Rae just rolled her eyes. She looked at Mary Jane and asked, "Do you have any idea how many times I have heard these same stories over the last fifty years?"

"No, but I can just imagine. Every time Ron has some of the old-timers in to BS, it is the same here. It must have something to do with their age."

That elicited a middle finger from Ron. "Mary Jane, why don't you take Rae downtown and show her the thriving metropolis of Wolfeboro. Larry is due in in about an hour and we will be disappearing down stairs for quite a bit. We can all meet at the inn for dinner."

After an hour Bob had completed transferring all the data into Ron's mainframe, including the program to break the code. Bob printed out the names of the assassins, and their targets. The list included the phone number to use and the code word to execute. Ironically, some of the assassins were targeting other assassins. That was their way of getting rid of the proof for high profile targets. Many czars, Congressmen and Senators were on the list, as well as several high ranking military officials, and some cabinet members. The stage was set to eliminate, on demand, any opposition the President felt he had. Ron speculated that this was to be used primarily to eliminate resistance in the event the President initiated martial law. It could in fact be used as the basis to initiate it.

Larry finally arrived and was taken aback by the data, as both his and Vince's names were on the hit list, as well as the head of every prime government agency. They theorized that, with the heads out of the way, they could put anyone they wanted in their positions due to the imposition of martial law. This was the blueprint to turn America into a dictatorship.

They all realized that the President wasn't smart enough to come up with this operation, and that begged the question just who really was running America.

They decided to have Vince fly up the following day, brief him on the whole project, and see what he could come up with, since he worked in Homeland Security.

———

"This had better be damned good," Vince said as he took a seat. "I was in the process of rescheduling the reconnaissance blimp to the west, as you wanted."

"Well, considering the fact that you are on your own agency's hit list, I thought you would want to be read in on it. Your scheduled assassin is Wilson Turner, your operations officer," Ron said with a smile.

"We have a major problem on our hands with this list, in-as-much as we don't know what its primary purpose is, or when, or if it is scheduled to be implemented. We all need to keep this on the front burner, and as soon as anyone on the list dies both you and I will have to take out our own private assassin," Larry said.

"We have speculated what the purpose of this list is, and it is our guess that somehow it ties into a declaration of martial law.

We feel it is either a reason to induce it, or to use it to eliminate the President's primary foes within the government, thereby paving the way for an orderly takeover. In the for what it's worth department, all of the Joint Chiefs of Staff are on the list. That would basically negate any likelihood of the military stepping in. At any rate, it has to be stopped, and I guess that is where we come in," Ron said. "The problem is how and when."

"We are back to taking my Boss out," Vince said, "as it is likely she is the only person besides the President who is fully aware of this. It would take a while to select a replacement that can be trusted, and it will take him or her a while to get up to speed on the whole system."

"And then again, we may want to leave her until the last minute, to create chaos when they are least capable to handle it," Ron said. "We may want to override the system and start taking people out that don't matter to us, and then release the fact that it is a killer squad orchestrated by Homeland Security under the direction of the President and make everything about it known to the entire media. That should create enough havoc to keep them all busy for a while.

"At any rate, we need to give this a lot of thought before we act, as the implications will be monumental. I will have my trusted associates in the CIA quietly snoop around and see what they can come up with," Larry said.

"Additionally, we need to see what the fallout will be on the ICE sex scandal. That could have a major impact on this whole operation if Vince's Boss is caught up in the fray. At any rate, it is going to be interesting.

"By the way", Larry commented, "the Chicago caper was priceless. I told you she would be worth the baggage she brought with her. What do you have in mind for her right now, Top?"

"I have her and Joe planning to take out the crooked election officials that you provided me a list of. It isn't much, but still a monkey wrench in the process. Every obstacle will help."

"Ok, guys, I've got to head back. I will definitely be giving some thought to my Boss' hit list, especially since I am on it. I suggest we meet again down the road and discuss this further. Until then, let's hope they don't try to initiate it."

Larry and Ron watched the Porter disappear in the horizon. Larry suggested that they go to the war room.

"And what occasion brings you down here, in the bowels of the operation?" Ron asked.

"Top, you should know by now I am full of surprises. The recent shake up in the Secret Service shifted many people around. This resulted in four extremely close friends of mine transferring into the Presidential Detail. They worked for me for years until the Secret Service recruited them several years ago. One of them is assigned as the head supervisor of the overall protection detail. I have an appointment with him Friday, just to feel him out. I think we can work with these four, as I know they are all disenchanted with the current administration, and I venture to say they have more loyalty to me than they do the President. This information has to remain between you and I. If all else fails, we may just be able to solve the problem easily."

"Shit, just to be able to get an up on scheduling and mode of transportation would be worth its weight in gold, in the event we decide to take him out.

"OK, Larry, you have been forthcoming with me. I guess I will reciprocate. Three years ago I had a plan in place to wipe out the entire Congress. I cancelled it the day before it was going to happen. All of the equipment and materials and personnel are still in place to conduct that mission in the event the elections go wrong. Shit, I have half a mind to do it regardless, as I feel we need to till the soil and replant. The career members are all in someone's pocket and aren't out for anyone but themselves."

"You do realize, of course, the chaos this will cause. We will be like a rudderless ship bobbing in the sea for whatever time it takes the states to conduct elections," Larry said.

"Not sure if you have noticed it or not, but we aren't doing too well with a rudder. It will be rough, but in the long run I believe we will be better off. Anyway, if that happened,it won't be until they swear in. It will be one hell of a ceremony.

"At one point I was planning on doing it during a State of the Union Address, but that would take out our entire Joint Chiefs of Staff, and a lot of infrastructure we will need to rebuild, so I scrapped that idea."

"That was damn noble of you, Top, a definite act of magnanimous benevolence on your part, of that I am sure. Got to give you credit, you're all heart when it comes right down to it," Larry said with a smile. "What else do you have going on?"

"I have a plan in place to take out the Old Kodak theater the night of the Academy Awards. As much as I want to deal with those socialist assholes, I think I am going to put it on hold. Too many major issues to deal with. All this would accomplish is muddy the waters and heighten security, which is something we don't need."

"Probably a good idea, Top, as no matter which way the election goes, we have our hands full in the next several years. I don't see any relief from the threat from Hezbollah, Hamas, and now it is rumored that al Qaida is in Mexico, also, and you know they are coming our way. We can worry about Hanoi Jane and her communist friends later; right now we have our hands full trying to keep track of the President's Communist friends."

"Yeah, I know, but it would be so rewarding to watch those mother fuckers go up in a plume. I will have Freddie put it into a holding pattern."

Chapter 33

Teriq ali Habib was patiently sitting in his office awaiting Raoul Pena. Teriq, owner of one of the largest import-export companies in New Orleans, was getting ready to diversify; it was just a matter of logistics.

Raoul Pena had been a shift foreman on the docks at the Port of New Orleans for years. It was an established fact that if you wanted anything that was going through the Port, he was the man to deal with. Little did he realize that the transaction he was on his way to negotiate had the potential of totally changing life in America. Basically, he didn't care, he never knew the contents of the containers he diverted. It was simply a business transaction to him.

"Mr. Habib, I want to apologize for being late, it's that traffic thing, as you well know. How can I be of assistance to you?"

"Raoul, you needn't apologize, we have conducted too much business in the past to worry about formalities. I have two containers coming in on a Norwegian freighter next month. Those containers have been around the world a couple of times on their route to get here, changing ships several times. I have been able to have a crew accompany them the entire trip, not an easy task, but as you know, every time a ship docks they lose part of their crew and pick up new members.

"Anyway, I need those containers diverted so they bypass customs. That my friend, is where you come in."

Raoul smelled money on this gig. "Some things are harder than others. This will place a strain on resources and logistics. Do you have flat beds with tractors to load them on?"

"Yes, I do, and worry not, you will be well reimbursed for the strain we place on your resources. Do you have a basic plan?"

"Depending on the water level, and backlog of barges, ideally we would trans load them onto a barge headed to Baton Rouge. Right now, there is a hell of a backlog due to the river level being low because of the draught. Anyway, the barge will go through customs at the port of Baton Rouge, but your containers won't be on it. This involves coming up with a dummy manifest, bribing the barge crew, having a ground crew with crane at the transfer point. Not an easy process, but totally doable."

Teriq realized that this diatribe was Raoul's way of padding the bill. Little did Raoul know that the cost didn't matter; the contents of the containers were worth any price charged. "I will keep you posted on the progress of the ship, and you start putting your part of the plan in motion. I am prepared to pay you half now, and the balance upon delivery. Obviously, it will be in cash. How much do you need now?"

"I estimate $25,000 per container," Raoul said, holding his breath for a response.

"Not a problem," Teriq said as he approached his safe and counted out the cash. Let me know if you run into problems and need more."

At the same time, Teriq realized that he was being taken to the cleaners. The per container cost was a bunch of bullshit. The work and risk was the same for one container as it was for two. Teriq decided not to make an issue out of it, as he realized that Raoul was an invaluable contact at times, and it was worth the price just to be able to call on him again.

———

Chapter 34

fter Larry left, Ron sat and pondered his entire situation. He knew that the majority of his problems would be coming at him from the south. It was at this time that Ron decided to relocate most of his warriors to Deming. Steve just located David Schmidt, another medic from ODA-335, and invited him to come up and see what they had to offer. The major attraction to having David aboard was that he was SADM, special atomic demolitions, and munitions, qualified. He will be invaluable in the event we ever have to employ our suitcase nuke, Ron thought.

Ron decided to ship Bu Dop Blue and Ray Maggi to Deming. This action would beef the southern component up, and put them in a position where they could react a lot faster than they were currently able to.

The Dief was able to go back with John. He was not operating at full capacity, but he could take some of the heat off John, and they would finally be able to start refresher training on operation "We the People".

Based on reports from Joe and Tracy, he was going to pull the plug on their operation, as it was not as fruitful as envisioned. They were due in tomorrow. As soon as Joe arrived he, Ray, and Bu Dop Blue would start segregating supplies, munitions, and weapons to accompany Ray and Blue to Deming.

As soon as they were ready to head out Ron would have Bert

come, pick everyone up, and deliver them to their destinations. This will be the beginning of a new strategy for the warriors. Serf would have enough people to have two teams of two, each one with a medic, and still have one left to staff the safe house.

"Good morning, Vince, how are you doing?"

"Okay, Sergeant Major, out with it. What are you looking for? You didn't call to check on my well-being."

"Now that you mention it, there is something you could do for me." Ron went on to explain his new concept south of the border. "We know Hezbollah, al Qaida, and Hamas are all working their way north. We think something big is getting ready to go down, but have no idea when or where. I am going to have Larry beef up his listening posts, and would like you to keep an eye peeled for anything you can pick up on the ground. We are beefing up Deming a bit, so that will give us a faster reaction time."

"That sounds like something I can handle. Is there anywhere in particular you want me to concentrate?"

"Not really. Cover a wide range. We can get there either with Larry's assets, or with the Albatross. Remember, they may already be on this side of the border. You have your work cut out for you."

"Ok, Sergeant Major, I'll get on it. I will probably deploy two blimps, one for each side of the border, as they have a high on-station time. I'll keep you posted."

"Ok, sir. Keep me posted. Right now, I have a shitload of calls to make. Got to keep the troops informed. They don't mind being screwed with as long as they know it is coming. Talk to you later."

"Hey Batman, what's up? I figured it was about time to hear something from you."

"Same old shit, Serf. Just want to run a couple of things by you. I am beefing you up by two more personnel, Bu Dop Blue and Ray Maggi. That'll give you an additional medic, so you will be able to support multiple operations.

"We need to get back into the picture across the border. Vince is dedicating two recon blimps to you; and Larry is beefing up the NSA and ASA listening posts. As soon as they get a hit we will deploy your crew.

"I am sending several RPGs with both HE and Thermobaric rounds. A case of grenades, a case of claymores, and an assortment of rifles and ammunition with them, so you will be able to stage out of there, if need be."

"Shit, Batman, I'll be farting through silk here. I won't know how to behave with all of this support. What I do know is all of this comes with a price tag attached to it.

"I will prepare one of the underground bunkers as a weapons storage area. Shit, I might put Rodney in there as a guard. When can I expect to see them?"

"I estimate within a week. I am going to have Bert bring them down in the Commander. Speaking of Bert, I guess I had better call him and give him a heads up on this operation. I'll keep you in the loop. Later, dude."

"Hey Bert, I have a mission and a deal for you. Which do you want first?"

"Like it really matters. Every time you call I run for the Vaseline. What's up, guy?"

"Okay, first, I need you to come and pick up a couple of people and some equipment and get them to Deming. I would have Joe do it except this is more than the Otter can handle.

"I'll likely have a new guy coming on board here; I have known him since the early 70s. Anyway, he has a pilot's license for multi-engine aircraft. I'll give you the option: try to locate another Commander twin, or you upgrade and give him your twin. Of course, I'll pick up the tab. The call is yours. That will take a lot of pressure off your operation, as David could pick up a lot of the slack from this end."

"That sounds like the best news I have had all week. I will start looking around and see what I can come up with."

"Great, just don't commit until I am sure he is coming aboard. On a more serious note, I am beefing Serf's location up, as I anticipate getting a lot more active across the border. With luck, we will be able to use Larry's Agency assets for deployment and recovery, but as you know, we may need to call on you."

"Ok, Ron. I am pretty open, so just give me a call when you're ready to move the crew to Deming. I'll talk to you later, guy."

———

Ron and Joe were watching Bert , Dief, Ray, and Bu Dop Blue disappear in the horizon. "Top, it seems a hell of a lot has changed in the several days Tracy and I were gone. So, what's up?"

"Hell, Joe, I don't really know, but I have a sneaking suspicion the shit is going to get hot and heavy very soon on several fronts. Some of it we have an idea on, some of it we don't have a clue on. Sit down; I am going to brief you on a lot of shit you haven't heard before. This is the main reason I brought you and Tracy home from your mission. I may need to deploy you on a moment's notice. I will brief her later."

———

Ron just finished giving David the tour of the Academy, along with a general briefing on what was going on with the

Warriors. "You do realize that there is a likelihood that you will be required to step outside the boundaries of the law on occasions, just know that it is for Lady Liberty."

"Hell, Top, you, Joe, Larry, the Dief and filthy Fred are involved. Do you think for one minute I would pass this up? When do you want me to start?"

"Basically, as soon as you are able to. I have Bert looking for a Commander Twin for you, which will make our life a lot easier around here. I am thinking that Steve needs to come up with one more medic, as I have plans for you and your skill sets that may conflict with his plans."

"I can start here as soon as I can get back to upstate New York and grab some stuff. I'll put the rest of my crap in storage."

"Shit, your truck is here. How about if Joe flies you, and at the same time he can help you pack, and bring you back?"

"Sounds like a plan to me. I can't fucking believe it—it has been forty plus years, and ODA-335 is again going to battle."

"By the way, if you still have any SCUBA gear bring it with you."

———

"Damn it, Top, we just get a new medic, and you take him away from me. What's up with that shit?" Steve asked.

"I really hated to do it, but his qualifications make him valuable in several different areas. He is the only SADM trained and qualified member of the team, plus he is scuba qualified, and his license is current. Put your feelers out. Shit, Steve, you know damn near every SF medic out there. I have no doubt you can come up with someone."

"I'll see what I can do. It seems like the tempo is picking up around here. Anything I need to know?"

"Actually, there is. Stock up on iodine, double your aid kits, and beef up on CBR supplies and detection kits and alarms."

"Well, Top, I guess that answers that question."

"Actually, Steve, that doesn't even approach an answer."

Ron had a plan he was working on ever since he got the word that David was coming aboard. He couldn't run it by Larry, as he would have a major problem selling it to him. He wasn't sure David would go along with it but he figured he could sell him on it.

———

Chapter 35

"Okay Top, what's up? You didn't call us both up here for tea and crumpets," Joe said as he and Tracy were drinking their coffee and eating their Danish.

"Well, I have to give you that. I have a major operation in the planning stages that I need you two working together on. Tracy, I know you are a loner, but this isn't a hit, it is a security over-watch mission. If you are called into action, it will be with silenced .300 Win Mags at a range of 600-1500 yards, over water. Don't worry, you'll have the finest night optics available. Hopefully, you will never have to fire a round. With luck, we will be able to pass this off on Hezbollah."

"So, just what is this target, Top?" Joe asked.

"I can't discuss it in any greater detail yet. I will brief everyone involved within the next ten days. Until then you'll just have to spend a lot of time at the range, working on tightening up your shot groups. Oh, you also need to get a lot of running in, as if the shit hits the fan you will have about a four mile run to a pick-up point, or about a thousand foot swim." I have a lot of recon to do before I can brief you; as I said, this plan is in the very beginning of the conceptual stage."

"And just why did you select the two of us?" Tracy asked.

"Simple, you're the best I've got. You are both excellent shots, and your judgment is impeccable. I don't have to worry about you doing something stupid. Too much is at stake on this mission to leave anything to chance. You both think on your feet.

"The only other people that will know anything about this is David Smythe and Filthy Fred. Under no circumstances do I want it brought up around Larry or Vince. I hope we can fly under the radar on this one and maintain complete denial."

"Top, I don't know what we have stumbled on," Larry said, "but we got some Arabic encoded chatter from an airborne LP south of Ruby, Arizona. Ruby is a ghost town in Arizona that they are trying to restore. It is nestled in The Coronado National Forest, which is not one of the healthiest of places for gringos to go traipsing through the countryside.

"I have already notified Vince, and he is moving a blimp into that area to see if he can find anything. It's tough terrain, unless you use the roads, and they are likely watched. We'll keep you posted. I will start checking on the availability of stealth air assets in the event we need them."

"Keep me posted, Larry. I may want to insert a two-man recon element into the area just to get a ground, eyes on, assessment of what's really there. In the meantime, I am going to get a grip on our personnel assets, to see what we can commit to this operation. Some of our wounded should be up to the task by now. Call me when you hear something."

Chapter 36

"Dave, you have no idea how happy I am to welcome you to the Geriatric Warriors. Or, as I prefer to call us, America's last hope. We do some wild shit here. Even though we are under CIA contract, for the most part we operate well outside the law. Larry is aware of most of what we do. He, like the rest of us, realizes that if it is going to happen, we are going to have to do it.

"Have you maintained your SCUBA skills since you retired?"

"Oh, hell yes. I am deeper into it now than I have ever been."

"That's good. I want you to take a trip with me next week to New York to perform a target assessment on the United Nations Building. You do remember the acronym CARVE, don't you?"

"Oh shit, let's see: Criticality, Accessibility, Recoverability, Vulnerability, Egress. That's a pretty ambitious undertaking, Top. It would take tons of explosives to do that job."

"Oh, ye of little faith, I failed to mention that another one of your jobs was to figure out the Soviet Suitcase Nuke I have in the bunker. I know you were trained on them in SADM school. I figure that should do the job."

"Top, have you considered the consequences of setting a nuke off in the middle of New York City?"

"Picky, picky, picky. It is a tactical, low yield device. They were designed to take out bridges, dams and the like. It will definitely take out the entire United Nations complex, but little else. Let's face it, you can only put so much in a suitcase. It will make a nice memorial on the banks of the East River for future generations. In the short term, look at what the UN is doing to the world. They are the World's leading proponent of Communism. They are staffing all their agencies with anti-American representatives. We are footing the bill for their activities and they are working against us at every turn. It is time for them to go.

"Once you figure out what we have in that suitcase, start figuring out an assault plan. Filthy Fred, Joe and Tracy will be on the assault team. Your job is to figure the logistics of getting the suitcase on position from a drop off point near Bayonne, New Jersey and getting back. You may want to bring a SCUBA rig and suit with you on our recon, just to get a feel of what you will be facing. Carry a spear and a fishnet with you, just in case."

"Yep," Dave said.

"And what does that mean?"

"We used to have a joke on the old team that said you were a bit bonkers at times. Well, I guess it has finally kicked in full time," Dave said smiling. "When do we head out to New York?"

"As soon as you submit a list of what you need and get a feel for what we have in that suitcase, I will brief the three of you and we will head out to New York. So I suggest you get busy, sir."

Ron was waiting for Gunny and Ronnie Mac. He had told Dave to round them up when he left.

"Deacon, what in hell do you want now?" asked Ronnie Mac.

"Just be patient. I am waiting for Gunny to get here; I don't want to go over this multiple times. Go pour yourself a drink."

Ron had no sooner said that and Gunny appeared. "Gunny, grab a drink and have a seat.

"Okay, I'm going to cut to the chase. Gunny, are you up to a mission in the very near future?"

"Hell yeah, Top, I hardly know I have been wounded. I would say I am up to 95% effective."

"Ronnie, if I have been reading you right, I think I have detected a yearning for a little activity on your part. Is that a reasonable assumption?"

"Well, yeah, I have been giving it some thought. What you got going on?"

"We have picked up some Arabic chatter coming from an old deserted ghost town in The Coronado National Forest in Arizona. The forest has become a major smuggling route from Nogales, Mexico. Vince is placing a blimp in the area and Larry is concentrating several listening posts to try to pinpoint them. If we come up with a definite location, I am putting a recon team, from Deming, in to see what's going on.

"Remember, we still have the ever evasive cargo containers that are rumored to be coming in from North Korea. We are reasonably certain there is merit to that claim, and we have to track down every lead we get to try to find it.

"If the recon team turns up anything, we may well launch an assault on it, and we will need every able bodied soul we have. Plus, there is a likelihood that David and Joe will be out of the net on this one. So, are you in, or have you just been paying lip-service to the urge to get back in the game?"

"Fuck you, Deacon, I'm in and you know it."

"Great, start doing a little PT to get your roly poly ass in shape, and I will keep you posted. See Joe and have him issue you an M-4 and an M-16 both with night optics, and get a little trigger time in while you're at it. I will brief Dewey about your absence. The Academy is getting ready to pull the plug and head to Columbia next month anyway, so it shouldn't be a problem.

"Ok, Top, are you ready for the nickel tour?"

"Let me grab a cup of coffee and I'll be ready. We can do it up here: Mary Jane is in Maine for the day. Ok, so what you got?"

"First, on the infiltration phase, a simple flat sled with control handles and diving planes along with a diver propulsion vehicle, DPV, is about all I can think we need to get to the target. I have one I have been using for years that will do the job.

"On our recon, I want to swim the area to get a feel for the depths involved. As long as I can stay above seventy feet, I have a LAR V Draeger closed circuit rebreather that would facilitate a clandestine infiltration, as it leaves no bubble trail. Considering it is already the end of August, I will be using a Viking dry suit to keep warmer.

"Once the device is in position and activated, I will use the sled and both DPVs to rendezvous with you at the pick-up point."

"That sounds like a good start to a plan. We will have to firm everything up during the recon trip. Joe and Tracy will be going with us. I plan to take two vehicles, as they have a lot of traveling to do. They are going to be your security over-watch, so they are going to have to select their location.

"What did you come up with on the device?"

"The good news is that the model we have is an RA-115-01s. The –01s suffix identifies it as submersible. It is a pretty straightforward device. It claims to have a yield of 5 kilotons, but from what I recall from school that it is more like 2-3 kilotons. It is more than ample to take out the entire UN complex, but not likely to do much beyond there.

"It can be configured to be triggered in several different ways. The one I suggest is by timer. Once set, it requires a constant supply of electric power. The original back up battery is shot; I am in the process of replacing that now. Once the device is triggered, the battery will last a week. I suggest we set the timer for no more than forty-eight hours. That gives us a safety factor and minimizes the amount of time where someone can find it. I still have to get accurate tide and current data for the region, as that can have a great impact on the entire operation. You know,

Top, there is a well substantiated rumor that Russia lost control of up to one hundred of these fuckers in the 90s."

"Oh, I know. We have captured four of them, one of which I was able to get my hands on. Larry took the rest to the CIA. Larry doesn't know about the one I have, nor does he need to. What is scary is that all four were recovered from Islamic terrorists. Makes you wonder how many more they have.

"That is why I am fairly comfortable in pulling this off. The CIA, FBI, and Homeland Security know they were recovered from jihadists. That should take the pressure off a wide-sweeping broad-scale investigation. They will be looking in a different direction. It is a win-win: we get rid of that cesspool of humanity called the United Nations, and the jihadists will be blamed for it.

"I will schedule a meeting with Joe and Tracy next week, just before we go to New York. See what you can come up with for tide data by then, as that will play heavily into the planning phase. We will be dropping down to see Filthy Fred. I am sure it has been ages singe you have seen him. He's doing real good for a pimp," Ron said with a smile.

Chapter 37

"Teriq, I need to come talk to you. I have some good news. When do you have time to meet with me?"

"Hell, Raoul, you can come over now, if you want. I will put some tea on."

"Where is the freighter your containers are on now?"

"It just got in, they are in line to go up the river."

"Great! The good news is that since hurricane Isaac the water level is back up in the Mississippi. Traffic is readily flowing, so it should not take too long to clear the backlog and schedule a barge to take your containers. Do you already have the flatbeds and tractors needed for this job?"

"Oh yeah, they're in my warehouse and storage area. I just don't know where to go with them."

"Worry not, friend. When the time is right, I will dispatch guides to take you to the offload point. You will never find it on your own. I will have a 12 ton cherry-picker on site to trans-load the containers."

"I expect to be able to move up river within two weeks at the most."

"Raoul, that will work great for me. The timing is working out perfect."

"On that note, I will say goodbye. The next time we will meet will be the afternoon of the transaction. I will see you then, my friend."

As Raoul departed, Teriq thought to himself that the only reason we would meet in the afternoon is so that bastard will be sure to get his money. Being a suspicious soul, Teriq decided to have a couple of bodyguards there, just in case.

His thoughts then went to storing the trucks until he got legitimate manifests for them in the event they were stopped on the road. That alone was going to be an expensive endeavor, as he would wind up having to bribe someone for 'legitimate' but false documentation for the contents.

Teriq checked with his warehouse manager and inquired about the new heavy-duty forklift they had ordered, to see if it was in yet. Its purpose was to move and load the warheads. He was told it would be in tomorrow. That meant he was going to have to rent a tractor-trailer to haul it, too.

Chapter 38

"Hey guys, I wanted you here before we meet with Dave tomorrow, as I want to discuss another mission with you. In light of the situation in the mid-East and the operation we are getting ready to kick off, the President may be pushed into a chain of events that will cause him to impose martial law. Frankly, I feel that that is something he wants to do anyway. What you have not been briefed on is the extensive hit squad the President has. The director of Homeland Security controls it. It is a very complex computer-driven system that we have been able to break.

"When we actually kick off the UN operation, I will want you to have the Otter with you. The two of you will start to shadow the Director of Homeland Security, and the first indication I get that Martial Law is going to be imposed, you will need to take her out. That will temporarily disable that system. At the same time Larry, Vince, and I will be able to call on hits for people we want out of the way. Ultimately, they will all be traced back to Homeland Security, and possibly establish a link to the President. At any rate, this will minimize the effectiveness of any degree of martial law he does impose, as he was targeting those who would have been a problem to him.

"With what's at stake, do either one of you have any problem with this?"

"Not really," Joe said. "I just question how difficult she will be to get to."

"That is the only question I have. She is a pretty high-profile bitch," Tracy said.

"Ok, all means are open to take her out, if need be. That covers shooting, accidents, ricin, throw her off a fucking roof if that's what it takes, just kill her! Now, to make your job a little easier Vince will keep you posted on her schedule on a regular basis. She won't be making a move you don't know about.

"I will have Bob on standby to hack and jam her signals if she starts to initiate the process before you can get to her. Ponder it, and we will meet with Dave tomorrow."

"Wow, the Deacon calling on my secure line? Must be something going. What's up, Top?" Larry asked.

"Larry, I am not totally comfortable with the safeguards we have on the Homeland Security dilemma. I briefed Joe and Tracy on it today, and they are putting their heads together. You see what's going on in the world right now, the situation is almost to the point that the President could sell imposing martial law.

"You had a long distinguished career. Who do you know in a position of power that we can talk to and explain what America is really up against now?"

"Damn you, Top, I knew this was coming. I am a very close friend with the Secretary of the Army. He and I go back forty years. What's on your mind?"

"Is your relationship to the point that you could get him to the Lodge where you, Vince, Bob, and I could brief him on what's really happening in America? Show him the Homeland Defense assassin system, and see if he could influence the other chiefs to come down for the same briefing. I am suggesting the imposing of a military coup d'état, if need be. I figure it will be a little easier when they realize they are all earmarked for assassination."

"You crazy mother-fucker, have you gone totally nuts? Have you considered the ramifications of this path you are suggesting? It would be an epic change to everything we have in America. That's if they went for it. If they don't buy into this, we are all going to be wearing orange jumpsuits for the rest of our lives. It will only take one to dissent and the shit will hit the fan."

"Larry, remember, as long as we have access to the system we can take care of a dissenter. Now, I am going to throw it right back in your lap: what if we do nothing? We will become a nation of subjects. You know the number of FEMA internment camps they have built. With luck, we can share a cell, as you know who will be the first rounded up."

"Have you mentioned this to Vince yet?"

"Fuck, no! He is going to piss and moan longer and louder than you did."

"Hey, I'm not done yet. I still haven't bought into this."

"Hell, I wouldn't expect you to, I have been pondering this for months. I just brought it up today, as I am not sure we are going to have an election in November. I don't put anything past him. Give it some thought, but realize we are running out of time. Go visit your friend and feel him out; you may be surprised."

"I'll give it some thought, no promises."

"That's all I ask for, for in the process of thinking about it you will see I am right. Have a good day, Boss."

Chapter 39

Dave asked Ron to have the brief in one of the classrooms in the Academy, which was no problem since this was the mountain phase of the course and the Academy was deserted.

When Ron, Joe and Tracy arrived, it was obvious to Ron that Dave hadn't lost a step when it came to putting on a dog and pony show. In the front of the classroom, Dave had two tables pushed together with something that was covered by a tarp on them.

There was also a massive Nautical chart of New York Harbor affixed to the chalkboard. The first thing Dave did was to show off his pride and joy, the "Treasure Hound". "The 'Hound' is a compact, towable, self-powered sled created for underwater exploration, using improvements developed during years of treasure hunting along the Texas coast. It is powered by dual DPVs (which can be detached for individual use), a bed of special lithium batteries for power and mission endurance, a color nav panel, Lexan windshield, IR spotlight and monitor for finding my previously placed treasure site marking devices, compact SONAR unit, LED running/marking lights in red, green, white, and IR flavors. Much of the technology, and some equipment, was borrowed from buddies on the SEAL teams in Virginia, and all is sterile.

"The sled is a unique creation. It has everything needed for treasure hunting, which has been my passion ever since I watched "Sea Hunt" with Lloyd Bridges. I, like Ron, was raised in an era of 'larger than life' role models like Mike Nelson, Matt Dillon, Sky King and the like, I learned to respect competent leadership, take responsibility for my own actions, and love the America that existed at that time. Now, because bad people are causing the implosion of our beloved country, a favorite quote echoes in my head continually: "The only thing needed for evil to succeed, is for good men to do nothing."

Next, Dave went to the chart and started to explain his concept of operations, along with some well-thought reasons to be in the area.

"After we load the 'Hound', we can cover it on the launch trailer with a tarp, and move to the insertion site. Or, you can be at a particular location in the harbor with a towline hanging in the water and an IR chemlight attached to it that I can spot, hook-up to, then pull a string to signal you that I'm ready. Better something simple like a string, in case you are being eyed by Harbor Police or the like, and can't communicate overtly.

"When you deem the time to be right, you can head out at a leisurely sight-seeing/fishing pace, towards Governor's Island. Pass to the east of the island, then turn west and release me between it and Diamond Reef, which is 28' deep. You can head back down the channel to take romantic/patriotic night pictures of the Statue of Liberty to hopefully sell to your favorite magazine that accepts freelance work. As you pass the northern part of the island, you can put another weighted IR chemlight on the tow line and let it slide down to me, giving me the "release in five minutes" alert.

"If you will note the chart, you will see I have designated checkpoints along the way. They are for my use. I have tons of navigation on the sled, but I like to trust my eyes, too.

"By using a combination of GPS, Loran and map data, the mission will be programmed into the nav panel, which provides a relatively simple mission profile. The trouble with night operations, especially in this area, is 'flying blind' and the things you meet that you don't expect. The problems arise when you add those unexpected factors, such as boats, aquatic wildlife, garbage, and 'things that go bump in the night'.

"In the event of an issue with the authorities, my cover story involves diving an old shipwreck in the "Hell Gate" area of the river north of Roosevelt Island, the location of which was tentatively revealed during a conversation in a local pub. After red tape and associated dealings with government bureaucracy, this unofficial and slightly illegal wreck dive was the attempt to find the wreck. Better to have an outrageous but probably true cover for status, action and location, than to try and tap dance around the issue if questioned by the locals or authorities.

"Well guys, that's my story and I'm sticking to it. Any questions?"

"What other problems do you foresee?" Ron asked.

"The only major issue that could present problems is the current. It can be a real bastard to deal with, but with dual DPVs I should have no problem. The other problem could be presented by the electric turbines close by. They are the brainchild of "Verdant Power". They are expected to generate enough power for a few boroughs and ease the load on the main power grid, but the force of the current was breaking blades off the turbines. Once one of the three blades was broken, the resulting lop-sidedness began to cause the entire unit to self-destruct."

"That was an excellent presentation, Dave. When can you be ready to hit the road and kick this operation off?"

"Give me a couple of days to get everything checked out and ready to roll."

"How about you, guys, are you up to this?" Ron asked Joe and Tracy.

"Ready to rumble, Top," Joe said. Tracy echoed the same sentiment.

"Shit, I guess it's a done deal, then. I'll contact Freddy."

Chapter 40

The recon went off without a hitch. Joe and Tracy located a perfect firing position on the southern tip of Roosevelt Island where, with luck, they would be retrieved from, as would Dave.

The best news of the trip was that Dave discovered a massive storm drain that ran directly under the UN headquarters and he placed a piece of IR marker at a couple of places on the grate. That would assist him on his return. The storm drain took a lot of the risk out of the operation. The grate had a lock on it, but Dave's bolt cutters could handle the lock with ease. He made a note of the size and type of lock and bought one to replace it when he was finished.

The overall contingency plan called for Joe and Tracy to E&E to the north end of the island, where they would be picked up by Freddie. Beyond that, it was swim their ass off. Dave would have to make his way down to the Bayonne golf club, where he would hook on to the Zodiac. Quite a trek, but with luck the tide would be pushing him.

Joe was fueling the Otter for this afternoon's trip. He and Tracy were going to New York a day early as they had to rent a car and go make a last minute check of their shooting position. They would have to take the park tour to get in, as it was open during the day.

The Deacon was fiddling with the Zodiac, making sure he had ample fishing gear to pass off as an old man fishing. He also checked on his fully automatic M-4 with 2 CMAGs behind the false back on the center console.

Dave was checking the programming on his navigation rack, to insure that he would wind up on target. He had the most to check out; there was a lot of stuff on that sled. He also wanted to go through the sequencing of the timer for the device, as this was a one shot operation.

Tracy was packing. In addition to her clothes she packed her regular two pistols, as well as the .300 Win MAG. She also packed a burn phone in a double zip-lock bag, in the event their swim became a reality. Other than that, she was pondering giving Joe some pussy during the trip. It all depends on how he behaves, she thought.

Ironically, at the same time, Mary Jane was considering screwing Ron's ears off tonight.

Ron made one last call to Vince to check if he had been able to pick up anything on his latest recon mission. "Not even a blip on the sensors, Sergeant Major. Haven't even picked up any wildlife, either. I talked to Larry this morning and he is in the same boat."

Ron decided to call Larry, to establish his location more than anything else. "Hey Boss, been wondering if you ran what we discussed by your friend yet?"

"I ran a hypothetical by him, just to feel him out. I think I want us to brief him first, to check on his reaction. We will take it from there."

"Okay, just so you know, I am dispatching Joe and Tracy on an over-watch mission on the Director of Homeland Security, in case the situation presents itself where we need to take her out.

I am sure someone else may be read into the system, but it will take him a while to come up to speed on it, and that may well be enough time for us to preempt it and have a selective kill-off."

"Top, it sounds like you are playing Russian roulette with three rounds in the chambers. Keep me posted before you jump off the deep end."

"Ok, Boss, that's a deal. Talk to you soon."

———

Ron and Dave gave the sled one more thorough check prior to covering it and placing it in Dave's truck. Ron carried the suitcase nuke in the Touareg with him, as he was the most heavily armed and more maneuverable in the event of a problem. All the way to New York Ron questioned himself about what they were getting ready to do, and he kept coming up with the same answer…go for it, you'll never have another chance. They got to Freddie's joint at about 1500 hours. As expected, Fred was ready to go, as were Joe and Tracy.

They all had a silent drink, and then drove to the departure point, just east of Keansburgh, New Jersey.

They pulled into the little cove, and Ron and Joe unloaded the sled from Dave's truck while Dave got suited up. It was a long trip to the Bayonne golf club, where he would hook on to the Deacon, but Dave had the tide pushing him the entire trip. One last check of the equipment, and Dave slid out of sight in the breakers, with the suitcase secured between his legs.

———

Upon Dave's departure, Freddie drove Dave's truck to Blackwell Park on Roosevelt Island, where he would wait for Joe and Tracy, in case they needed him. In the event they didn't need him, he was to drive to the rendezvous point located in the jetty just north of the Bayonne Golf Club, where he would link up with the rest of the team.

After what seemed like an eternity Dave spotted the IR chemlight tied off to a towing clevis attached to a tow rope that was in turn attached to Ron's Zodiac. Dave screwed the clevis onto the towing pintle on the sled. He then gave three gentle tugs on the rope.

Dave watched Ron's line and lure as it appeared to swim toward the Zodiac. Immediately thereafter, the jet drive on the Zodiac came to life and they started to ease towards Governors Island, trolling two lines the entire trip.

The sled settled down to the cruising depth of 15 feet, under tow, and Dave began following the dark red track on the nav screen. Putting on his 'war face' and entering a highly focused 'mission mode', his respiration and heart rate began to slow as the Draeger was functioning smoothly, hissing with each inhalation and exhalation, even with the additional modifications made to it to increase bottom time. A smaller rebreather rig and a single tank compressed air unit rested beside the nav panel for emergency backup. On the left side was a compact underwater metal detector, IR marking devices, including chemlights, Glint tape panels, strobes, and innocuous looking things that would show up under IR light but not attract attention if seen in a water environment. On the right, a Hawaiian sling spear gun for emergencies, a utility tool, flashlight, pry bar, bolt cutters, and the ubiquitous Leatherman Tool that was carried everywhere. Everyday items that became priceless the moment you need them but don't have them.

Ron couldn't help but notice that there appeared to be a closeness between Joe and Tracy he had never noticed before. This gave Ron a bit of concern, as functioning in their capacity you needed to have a totally clear head, and be completely objective. There could be no room for personal feelings when working as an assassin. Ron decided to keep an eye on them as time went on.

They were going around the north side of Governors Island, heading for checkpoint one—the Brooklyn Bridge. It was here that the Deacon would stop, giving Dave the opportunity to unhook and go on his own power for the mission.

Dave felt the rope go slack, and he knew what this meant. He unhooked from the Zodiac and gave a double tug on the rope, which then disappeared in the dark. As Dave looked up he saw the Brooklyn Bridge looming above the surface. It brought up a flood of memories of fun times in the Big Apple while on the Golden Knights, jumping into Coney Island and later into Yankee Stadium for the second game of the '82 World Series. Ok, time to wipe the shit-eating grin off the face and get back to work as the sled continued to hug the coast of Manhattan Island.

"The Swim" was on. As on earlier SCUBA operations, the main mission was referred to as "The Swim", regardless of whether it was to explore a located wreck or place a special charge on the bottom of a vessel, bridge, dam, or in the case of "The Swim" in Columbia, a drainage system that would 'flush out' a murderous drug lord.

As soon as Ron felt slack on the line, he retrieved it, throttled up, and headed to the east side of Roosevelt Island. Joe and Tracy both donned their night vision goggles and directed their attention to the Island to see if they could detect any sign of life in the South Point Park area. They went on to the north the entire length and circled around to the other side of the Island. Satisfied that the coast was clear, Ron killed all running lights well ahead of the beaching area, coasted in to the designated area and dropped Joe and Tracy off.

The sled was a little heavier this time, with the added weight and bulk of the 'suitcase' which was riding between Dave's legs as he lay prone on the sled. Some tweaking with weights and balances produced the same stability and neutral buoyancy as before. The watertight plastic cases, available commercially, were perfect for this type mission, because they could be packed to have negative buoyancy that would cause them to sink if jettisoned in an emergency. IR markings would make them easy for the sled to locate and retrieve.

The mission profile for The Swim began as the recon did, with the link-up and approach running smoothly. Following the nav panel's red line up the river, Dave prepared to start looking for the checkpoints and hitting the stopwatch to determine speed and know when to look for the next checkpoint.

Something was different tonight, though. Like Spider-man's "spidey-sense", there was a feeling that the river was agitated about something, but Dave couldn't put a finger on it. Reminded him of The Swim in the Danube when some very bad people were dragging the river with large treble hooks in an effort to catch him and stop The Swim. Once started, NOBODY stops The Swim, unless called back by Larry or the Deacon. He grinned as he remembered how the target went up in a ball of flame, as did the bad guys, thanks to the small Limpet mine he left on their hull, generously affording them the opportunity to give their lives for their country...

As he passed checkpoint four, the feeling got worse: a vibration? The sled was 'shipshape' and tight; no loose equipment here. Even the Deacon had examined the equipment with his trained eye to make sure all was secure and ready for the mission. Had to be something in the environment—pleasure boat with a bent prop?

As the sled approached checkpoint five—the turbines—Dave dove to hug the bottom to avoid turbulence from the turbine blades, even though the tide wasn't at its strongest yet. About halfway through the field the vibration suddenly grew louder and louder, then with a crescendo of mechanical noises, all hell broke loose. Sensing a change in the water pressure on his ear drums and chest, Dave tensed as he heard the sssss-sh-sh-sh-sh-SH-SH-SH-WHUMP just before the newly detached turbine blade sliced through the water and landed on him and the sled, pinning both to the muddy bottom.

Trying to maintain control through the intense pressure and pain, he powered down the sled and assessed the situation. Breathing was becoming more difficult and movement was restricted. All he knew at this point was that there was a large, heavy mass on top of him and he wasn't physically able to lift it or carry on with The Swim. Shit. Going through his mind was the obvious: "the Deacon's gonna be pissed if I die and don't carry out the mission. Can't let him down. Besides, he will probably be so mad that he will find my body and kill me again. That would ruin my whole day."

Ingrained in every Special Forces soldier is "mission first", and in that mindset 'improvise, adapt and overcome' were watchwords to live by. Thinking a mile a minute, Dave went over everything he had within reach that could be used to free himself and continue the mission. No luck. At least the Viking dry suit would keep him warm against the cold water, especially since he was below the thermocline and bitter cold. A thermocline occurs where the upper layer of water warmed by the sun meets the lower, colder water and can deflect sonar 'pings' making a vessel below it invisible to sonar. Strange that the mind would wander to thermoclines when facing a situation like this.

DRY SUIT! Dave flashed back to scout swimming training on Mirror Lake at Fort Devens, where they used Viking dry suits to protect against the cold water. A simple unisuit of vulcanized canvas with integral boots, the Viking has pliable rubber at the cuffs as well as at the neck, where you climb into it. He had always liked the Viking for its simplicity and durability and now its versatility. Always one to push the limit with equipment and vehicles, while at Mirror Lake, between swims, he had taken deep breaths and exhaled into the suit, making it inflate like a raft.

Improvise. Discovering that he had enough reach to get to the small compressed air cylinder, he put his plan into action. After inserting the regulator into the neck of the suit, he opened the main valve and depressed the 'purge' button, forcing the jet of air into the suit. As the suit slowly inflated, the weight on him eased off to where the pain was manageable and the breathing was easier. As the weight shifted, he was able to reposition his upper body to cause the object to start to slide off him and the sled. Powering up the sled, he gave the DPVs full thrust to drive out from under the load. A sudden lurch revealed no power on the left, which he compensated for with right rudder. Now a huge balloon, he had to grab his dive knife and stab the suit to let the air out and decrease buoyancy or he would shoot to the surface into view, developing a nasty case of 'the bends' on the way.

A quick check revealed that it was, in fact, a turbine blade that had pinned him to the bottom, and that the left DPV was damaged when it had hit an object on the bottom. The object, he discovered to his amusement, was a washtub that had been filled with concrete and had the remnants of two human legs protruding from it. Cement shoes—guess those stories were true.

Adapt. Since the port side DPV was inoperable, a simple tweak of the rudder and dive plane was all that was needed to regain control and continue the mission. The design of the sled had allowed for this contingency and it was performing as expected. Equipment was shifted as needed, dry suit adjusted, and The Swim continued. The cold water that entered the suit through the deflation hole made by the knife actually felt good on whatever wound was there, causing the pain to subside, but also creating a potential problem with hypothermia.

Overcome. Take a deep breath and drive on. After passing the final pipeline checkpoint, the flashing of the IR 'firefly' left near the drain came into view on the monitor. The sled was anchored as before, equipment removed, and attention focused on the lock on the grate.

The lock didn't pose a problem for the bolt cutters. Dave entered the drainage system until he reached the first ladder that he could climb up. He fastened the nuke and flippers to the ladder and climbed up, until he surfaced. There was still 12 to 15 feet of ladder above him. He went all the way to the top peered out, and realized he was in the pavilion in the middle of the grounds of the UN complex. He inspected the lock on the cover to the drain, it was rusted solid. Dave smiled, as nothing could have made him happier.

Dave climbed back down, retrieved the nuke, and then returned almost to the surface. He checked to insure the timer was still functioning … all was ok. Yep, thirty-two and one half hours until detonation time. Dave now closed the suitcase and purged it. Securing it between the wall of the shaft and the ladder was easier than he expected. After placing it on a pair of braces that held the ladder to the wall, he securely tied it off and, for safety, handcuffed the handle to a rung of the ladder.

Dave worked his way through the drainage system back to his sled. Basic mission complete. New mission…Survival… he thought as he recognized the first signs of hypothermia starting to set in. Get rid of ballast to allow sled to rise above the thermocline, where the water was much warmer. Once the sled stabilized in the thermocline, Dave attached an IR chemlight to a bobber attached to a line he controlled, and released it, hoping it would be seen by Joe or Tracy, as planned. Oh, shit! he thought, I know Joe. What if they are fucking and not paying attention to me? I am not sure how long I will last at these temperatures and I still have no idea of the extent of my injuries. Fuck it, time to get proactive; I have to get out of the water soon.

———

Joe and Tracy, having had a totally uneventful stay in their selected position, were starting to get a bit worried, as the operation had exceeded its expected duration by almost an hour now. Tracy was the first to spot the IR chemlight bobbing in the water.

Joe immediately called Top to tell him to come and get them. "The bobber was up."

Ron promptly started back up river, first to retrieve Joe and Tracy, and then to hook on the sled. As earlier, Ron killed all running lights on approach to the pick-up point and coasted to shore.

———

Dave smiled as he heard the unmistakable whine of the jet drive on the Zodiac; he knew he would soon be in the boat. Dave heard it depart from the island and get steadily louder as it approached him, dragging its own IR chemlight attached to the towrope.

The plan was to hook up and proceed to link up with Freddy at the Bayonne Golf Club, but Dave had a different plan. He hooked the sled to the clevis, set the diving planers to maximum and then started a series of three yanks on the rope, at the same time freeing himself from the sled. He then climbed/swam to the surface and started boarding the boat from abaft. Joe immediately saw Dave was injured and helped him get aboard.

Dave gave the Deacon a quick rundown on the operation, while at the same time Tracy called Freddy and told him to meet them at the rendezvous point.

Dave told Top that the diving rudders were set on full to keep the sled submerged just from the current, in the event they were stopped. "Oh, by the way, it won't be too long before a team arrives at the turbines to assess the damage to them, so we might want to get to fuck out of here," Dave said.

It was slow going to get to the golf course. At one point Ron was considering cutting the sled loose and just replacing it later on, when needed, but he knew that it was more than just a sled. It was a part of Dave's history and, while he might agree to ditching it, a deep scar would be left in Dave's soul at its loss.

Fred was there, waiting for them. They loaded the sled up and Ron told Fred to take Dave with him and meet them at the inlet where they launched from, as that's where all the other vehicles were. Freddie had a couple of his goons watching them so they had something to come back to; after all, this was New Jersey.

Finally with everything loaded at the inlet, Ron pulled out a bottle of Cognac and toasted everybody for a job well done.

"Joe, you guys have less than 28 hours to get that plane to hell out of here, and out of range of any possible EMP issues. I fear that they are going to have major problems at LaGuardia; it is only about two miles straight line from the UN.

"With luck, the EMP won't be too bad, as the device is low yield and is being detonated underground.

"Freddie, I am sure you and your dancers will all be in good shape. How about you, Dave? Are you up to driving back to Wolfeboro tonight, or do you want to stay with Freddy? Realize we don't know what effect the explosion will have on traffic through the city; it could well wreak havoc on some of the bridges and tunnels. I don't think so, but you never know."

"Shit, now that I'm warm, and not hurt too bad, I am up to the trip. Let's get to fuck out of here."

"Guys, America thanks you. Although this is going to hurt a while, in the long run it is for the best. Joe, Tracy, keep in touch."

After a long uneventful ride Ron and Dave pulled into the Lodge parking lot at 1430 hours. Ron invited Dave in for a cup of coffee, which he accepted, although what he really wanted to do was go to bed.

Ron mentioned that he had considered cutting the sled loose, and got a glare from Dave. "Top, I love you like a brother, but we would have fought in the middle of New York harbor. The Hound is one of a kind, I have spent over twenty years working on her and tweaking her features. Some of her components can no longer be found. In my divorce settlement I gave the wife custody of the kids, the dog, she got my house, my Mercedes, I walked out of it with the greatest treasure I had, "The Hound" and my pickup."

"Glad I didn't mention it," Ron laughed. "I sort of thought there was a lot of sentiment attached to her; that's why I didn't pursue it. Now get your ass over and have Steve take a look at you, and that is not debatable."

"Yeah, I was planning on that. At least let him run an x-ray to see if I have anything cracked or broken."

"Ok, do that and get your ass to bed. I plan to do the same as soon as I talk to Larry."

When Dave left, Ron went over and poured himself a snifter of Cognac and then proceeded to dial Larry.

"Hey Larry, any word on your listening posts yet?"

"Not a thing. I am beginning to wonder if they just picked up on a stray signal."

"That could be. We'll give it a couple more days and I will have Serf return to normal operations. There is no sense on that crew sitting on their asses. I will have Bert insert them.

"I just heard from Joe and Tracy. They are in position and will start maintaining a schedule check tomorrow. You know she has to have a routine; all we need to do is figure out what it is."

"I will keep you posted if we turn anything up top. You may want to consider using agency air assets to insert Serf's teams instead of Bert. We can do it safer, and we have a degree of immunity."

"Good point, Boss, I will let you know when. Talk to you later." Ron hung up knowing that he had completed the loop on maintaining his whereabouts, since he'd called Larry from Wolfeboro yesterday and today. Little did he know that there were events in the making that would shift all suspicion away from him in the immediate future.

Ron was just getting ready to go to bed when Mary Jane arrived home. She looked at him and said, "Damn, that's a waste, going to bed alone," as she slipped out of her dress.

Chapter 41

Ron was sitting in the lodge, drinking a cup of coffee, and thinking that in just a little less than three hours hell was going to visit New York. He was between pensive and remorseful, as he fully realized the damage that was about to be wrested upon that magnificent city.

He justified it in his own mind by knowing that it was going to take out several hundred delegates, most of which were constantly working against the interest of the United States in virtually all of their endeavors. Ron had often stated that the UN was staffed from the cesspool of humanity. The majority of the people he knew felt the same way, but they would never state that in public. Fucking wimps, he thought.

At least the bomb would go off before visiting hours. That was the only consolation Ron could come up with for what was about to happen.

The only concerns Ron had were as the cameras on the George Washington Bridge; they would have recorded both him and Dave coming and going. He knew that was a stretch, but nonetheless a concern. He figured they needed to come up with a cover story, just in case.

"Hey Top, how are you doing?" Dave asked as he entered.

"Shit, I'm ok. How did you make out with Steve last night?"

"Well, fuck, I cracked two ribs and have a lot of localized bruising, but other than that I am okay. Hurt a hell of a lot more today than I did yesterday. I was running on pure adrenaline last night. Coming down really sucks.

"I have a feeling Steve knows what we were up to, just based on his conversation last night."

"That doesn't worry me. He's the one who snuck that nuke out of the batch we recovered, and gave it to me. You know Steve, after a spate of pontificating he settles down and goes along with the operation. Been like that as long as I have known him, and isn't likely to change any time soon."

Dave looked at his watch. "Less than two hours, Boss. Are you going to try to catch it on TV?"

"I figure we will lose all New York based signals. Actually, I don't know what to expect. It all depends on the actual yield of the device and the EMP it produces. The EMP is much further reaching than the blast or shockwave. The Enola Gay and Bockscar were almost taken down from the EMP generated by the bombs they dropped. The understanding of EMP was minimal at that time. There were some systems on both planes that were damaged, even though they were miles away when their bombs went off.

"Not sure how long the networks will take to bring in operational equipment, if they are even allowed to approach New York. We are in unchartered territory here. I have already pulled all of our computers off line, just in case. I have Bob monitoring the Homeland Security kill list, to see if there is any traffic on it. He will contact Joe if necessary. Other than that, all we can do is wait."

It was 10:31 am when the TV signal went dead. "It's just a waiting game now. I imagine every official from New York to DC is jumping through their ass about now."

Ron surfed through the local channels, and they all knew something catastrophic had happened in New York, but none of them knew what.

Bob's secure phone rang, "Hi, Bob, what's up?"

"Homeland Security just sent out a kill notice on the Chairman of the Joint Chiefs of Staff before I could stop it, and I can't get through to Joe."

"Okay, I will get on it."

Ron immediately called Larry. "Larry, I don't know what in hell is going on, we're not getting any news up here. Just wanted to tell you the kill list has been activated.

"Homeland Security just put out a hit on the Chairman of the Joint Chief. You have less than 12 hours to save his life. I can't get in touch with Joe. The assassin's name is Robert Jessman; he works with the Chairman. When things slow down call me with an update. By the way, remember, you are also on that list! Cover your ass."

"Okay, Top, let me get on this issue. Just maybe they will be receptive to that briefing now. I'll call you when I can."

Ron walked over and poured a shot of Cognac for both him and Dave. "The deed is done, ain't no looking back now!"

———

Chapter 42

Teriq was patiently waiting for Raoul. Needless to say, there was a degree of anxiety and trepidation on tonight's activities.

Through the window, Teriq saw Raoul pull up with another person, and they were coming into the office.

"Teriq, this is my associate, Willis. He will be your guide tonight."

"Hey Willis, glad to have you on board. So what's the drill for the night?"

"Your barge will be entering the river somewhere between 7:00pm to 10:00pm. That's as close as you will ever get for a barge departure time. Your two containers are right dead in the middle of the second tier. We put them there for balance after we unload them.

"After the barge passes Darrow, it will make about a 120 degree turn starboard. Just shy of a mile farther, there is a slew on the eastern bank. The barge will pull in there. I have an 18 ton crane on location that will unload the containers and place them on your trucks. From there you are on your own. It shouldn't take more than 20 minutes. You will need a couple of cars to transport the crew that accompanied the containers. That must be precious cargo, to have it guarded as heavily as you do."

Teriq went over to the safe and grabbed the pile of cash that he had pre-counted and handed it to Raoul. "You will notice there is an extra $5,000 there. That's for good service."

"And that will insure you always get good service, my friend," Raoul said. "Don't worry about Willis, he will grab a ride home with the crane operator."

Teriq had three sedans, Willis, and the two trucks follow him to the pick-up point. They were all well-armed, in the event any unexpected shit came down.

It was about 11:45pm when the lone barge killed its lights and swung into the slew. Obviously, the pilot had done this before. Willis worked with the crane crew, and before you knew it the containers were on the trucks and ready to roll. As soon as the second container was lifted, the barge slipped back into the river, headed for Baton Rouge.

Teriq led the convoy back to his warehouse and stockyard. He had the trailers backed into the warehouse. His job was finished as soon as he got the false manifests. It was obvious the nine men accompanying the containers were in charge at this point. They just had to wait for their contact from Canton, Ohio, to come and get them. The one who was obviously in charge, named Najib, asked to make a call. He talked less than three minutes, and then asked if Teriq had made provisions for his men. Teriq assured him he had and he took them to their makeshift quarters.

The next morning Najib paid particular attention to the forklift Teriq had procured for them. It was obvious from the smile on his face that he approved. He then proceeded to open the containers and inspect the contents.

The rest of Najib's crew were technicians who were trained on the operation of the SCUD D system. Although the Scud in the truck was from North Korea, they'd received their training in Syria, who had purchased a number of the Korean models before they started producing their own. These Scuds were the first nuke Scuds North Korea produced.

The documentation and manifest, along with a customs tag, arrived by courier that afternoon. Teriq took them to Najib, who immediately made a short call on the throwaway phone Teriq had bought him.

"We will be departing in three days," Najib said. "We have a long ride ahead of us. In the meantime we will continue to work on the equipment. I appreciate the assistance you have given us."

Teriq was surprised with Najib's mastery of the English language; he could have passed for a native-born American.

Late in the afternoon on Monday, a man identified as al Sa'd arrived at Teriq's office and asked to be taken to Najib. Teriq was expecting him, so he led him to the warehouse.

After a period of discussion, Najib told Teriq that al Sa'd was going to stay in a hotel in town, as he had never seen New Orleans before and this would likely be his only opportunity.

"Not a problem, my friend," Teriq said. "I will take him and set him up in a decent hotel, and will bring him back here in the morning."

"That will be ideal," Najib said. "I appreciate it."

Teriq and al Sa'd arrived back at the warehouse at 8:00am sharp. Teriq was surprised that the vehicles were lined up and ready to go. The only matter of business was the cash transaction for all of the equipment.

Teriq, al Sa'd and Najib all went into the office. Najib was thanking Teriq for all of his assistance. It was at this point that al Sa'd took a 9mm pistol from his briefcase. Teriq looked at Najib incredulously and asked what was going on.

"You see, my friend, in battle there are casualties. You are what Americans call a loose end, especially after yesterday's explosion at the United Nations. I choose to look at you as a martyr. In either case, the result is the same. You know too much." At this point al Sa'd shot Teriq in the head.

A couple of the technicians came in, carried the body over to an empty barrel, placed him in it, and sealed the top. Najib called one of them over and told him to drive Teriq's car so it wouldn't draw attention. The convoy then departed, as it had approximately 1100 miles to go, which was no major problem as there were plenty of drivers to allow them to drive straight through.

On the second day of travel the convoy pulled into a deserted gravel pit about 20 miles south of Canton, Ohio. There were rows of trees planted to control erosion, and that was where they pulled into, to avoid detection. The crew immediately went to work unloading the forklift and the Scud carrier/launcher. The forklift was busy getting the warheads out of their truck, while the head engineer was making a last check on the coordinates needed to key into the guidance system on the Scud missiles, to insure they arrived at the right place.

The targets, Washington, DC, Chicago, Il, and Philadelphia, PA, were keyed into the appropriate missiles, with Washington, DC, being the first.

Ron Dahle

The crew all prayed at 5:00 pm and then went directly to the task at hand. The first missile was already loaded, and the second was on the forklift ready for immediate reloading, as they knew they didn't have a lot of time to spend in the area once the first launch took place.

It got very quiet, then al Sa'd hollered "Allah Akbar" and the first missile was on its way to Washington, DC, carrying a 20 Kiloton warhead. Immediately, the second missile, destined for Chicago, was loaded, and was ready to deploy. Again, al Sa'd hollered "Allah Akbar" and the second missile started to take off, when everything went wrong. At approximately 25 feet from the launcher, it exploded in a massive fireball, killing everyone present and setting the other missile off. Neither warhead went off, but the fuel alone was all it took to end the mission. The last thought in Najib's head was the satisfaction of having succeeded in getting the missile destined to Washington, DC, underway and knowing that he was going to Paradise.

Look for *The Grey Zone.* A continuation of the Churning Cauldron series. Featuring the Geriatric Warriors.

———